THOSE WHO BUY STARS

THOSE WHO BUY STARS

A NOVEL BY
ANCA MIZUMSKY

Current edition translated by the author,
accompanied by a *glossary* containing specific, rare words in the text

All rights reserved. Published by New Meridian, part of the non-profit organization New Meridian Arts, 2024.

Originally published in Romanian,
Cei care cumpără stele, Editura Trei, 2022.

LIBRARY OF CONGRESS CATALOGING-IN-PUBLICATION DATA

Those Who Buy Stars
Authored by Anca Mizumsky

ISBN: 979-8-9880234-2-5
LCCN: 2024932593

To my grandmother, Athena

FIRST PART

GENOA

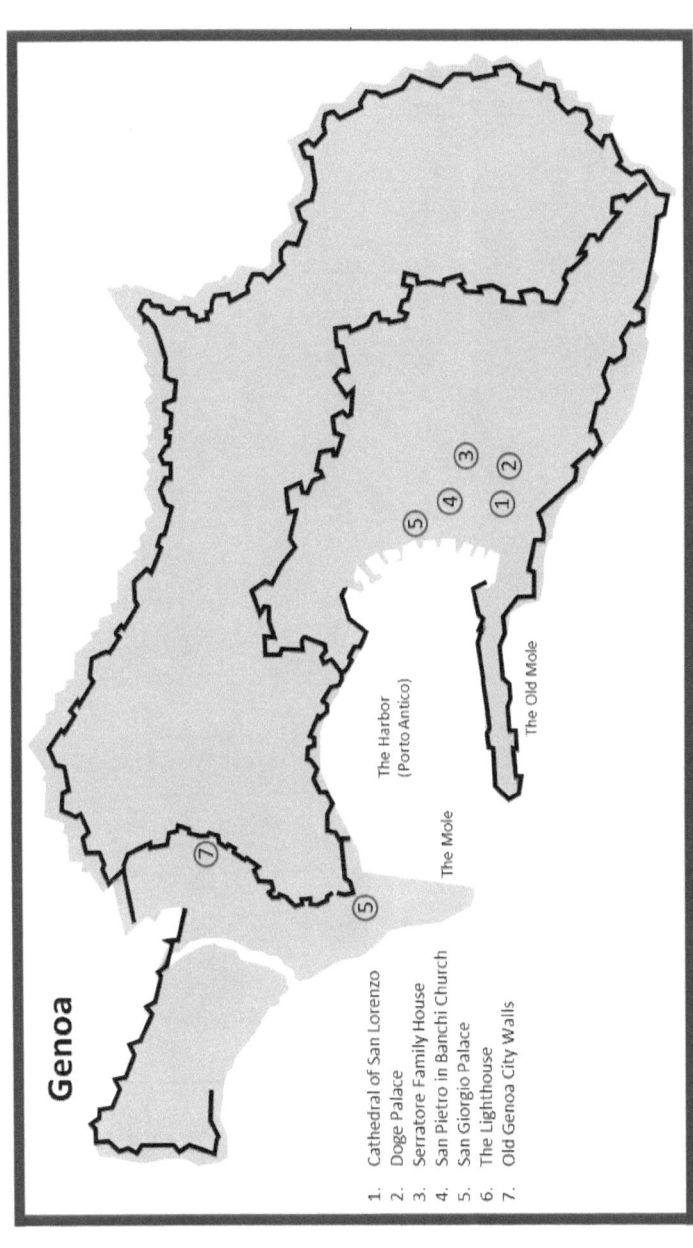

Genoa

1. Cathedral of San Lorenzo
2. Doge Palace
3. Serratore Family House
4. San Pietro in Banchi Church
5. San Giorgio Palace
6. The Lighthouse
7. Old Genoa City Walls

The Harbor
(Porto Antico)

The Mole

The Old Mole

MUSTAFA

He got up from his chair and looked at the bruise on his hand. It was the size of a silver coin on the inside of his wrist. He rubbed it a little with the nail of his thumb, but the bruise wouldn't go away. They had been appearing more and more often lately, mainly on his hands and feet. All he had to do was pick up the casting cylinders or the two crucibles in which he mixed the jewelry alloys, or pick up the water pails with which he cooled the soft glass of freshly burnt enamel, and the bruises would immediately appear.

What will be, will be, he thought to himself and stood up. He decided not to argue again with Meryem, who had been relentlessly insisting that he should visit Leib Peres. He'd lie to her again that he was going to the apothecary, but he wouldn't go, because he refused to give that fox-faced guy any money. Whenever Mustafa entered that apothecary filled with magnesium, camphor, nux vomica, aconitum, mercury, laudanum, senna, ambergris, and other things that only the Sephardic Jew knew, it seemed that a spontaneous swirl of yellow mist erupted from the ground beneath his feet, enveloping him and poisoning his blood.

What thoughts I have this morning! Mustafa sulked and started to gather his things. First, he put down the two large volumes of the *History of Muhammad ibn Jarir al-Tabari* and took, just in case, the Turkish translation of Abd al-Rahman al-Sufi's manuscript, *The Book of the Fixed Stars*. His Arabic was not good enough, and he wanted to talk to Khalil. Then, he searched the corners of the house for a box of semi-precious stones, which had been sent to him the day before by the Imperial Palace, for the *tespih*. In the First Courtyard workshop, over forty jewelers and their apprentices had polished the stones and sent them to him so he could thread the prayer beads and make the clasps. He opened the box, picked up the lambskin in which they were wrapped, and spread it on the table. In front of him lay, rounded to the same size, small beads of translucent deep red carnelian, lapis lazuli, hematite, jasper, chalcedony, nephrite, and quartz. Perfectly aligned in several rows, sleepy in their leather scrolls, all the beads were strung together on a wire, as in an insect collection.

Those little globes of minerals had waited for millennia in the belly of India, Arabia, and China, had been unearthed in uneven, rough boulders of rock, transported by sea in vessels that smelled of fish, human excrement, and filth, by land in chests bound with thick ropes soaked in horse sweat, and now they lay before him, tamed.

He sighed, took the scroll, carefully tightened it, put it back, picked up the cloth bag where he had placed the books, and went to the kitchen. Meryem was not at home. She'd most likely gone to the fish market early that morning to speak with Musa. Mustafa understood what was bothering her, but he chose to remain silent, despite hearing her toss and turn from one side of the bed to another each night. Her body, weighed down by pregnancies and age, draped across the bed every night like a sack of wet wool, woke him when she tossed and murmured in her sleep. That was how Mustafa had come to watch over her, covering her three rolls of fat, one larger and two smaller, which bulged under the cloth of her nightgown and rose in rhythm with her breathing when she slept face up, with a thin sheet in summer or a quilt in winter.

He went out back and pulled the garden gate after him. It was early but still very warm for mid-April. Constantinople woke up to the usual hustle and bustle of the morning: the shouts of merchants, the voices of boys carrying trays of tea into the Grand Bazaar, hooves and dust, and people from all nations on the face of the Earth talking at once and gesticulating at the same time.

Because of the sleepless night, he didn't hear the muezzin and hadn't perform his pre-dawn prayer, again. Late, he kneeled with increased difficulty on the prayer rug. His belief in Allah Most High, the One, All-powerful, stood as strong as always, but he struggled with the stubborn muezzins and imams, their interpretations of the Sharia, and their rules.

After they forced the closure of the Astronomical Observatory, Mustafa was furious at all the self-righteous clerics who hung out at the Imperial Palace every day, poking their noses into everything. And he wasn't necessarily angry for his own sake but for Khalil, his lifelong friend.

You could be flogged for heresy, he smiled to himself. If thoughts were transparent, Muslims and Christians alike would be horrified at what they saw. But thoughts are not transparent; they are opaque, gelatinous, and sometimes as hard as the semi-precious stones in his workshop, and so he would continue to lay his arthritis-ridden knees on the old prayer rug and remain silent.

The slope up to the Seraglio seemed endless, and when he finally saw the imperial guard's janissary, he asked for a glass of water. As it was brought to him, he studied the slender figure dressed in a red and blue uniform.

Where was he born? Rumelia? Armenia? Bosnia? The Imperial Guards were made up of Christian boys, who were taken from their families at an early age, raised in the Muslim faith, and who then served exclusively the Sultan. The one in front of him couldn't have been more than twenty-two years old, but he already looked old, with a sharp mouth, lips like two blades, and eyes deepened in their sockets.

Mustafa stopped looking at him and handed him the empty cup. There is no justice in this world, but what is justice? He passed through the Middle Gate and entered the Divan's Court, walking along the wide alleys lined with cypress trees without straying too far. As he waited for the Head Guard to come and show him to his private quarters, he realized that the Seraglio was too quiet. What had happened? Normally, there were the voices of cooks, grooms gleaming horses, or gardeners chatting, but today there was nothing; everything appeared hushed, forgotten, and walled up.

"The Sultan is not here," the Grand Vizier's secretary, who came to see who was looking for His Highness, told him with a wan expression. "He left in the dark, about four in the morning; he could not sleep. He decided to stay a few weeks at the Edirne Serai."

Another one who couldn't sleep! Mustafa murmured a few polite words of approval — "The Sultan's health is more important than anything else; may Allah protect His Highness" — and departed, this time with quick steps, despite the weight of the cloth book bag still hanging on his right shoulder. *Surely, something had happened. When you live in a palace between the Golden Horn, the Bosporus, and the Marmara Sea, you don't have to go anywhere else to rest.*

He sighed in relief. Lately, the meetings with the Sultan had become increasingly unpleasant. In their youth, they shared a passion for jewelry and Persian miniatures and had become friends. The silent goldsmith, who was not even one of the palace artisans, who only came occasionally when called, was in fact an enigma to the servants and the advisers who met him. Modestly dressed and not seeming to pay much attention to imperial etiquette — he respected it to the limits of basic politeness — he would spend hours alone with the Padishah in the gardens or in his study, discussing the proportion in which sulfur, copper, silver, and lead were to be mixed for the black inlays on the rings of the Safavid dynasty, or the art of twisting thin silver wires into the arches of Byzantine earrings, in which the filigree was usually finished with granulated borders.

The Sultan had a taste for not only jewelry but also enameled vases, swords embellished with rubies and diamonds, sandalwood inlaid with pearl for harem bedroom furniture, Egyptian anklets, Venetian coffers with mother-of-pearl walls, and even the relics of Christian saints. The latter, plentiful in the basilicas or brought to him from every corner of the empire, draped in red silk and fastened to their gold reliquaries with invisible, precious pins.

The emperor collected antiques, and the only one he really trusted to evaluate them was Mustafa. Over time, as they saw each other, the discussions had come down to one point in question: which combination of gemstones, if you wear them together, would make you immortal. When they first talked about it, Mustafa was still going strong. He had worked in the Covered Bazaar in the alley of the goldsmiths; he had two young daughters, Atife and Yesim, and his wife Meryem was still singing around the house.

He decided not to go to Khalil's because of the sweltering heat and the mounting feeling that he could not breathe. He felt tired. *You've grown old, Mustafa, you've grown old.* People grow old. Only this town was forever young, with its smell of cardamom, mint tea, and the blood of young rams slaughtered in the bazaar.

He entered through the same back gate of the garden, hoping he would be able to steal unnoticed into the workshop. Indeed, Meryem hadn't returned. Last night's food had been left on the edge of the stove; the woman hadn't even washed the dishes. "She'll lose her mind because of Musa," whispered Mustafa, and went upstairs. For a long time, he hadn't tidied up his workshop, which only he was allowed to enter. The scrolls on which he drew the patterns, the wax cups for the molds, and the stencils lay in piles in the corners of the room.

He left the tote bag leaning against one leg of the table, sat down on the only chair in sight that had a backrest, and put his head in his hands. Thick, woody veins protruded more and more obviously at his wrists. From the weight of the books he had carried and the heat, it seemed to him that the bruise on his left hand had enlarged. Now, it looked like a wound. *I'll go to Leib Peres later; maybe he'll have some remedies to give me. I have too many bruises.* He laid his head on the table, hoping to doze off, at least until Meryem returned.

MERYEM

She carefully tightened her shawl and approached the quay. The sun had yet to rise, and the coldness hung above the dark sea. She knew that fishermen went out long before midnight to fish by firelight. Especially on moonless nights, light-hungry fish would surface, drawn to the flames of the cauldrons burning with coal and pyrite. Gathered in lively trains of transparent dresses, they would rush into nets like a flock of birds, flying hypnotically in the phosphorescent foam of the wake. Fishing by torchlight was a hunt based on the worship of floating gods, in which the victims drawn to the fire stood no chance against moving, unreal silhouettes. At sunrise, buckets of seawater filled with mackerel, gobies, sardines, and sprat were brought ashore. The silver spines of the survivors rolled, jumped, and divided into groups, and the fishes' eyes, like liquid mercury, silently begged for the right to live, even with their last strength. Some lived for hours and still wriggled in their wicker baskets when they reached the fish market. They would end up thrown onto large blocks of ice, and then be covered with fig leaves.

Meryem didn't like the spectacle of agony, of expected death, of hideous prolongation, but she had no choice. It had been more than a week, and she desperately needed to speak with Musa. To speak, to beg him, to weep, it no longer mattered. The burden of so many sleepless nights was taking its toll on her, and she wanted to know, one way or another, what her youngest son had decided to do and whether he would return home or not.

The long, blackish fishing boats entered the harbor one after the other, roped together, but Musa's boat and Emrah, his childhood friend, were nowhere to be found. The boys had come ashore earlier than usual, left their catch of fish, and departed.

The woman couldn't believe she couldn't see him once more, so she stayed for a while longer, arms wrapped over her torso and shoulders slumped, indifferent to people who walked by, raising their eyebrows at her. When the last bark was pulled to the docks, she realized how late it was.

She left the port and climbed the wooden stairs to the harbor's gate. The day had begun long ago, yet she had not prepared any food or done the dishes. Pale threads of dust beads clung to her; her back hurt. Meryem walked slowly, staggering from time to time. Near the cemetery fence, she stopped for a moment under the foliage of a lemon tree. When they had been brought into exile by Mehmed II, the Conqueror of Constantinople who found himself master of a depopulated city, her Armenian grandparents settled at Kumkapı in the Fatih district.

Wise and tested by life, the displaced Nazar Harutyunyan swiftly comprehended that he would never lay eyes on the Caucasus again and that the shores of the Sea of Marmara were just as good as any other sea. He named his first son Ibrahim and, together with his whole family, voluntarily converted to Islam. In the end, Meryem's grandparents rested in Kumkapi's small cemetery, where tall grass covered the stone slabs, with oblivion, sharp leaves and dust, and the memory of the steppe mixed with the salty air of the city of Constantine and Theodosius and Suleiman and Mehmed. Once again, the plants' blood, alive, triumphant, and relentless, buried all the dead in a row.

Mustafa taught Meryem how to read and spell a long time ago. Every time she visited the cemetery near the house, a place where she had no one, she always brought her grandfather's first Koran: an old book that Meryem kept on a shelf in the kitchen, and which was often covered by a white powdery layer when she sifted flour. Usually, she didn't open the holy book as she sat deep in thought in the cemetery; she just held it open in her lap with her eyes half-closed. In those moments, her dead mingled with the living, the distant cemeteries with the near ones, and the world no longer frightened her.

This time, Meryem decided not to go in. She felt uneasy as the tall grass whispered an unsettling oval sound downwind. She slipped past the cemetery wall and turned toward the house. She opened the door and saw that Mustafa was in his workshop. He had returned from Seraglio early. She didn't ask him why he was already home, because it was their understanding that she would only go into his workshop when he called her. She began to clean up the kitchen and, a few moments later, was surprised to find him wrapping his arms around her shoulders.

"What happened? Where have you been?"

She couldn't tell him she had gone to the harbor to find Musa, who had been causing her pain by dropping out of school, leaving home, and saying hurtful things. Or couldn't admit that, as the years passed, she found it increasingly hard to get along with the stranger she had borne.

She turned, looked Mustafa in the eye, and answered without blinking, "The graveyard."

It was past noon, and the light outside flickered slightly. Mustafa lowered his arms from around her and disappeared into the shady silence of the house.

TOMMASO

Like his father and his grandfather before him, Tommaso started in the silk trade. Spools and spools of fine silk, spun by silkworms, adorned the shelves of the shop in Genoa. Ever since he had learned to crawl, he basically lived in the shop, among all kinds of textiles, tailoring tools, and sheets of paper used for sewing patterns, held by carpentry glue to the lay figures. It took a lot of imagination to see in them the silhouettes of the curvaceous, full-bodied rich Genoese women who ordered their dresses from "Iacopo Serratore and Sons, Merchants, and Craftsmen," but imagination had not been a problem for Tommaso throughout his life.

Iacopo Serratore bought and sold wheat and wine, paper and silk, spices, and wax, without moving from his office on the first floor of a house in Piazza dei Banchi, because Iacopo Serratore wrote letters for every order, shipment, or request to officials. The first one was addressed to the person who transported the goods; the second to the person who received them; and the third one to the person who controlled the first two. Sometimes, in the case of a more complicated transport or sale, the letters flew in different directions, intertwined in a net, meant to let him know if anything happened to his goods.

The merchant Iacopo Serratore succeeded in business, because he commanded a secret army of letters, a habit not passed down to his middle son. Tommaso felt he could leave the house at any moment, a desire born when he was only a toddler and starting to migrate from the cradle room to the tailor's shop. He didn't resemble either his extremely ill younger brother Matteo, who captivated everyone's attention, or Francesco, the eldest son tasked with inheriting and managing the family business. His advantageous position as the middle child enabled him to spend the first part of his childhood observing the things around him, especially the hands of the apprentices in the tailor's workshop. They allowed him to play with the pincushions and fashion his own little fabric puppets.

He quickly learned to sew, to create puppets by filling with woolen yarns the brocade left over from the loose sleeves and hems of cloaks, to make buttonholes and borders, laces and seams, to dig out the silver threads knotted in the canvas with just his fingertips. When he was eight, he had seen his older brother pull a plank out of the floor and put his coins in a locked wooden box, so he pried out a plank from the floor of his room too, under which he hid his cotton-filled felt dolls. At first, he just played with them, like a puppet master in a theatre, but this bored him, and before long, he began to dress them up in day dresses and evening gowns, tunics, puffy pants, and hats. By night, he dreamed them up, and by day, he created them — deep slits and oversized sleeves embroidered with ribbons and trimmings, slender necklines, and velvet in different shades and colors.

Before long, Tommaso could close his eyes and name by touch any type of material or stitch. And, of course, all this would have continued if, when he was fourteen, his older brother had not died of a lung disease and he had not unexpectedly gone from son number two to number one. All of a sudden, his responsibilities expanded beyond overseeing the shop occasionally, measuring materials, or closing customers' accounts; he had to know all the ledgers his father kept, write contracts, pay workers, and make trips. He made his first journey at sixteen.

Serratore Senior disliked the sound of guns. To him, only the voice of money mattered, and he could do business with anyone. As such, on the very few times he did leave town, he would go to Venice to buy damask and brocade — the best in the world.

They had arrived on a foggy day, and the teenager mostly saw nothing, but he smelled everywhere the scent that had entered the wood of the boats, the foundations of houses, the skirts and cloaks, porticos, and tapestries. Since then, he had never forgotten the greenish moss of the lagoon — not even in the hot, dry, crumbling days of later Constantinople — nor his first encounter with a prostitute. By the time he'd stepped onto the water-rotted steps of the villas, where gondoliers helped you with bored attention, he'd known nothing but the hurried embracement of maids through the cellars — like unfinished deflowerings.

His father chose the prostitute, told the woman to take care of the boy, paid her, and left, leaving him alone with her, more scared than curious, in the poorly painted red room, with dampness along the window frames. The middle-aged woman came over, pulled down his pants, grabbed his penis in one short movement, and began to move it gently, caressing it tenderly until it swelled, and brought it close to her mouth. The boy watched in horror as she opened her mouth, the bluish gums, and he closed his eyes helplessly. She repeatedly touched him, with an ever-deepening movement, until a thin stream of semen spurted through her chapped lips. Then, she gave the boy a cloth to wipe himself with, slammed him down on the unfolded bed, and sat on her haunches on top of him, rocking like a ship on the waves.

In no hurry, she opened her dress even wider and, grabbing both her tits with skilled and voluptuous movements, bent down and buried his face in a mountain of hot flesh. Then, slid over him rhythmically. With the eyes closed, nearly suffocating, Tommaso entered the woman's body — and swooned. Something that never happened again, not with Giovanna.

Giovanna was the youngest daughter of Eduardo Taviani, a *popolare* from Mollasana who, by virtue of diligent efforts and the ability to cultivate his relationships, attained a position in the management of Genova's commercial bank. Since its establishment in 1407, Casa *delle Compere e dei Banchi di San Giorgio* had surpassed the political power of the Doge and become one of the best-known banks in Europe.

Unlike Florence, Repúbrica de Zêna, La Superba, as Petrarch called her, had a strong aversion to the exercise of authority by the old aristocratic families and loved money. Everybody looked with kind eyes at such alliances between families if they were meant to increase wealth. Both Eduardo Taviani, the banker from the lower class, and Iacopo Serratore, a merchant from father to son, knew very well how to do this.

The future parents-in-law arranged the marriage, and Tommaso accepted, without giving it much thought. They told him the girl was beautiful and very clean, that she would make healthy children, and that she could read and write. More than enough for him. He saw her, all in all, three times before the wedding, but in the short time they spent together as married people, they didn't fight once.

Tommaso liked everything about her: the coyness with which she approached him with drooping eyelashes, the taste of the *pasqualina* cake and the *farinata* baked by her hands, and the quiet silence with which she let him possess her without helping in any way, just touching him gently as if she were not in the room.

Two and a half years later, when she passed away while giving birth to their daughter, Tommaso struggled to realize if he truly missed Giovanna. They rarely spoke when they were alone in the bedroom, and they spent most of their days apart. Many years after, by candlelight, their bedroom's curtains would periodically slide back and forth. Nothing more.

He arrived back in Genoa ten days after his wife's funeral. When he first saw the newborn, the child slept peacefully in the nanny's arms. She seemed the most fragile and unnaturally white human being he had ever seen, and the name Ariadne, meaning the most holy, came first to his mind, as if she had been made with the Spiritus Sancti.

Tommaso spent almost two months with his daughter without ever holding her, then left the baby with his mother, who now remained the only Signora Serratore, and he traveled even more. Whenever someone asked him about Ariadne's mother, he would say "my first wife," although he never married again. All his carnal encounters would take place with courtesans and widows from various countries, but none of them would ever again have the intensity of that night in Venice when a prostitute with dark mauve gums, who could have been his grandmother, made him faint.

ARIADNE

Iacopo Serratore used to lock himself up in his bedroom every evening with a jug of *pigato* and draw maps. After tidying up the tomes in which he kept his accounts and locking the shop door, he would check the locks and padlocks of the workshop once more, and then, undisturbed by anyone, he would spend a few hours before bedtime drawing.

His wife, Lucrezia, couldn't even recall how her husband began making charts, but she guessed he bought books from Pietro Battifoglio's shop. For a man so reluctant to leave Genoa, she found it almost incomprehensible that charts had become so important.

He had no contact with any cartographers and did not discuss it with anyone. His limited education in this field comprised two compendia enthroned on the table in the first-floor room: a copy of *Abraham and Jehuda Cresques's Catalan Atlas*, published in 1375, with the cosmography and astronomy section full of bizarre illustrations, and a copy of one of the four volumes of *La Fleur des Histoires*, where the Mappa Mundi depicted the Ark of Noah on Mount Ararat. Apart from them, no one would have any sign that Iacopo Serratore knew how to find his way around a map, let alone draw one. In fact, Iacopo Serratore drew maps because he never thought he could paint.

Every weekday evening, and sometimes on Sunday afternoons, he sat down at his writing table with a piece of parchment draped over his knees and would begin to copy the map in front of him, with a thin pen, using different colored inks. At first, his maps looked strikingly like the originals, but as Signor Serratore's father grew older, they changed. Because of poor eyesight, he relied on a magnifying glass to read letters and contracts, but when it came to drawing maps, he could no longer use it. With one hand, he held the pen, and with the other, the scroll, which kept slipping, and from that slippage, worlds migrated, shifted, and changed shape. Where he found an island or a mountain peak, the old man usually placed an ocean.

Especially when feeling tired or during the late winter afternoons when darkness fell early, it was easier for him to sketch a single map encompassing both the Sky and the Earth. He used to position the continents with high plateaus, the Euphrates, and China, either in the sign of Taurus or Capricorn. The muddy plains during *akhet* when the Nile spills over, the olive-laden hills of Smyrna, and the entire territory of Andalusia, landed all usually in Libra. The map always had a large reserve of islands that no one had yet discovered and which populated a new zodiac sign — the thirteenth and sometimes even the ones after that. Because of his superstitions, he never reached the sixteenth zodiac sign. Just didn't like the number six.

Year after year, the oval Genoese map with its upside-down sky became more and more Iacopo Serratore's world. Ariadne inherited this upside-down sky when her grandfather died. At that time, only four years old, she had already begun to explore and take possession of the house, just as the European royal families of those years sent messengers to plant a flag in distant territories that they later appropriated.

The grandparents' house was a two-story house with mullioned, unglazed windows and heavy wooden doors set in iron staves that opened with difficulty and created a sad and massive medieval feel, even if they weren't very old.

From the front windows, you could see the narrow streets that overlooked the Porto Antico and the Chiesa di San Pietro in Banchi, divided in two: on the ground floor, the Lomellini family's goods warehouse, open all week, and above, the church where the neighborhood merchants and their families crowded every Sunday. From the rear windows, you could feel the sea air mixed with the steamy coolness of the Apennines in summer and the cold gathered from the forested hills of Genoa in winter.

As the little girl walked down the hallways of the old house, it was as if she was floating down channels dug just for her. The most important ports of these canals: the room where she slept, her grandparents' room, and the attic where, dirty, covered with dust and unraveled cobwebs, her father's felt dolls still reigned.

In the beginning, she played with the dolls. Then, she forgot them, like she did other new toys she received each time Tommaso came home. She stopped playing with them, but she transformed them with unbridled enthusiasm. The same enthusiasm for change with which she would drive everyone mad in the future. Without thinking too long or wondering if the dolls belonged to her, Ariadne drew carmine mouths on them halfway down their cheeks and, with cartographic ink, eyes of all colors. In time, she became the owner of a colorful theatre through her own will; the others had no say.

After the old's man death, her freedom grew even greater, and she conquered the amateur cartographer's treasure trove, with no resistance. Signor Iacopo Serratore didn't bequeath his manuscripts to anyone in particular, and in any case, who would be interested in a pile of invented maps? No one could navigate by them. No one, with one exception. His only granddaughter.

At first, the little girl didn't touch them; then, as with dolls, she began to modify them — sea snakes with chicken legs and glowing eyes; orange birds with two heads, one green, one blue; a sad greyhound with a crown of tin slipping off its head; or all sorts of many-legged insects with crenelated bodies whose scale would have far exceeded that of an elephant, if Ariadne had ever seen an elephant. All around the freshly populated maps of flora and fauna, she drew a lacy border in recognition of the real life around her.

Those living in the house rarely stopped by the library, and in consequence, they didn't find anything related to the strange planet that spread like a mushroom culture, and the only witness of the transformation, the grandma, saw nothing wrong with it. Often, Lucrezia couldn't manage to tell the difference between reality and the maps' world hidden in the library, as long as her own son, Tommaso went away for more than two or three years to strange countries and towns, where people lived in round tents, moved around, dressed strangely, and spoke in unintelligible words.

Things changed for the better, to Ariadne's amazement, when one clear May morning, without telling anyone, Signora Lucrezia Serratore did not come downstairs to make breakfast, did not wash herself as she used to in a little white ceramic bowl festooned with blue flowers, and did not shout to her granddaughter to stop sailing around the house. Lucrezia

Serratore peacefully passed away in her sleep, leaving her granddaughter and Uncle Matteo as the exclusive possessors of the entire house. Fully free, Ariadne Serratore had just turned ten.

At the opening of their father's will, Tommaso and Matteo had decided that the older brother would travel and bring in new contracts, while the younger brother would remain in Genoa to look after the shop, workshop, and warehouses. Matteo felt wronged and showed this whenever he could, especially in front of his niece. It seemed to him that Ariadne confronted him with her incomprehensible occupations, her disappearances, and her sharp looks. He scolded her without interruption and she, more often than not, answered him back.

In the end, they found a middle ground. For the whole day, Matteo would only come into the house to eat, and the niece would never show up in the shop at any time — a very easy thing for the girl to do. She had no wish to be around her sullen uncle, tormented by gall bladder crises. The joy of the truce lasted only ten months. That's how long it took the distant Tommaso to return and put his affairs in order with the Piazza Banchi house and his daughter's life.

As a result of his prosperous business ventures, the man who took on the role of the head of the Serratore family accumulated a substantial fortune, ensuring a sizable dowry for his only heiress. He could think of any marriage for her: a rich merchant or, why not, the son of a nobleman. As such, the young heiress needed a proper education. It wasn't a rebellion of the felt dolls — subjects living in the house's kingdom where the girl reigned as an absolute monarch — that put an end to Ariadne's happiness, nor even her uncle's petty efforts to push her away, but her father's thirst for her education.

As a result, on the February morning that she entered the gate of the convent of Santa Maria della Croce, greeted by Sister Cecilia, who smiled and gently took her by the shoulders, Ariadne felt that her world had ended. Not the world of her grandpa's library, nor the world of the attic, nor of the workshop with the young women — the whole world, the whole planet plus the farthest universe, had all come to an end at the same time.

After shutting herself up in her room for a few days to mourn her fate, she came to understand that she could not resist the enlivenment that flowed through her mind — the same flow of livelihood that reminded her of the earthworms squirming madly when she poked them out of the damp soil of the back garden with the tip of a stick. Curiosity won out, and Ariadne started to navigate again through corridors and gardens.

MUSA

Crushed, huge, chalky pieces of the Byzantium walls lay strewn everywhere. In his desire to sail up the Danube to Vienna and control the Mediterranean basin with Ottoman *feluccas*, Selim the First had, after a thousand years, removed large pieces of Theodosius' wall and enlarged the shipyard from Galata to Sadabad.

Since working in Tershane, every time he passed the dry, broken walls, stacked like a pile of coral flotsam pulled from the sea and abandoned, Musa would wonder how many people had walked past those walls over one thousand years, and what their lives had been like.

After leaving the fish, he washed and parted with Emrah. He took off for Haliç, even though it was Friday morning and he had half the day off. Everyone attended the collective prayer, *Cuma Namazı,* except two old sailors from Izmit guarding the docks. He hadn't had a close-up view of the minarets' walls in over two years, and all he wanted at that moment was a few good hours of sleep.

He'd made a bargain with Emrah when he moved in: in exchange for half the rent, he would help him fish at night. That way, Musa would have enough money to buy food and, rarely, a sailing book. But because of this, he was always exhausted. From time to time, he thought wistfully of his childhood room, full of flags, and his bed at home, mended, smelling of dried chamomile and pine and covered with a white woolen blanket. Musa worked in the shipyard right next to the warehouses full of timber, hemp for the halyards, brought from Samsun, and cotton from Egypt for the sails. Every morning, they had to soak the long trunks of oak, fir, and ash, stacked row upon row, in water before everything else. Otherwise, they couldn't bend them.

At the warehouses, with two buckets of water in his hands, Musa began his day by watering the wood chosen for the hulls. By the end of the day, he had swept the workshop, prepared the cotton sails, assisted in caulking holes between the planks, and completed a slew of other simple tasks that bored him. Soon enough, he worked side by side with the craftsmen on the arbors, sleepers, decks, and masts. Every day, Musa imagined the wood's journey from sap-filled trunks to the supple, elastic, rounded arcs of the hold, slowly advancing underwater like the thighs of a giant woman.

They were starting to craft a Venetian brigantine, commissioned in Constantinople by a Greek shipowner. Half of it had its planks fitted, and the other half looked like a wooden skeleton of a fish, through which he could see white, semi-finished clouds and air lint.

Musa found an old blanket at the carpenter's shop and went into the unfinished ship that was leaning on its side. Since there was no one around, he stretched out on his back, trying to fall asleep. Through drooping eyelids, he could see the sky overhead, divided by the scaffolding into smaller skies. He knew that the wooden planks on which he rested his head would grow old, absorb salt, take on a calcareous covering of barnacles, scrape against rocks, and be worn away by sand, but, on that particular day before it took to the water, look smooth and perfect. If the boy were a Christian, he would say he felt like a grain embedded in the unfinished ship like Jonah in the belly of the whale, but he hadn't read the Bible, and Jonah's name meant nothing to him.

On the other hand, he wasn't a Muslim either. Mustafa and Meryem had baptized him, taught him the suras, as far as they knew, and sent him to the madrassa to teach him better. At first, he tried, and he even liked some of them, but as time went by, he stopped opening the Koran — which led to big arguments with his mother. After one such fight, when he first ran away from home, he ended up working in the shipyard.

"I've worked so hard to raise you! Your father and I worked from morning 'til night. I only have you; why are you doing this to me? Why are you embarrassing me?"

"How am I embarrassing you?"

"You don't go to school. Allah will punish you for not listening to your parents."

"I think Allah has better things to do than to punish me for not listening to what you say, and this only if he exists."

"What?"

The edges of her mouth had spread across her face to the wide-open eyes in which indignation had been replaced by despair.

"I think there is something, *anne,* but it's not in the mosques, the basilicas, or synagogues. It's not within walls, Mother, and it is not in those soiled books that clerics walk around holding in their hands while saying that they are holy."

Meryem's shadow was lumping and wrinkling as her sadness traveled from her face to her body:

"Who put these ideas into your head? Who? Emrah, who's starving with his fishing? Adem?"

Adem lived at the end of the street with his mother, who washed clothes in people's houses and spread gossip. Meryem didn't like that widow at all.

"Khalil, the Arab? Your father's friend, with all those stars in his head?"

"Khalil teaches me how to navigate by the stars without asking me for a penny. Emrah is orphaned and poor, and he's doing the best he can with his life. And about Adem — his mother is holding the purse strings..."

And he wanted to continue: ...like you try to do to me. But he didn't say it aloud.

"Anyway, you have never liked my friends, so why are we talking about this yet again?"

"Why do you want to know how to navigate by the stars?"

"Never mind that; listen to me. How many different peoples are in Constantinople? Turks, Arabs, Greeks, Kurds, Armenians, Albanians, Bulgarians, Serbs, Tatars, Christians of all kinds, Maronites, Copts, Papist Christians, and many others I don't even know about. By the goodness of the Padishah, they all live under the same sun in this city, and everyone has at least one place to pray, if not more, and all the places are swarming with preachers. If you listen to them, one says something, another says something else, and often, things are out of whack. So how do you know which is the true God?"

"Allah is the true God, and Muhammad is his prophet! *His are the heavens and the earth. Who could intercede with Him without His mercy? He knows what is before them and what is after them, and they do not comprehend from His knowledge except what He wills. His throne is wider than the heavens and the earth, the keeping of which is no burden to Him, for He is the High One, the Great One.*"

"I know how to recite verses by heart, *anne*. That's why you sent me to school — to teach me to say the suras by heart — but I keep asking you: how do you know? You, Meryem, the woman Meryem, without others influencing you, how do you know? Because some people who wrote some texts told you? Some people who lived at the time of the Prophet Mohammed or the Prophet Jesus or other prophets, or long after they were dead? God didn't write the Koran, the Tanakh, and the Bible but ordinary people, Mother! Why won't you understand they could be wrong without even knowing it? Anyway, I don't need anyone from mosques, synagogues, and basilicas to preach to me. I don't need to pray five times a day or to listen for hours and hours to an old mufti who beats his wife black and blue. I have my God."

Meryem's silence stretched between the two of them, heavy, uneasy.

Over the future years, Musa would travel over seas and countries, marry, have three children, and do things unseen and yet unheard of. But he felt closest to God that Friday morning when everybody else was at prayer and he was asleep in the belly of an unfinished ship, from afar looking like a Christian prophet he had never heard of.

The next day, when several people told him that his mother had waited for hours at the fishery entrance, he decided to return home once again.

ELEONORA

The Franciscan convent had tall, oval windows, finished at the upper edge with stone garlands, filled with rosebuds, chubby angels, and the long faces of saints. With their statues so close to the ceiling, only Sister Cecilia could catch a glimpse of their marble eyes. Sister Cecilia used to wander by each pedestal every day and say, "Good morning, Saint Thaddeus. Good morning, Saint Urban of Langres. Good morning, Saint Augustine." Seen from a distance, her almost comic silhouette seemed to worship the air. Only she knew what she worshiped.

During the time when the Christian Church had not yet split into the Western and the Eastern empires, a hermitage occupied this place. A handful of men, dressed in sackcloth tied with rope, toiled in the January frost and the August heat. They toiled with vegetables and pack animals, through the seasons, with the scorched earth from which they made bricks, with the diseases that ate away at their bones, with fevers and headaches, and sometimes while they exerted themselves, they felt a suppressed longing for their families. Their hard work, combined with devotion to Christ, would slowly transform the hermitage into a full-fledged monastery.

By the time these lovers of Saint Francis of Assisi had become masters of the place, people from several duchies already knew the monastery. Despite the poverty espoused by the Order, the settlement had plenty of land, an orchard, and several hills with vineyards, a domain which no one had taken from them.

A century later, following its transformation through a papal bull into a convent of nuns, Santa Maria della Croce flourished into a prosperous and remarkably autonomous convent, especially given the Church's austerity. Its independence was grounded in the Genoese rebelliousness as a sovereign city-state and the serendipitous circumstance of that time of the French Pope living in Avignon.

The papal bull stated not only the name of the person who was to take over the monastery with all its lands — the pontiff's aunt — but also the terms under which the monks had to move out and relocate. In less than two years, the whispers of young women replaced the harsh voices of men, and the long linen ropes, from which had hung long brown monastic robes and breeches, were then filled with white nightgowns, long-washed with lye, covering the breasts of girls just past puberty, both as a uniform and a shroud.

Despite nobody knowing where it had come from, one thing did not change: "Santa Maria della Croce." Many years later, Ariadne would conquer the convent with this name just as easily as she took over her grandparents' house.

Apart from Sister Cecilia, who spoke to the saints placed near the ceiling of the central nave of the basilica, Ariadne befriended Elena, a girl her own age, as well as the Mother Superior.

To the Serratore heiress, the Abbess reminded her of her grandfather, not because she drew maps — she didn't — but because she had a large library where she spent most of her time, in the uninhabited wing of the convent, next to the rooms where they dried and stored the herbs.

Chelidonium majus, Artemisia absinthium, Mentha, Crocus sativus, Cassia, Helichrysum petiolare, Pulmonaria, and many other dried roots, leaves, and twigs filled the shelves. The Mother Superior's hands had prepared each small jar or pot. Only she knew the secrets of poisons or the best use of powders, decoctions, tinctures, and ointments. Nevertheless, the collection of jars bearing labels in Latin was not the Abbess's greatest secret but another one, known only to Matilda, Agnes, and Clara, the kitchen's old nuns. Eleonora liked wine.

She didn't drink too much, but she drank night after night. By lights-out, when all the convent went to sleep, she would pour herself a cup and, by the flickering candlelight, in her childish, heavy handwriting, she would write wine labels. Her small letters had a curling braid wrapped around them like the shoot of a vine, and the large letters, sharp at the ends, often crossed over to the next page.

When Eleonora first started out as Mother Superior, she wrote on the label the year, the name of the vine variety, and just a few words, such as "Aglianico, Campania province, raspberry, black cherry, and spice aromas. Don't drink it before five years." But then, as she added herbs to the burly, man-high vessels in which she kept the wine, she began to add words and, by the end, whole phrases. So, the texts that were stuck to the curves of the fired clay amphorae looked like a cross between the local news and snatches of heroic poems, such as the *Song of the Nibelungs* or the *Song of Roland,* but in their Renaissance version, brought up to date by the Mother Superior.

The epics in the wine cellar had subjects such as the Peace of Lodi, concluded between Milan, Naples, and Florence; the death of Catherine of Aragon, daughter of Isabella of Castile; the Ottoman siege of Buda; and commentaries on Copernicus' *De revolutionibus orbium coelestium.* She liked to mix all these texts and interpretations with simple household notes, such as, "We hired craftsmen to repair the bedroom roof, restored the altar's *predella,* ordered six new oaken barrels, and bought beehives."

Eleonora used expensive, high-quality paper for the labels and precious ingredients for the ink she made herself. Like any experienced scholar, she respected her work and could not let the dense wines, bottled and sealed, sometimes for ten to fifteen years, have cheap labels.

She obtained her favorite ink by grounding lapis lazuli into a powder using different mortars and adding vinegar until it reached the consistency of pollen. The result: a bright, noble-blue ink that Eleonora thought paired nicely with her favorite winter evening wine — a Barolo di Bussia — complex, opulent, oily, with aromas of apricots, overripe pears, and licorice.

On one such winter evening, Ariadne, on one of her usual night walks, had accidentally opened a door she had never noticed before and discovered Eleonora. The tall woman in her fifties was trying to find a place on a table full of papers, quills, and melted candlewax while holding a mortar and a pestle in her hands. The door creaked softly on its hinges, without a knock, and the Mother Superior, dressed only in a nightgown, with her grey hair in disarray, turned in wonder, staring for a long time. The girl seemed to walk in her sleep, not leaning on anything, and her eyes, half alive, half staring, had large violet circles around them.

The Abbess put down the pot and said in a low voice, not knowing whether she could be heard or whether it would wake her, "Come in, child, and close the door tightly before someone sees you."

ELENA

A few months after she had started living in the convent, Ariadne woke up one morning in a spot of warm, sticky blood. Without making a sound, she reached out and grabbed the woolen shawl at the head of the bed to clean up the blood. The only thing she could think of was *how to stop the blood? how to stop the blood?* Then, she sat up in bed and thought about what she would have to do. She wasn't in any particular pain, but she didn't move, so as not to soil the bedsheets.

When Elena knocked softly on the door, as she did every morning so they could walk together to the refectory, Ariadne was still lying in bed, waiting. She said, "Yes," in a muffled voice.

"Enter…"

"What happened?"

Elena looked briefly at the soaked lump between Ariadne's legs, carefully pulled back the blanket, and grasped the shawl, drenched in blood, as if it were a dead stillborn, and vanished with it.

"Don't worry, you're not sick."

Ariadne was still silent, sulking. Elena took the basin — the same one in all the rooms — from the small table near the bed's headboard, carefully placed the girl's legs in the cold water, and began to wash her.

"Stay here. I'll be back in a minute."

Then, she rushed to her room and brought long, rough bandages, which the nuns forced them to wash in water that seemed a milky gray from the wood ash. All the girls had cracked fingernails and red stinging hands, especially in winter, when the cold in the laundry swept through walls and people alike.

"Stand up," Elena briefly commanded and passed the thin strip between her legs, then around her waist, and tied it in a knot.

"Didn't anyone tell you anything?"

Ariadne shook her head briefly, still gripped by silence.

"It'll happen to you every month."

In Ariadne's head swirled the white marble statues, which surrounded them: all those women with their legs covered with folds of stone. Untainted by menstrual blood, untainted by the blood of deflowering, untainted by the blood of many births. Is that it? Is that what faith protects you from? From the faintly sweet-smelling blood that covers newborns? From the first milk that gushes forth?

Vivid and unstoppable emotions surged through Ariadne's body, making her feel like it was no longer her own, as it both defended and repelled her. The morning of her first period, she collapsed sobbing on the bed in front of Elena. As if in a delirium, she saw herself alone, petrified like the marble statues, devoid of blood, of leaks, of saliva, kissing the feet of a crucified Christ. *I am the Way, the Truth, and the Life.*

Suddenly, she saw the escape! She would become a nun and spend her life around a pure Christ, surrounded by bleary-eyed saints and living women who didn't smell.

This way, I'll be safe, thought the twelve-year-old girl, raised without a mother, as she continued to sob. Her own body, curled up with her knees to her chest, tied as if in a web by the blood-stained rags between her legs, frightened her.

ELEONORA

She liked Ariadne from the first day, when Tommaso Serratore, a tall, sad-eyed man, brought her to the convent like a precious treasure. She watched how he carefully opened the carriage door and carried her across a puddle. The Abbess and don Serratore met only twice before. Once, so that he could see the convent and ask permission to bring Ariadne here, and the second time, in a hurry, when he came with the signed papers. The girls' residencies, sometimes spanning many years, required the written approval of parents, relatives, or any guardian. The nuns would take care of their education, and the family would pay a monthly sum.

Tommaso had agreed without negotiating. He had only an issue with the convent being too cold, so he asked if he could pay extra to heat his daughter's room twice a day in the winter. Eleonora turned him down gently but firmly; she wasn't going to favor anyone in the convent. "And besides, that's part of education too, isn't it?" The merchant hastened to approve, slightly embarrassed, and that was the solitary consequential subject they delved into. Otherwise, they exchanged pleas-antries and details about the history of the monastery, and in less than an hour, he departed.

Over the next six years, while Ariadne stayed at Santa Maria della Croce, Eleonora and Tommaso would become best friends. Without fail, he would notify her of his arrival by sending a letter in advance, and she would eagerly await his arrival to take his daughter home, usually for a fortnight or so.

No one knew when the merchant would come or go, and once, he was away for almost two years. When he did show up, both the Abbess and the girl looked at him in awe. He seemed just as tall but thinner than they remembered, and he'd gone gray. Eleonora poured him a glass of wine and asked what had happened in the meantime.

"I'll move soon."

"Move? How can someone who only lives at sea move?"

"I won't stay so long at sea or anywhere else. I'm going to buy a house in Galata. I'm in a deal with some Englishmen, 'Company of Merchant Adventurers to New Lands,' and I'm going to represent them at the Sublime Porte — a sort of commercial consul. But that's not the main idea. We're trying to discover a new trade route to the Moluccas for the spice trade, and maybe one through the North Seas to China. I suppose I'll spend most of my time in Constantinople."

She suspected all sorts of intrigues behind the decision — the English interests in the Indies, the new Spanish and Portuguese territories, or the Ottoman Empire's customs duties — but she did not inquire further.

Things like that bewildered her, and besides, she felt happy in her small monastic world. Any news that reached her had value only if she could embellish it by writing it in bright blue ink on wine labels. Eleonora wouldn't let anyone spoil her peace through politics, and one would have to burn down the convent, like the library in Alexandria, to get her out into the wider world.

"And Ariadne?"

"I'll take her with me."

Eleonora looked at him in amazement, for she had seen with her own eyes the passion with which the young girl embraced the legs of the crucifix on the left of the altar, how she rubbed her forehead against its painted wood, and the ardor with which she watched Sister Cecilia some mornings, wiping the sky-blue statues.

"She didn't tell you?"

"What?"

"She wants to become a nun."

"I suspected...."

In their few weeks together, he also observed his daughter's closeness to God. She never parted with her rosary; even outside the convent, she chose faded, unadorned colors for her clothes. Her hair, combed austerely and gathered into a ponytail around her head, gave her the sad, unfinished, virgin-like appearance of a vestal born after Rome's fall.

He said aloud, looking her straight in the eyes, "Will you let her?"

Then, his thoughts continued, "Will you let her, you who live among books, varieties of wine, and all sorts of plants that no one has heard of, that only I know how to find in the corners of the world and bring to you, just so you can have something to do and attain your peace of mind? Will you let her? You, who taught yourself Latin and Greek, not only to translate all sorts of compendiums but above all to fill your mind with something? With how many things? Will you let her, you who never accepted a man in your youth? Is this the life you want for her? You said Ariadne is like a daughter to you."

Eleonora would not look at him — did not make a gesture. She looked away, over his shoulder, toward a window, and her thoughts flew far away from the botanical treatises that surrounded them, far away from sea voyages to mysterious islands of spices. All these inherent escapes for Tommaso comprised a life always out of her grasp. Her aching, shuddering thought was of the flesh, the flesh of the man nearly twenty years younger than she, who sat before her on a high-backed chair, flesh she had never touched but only imagined, every time penetrating her, unrelentingly subduing her to his desires, melting her brain as an adversary only dreamed of, crushed and macerated in the ether.

"No, I won't let her become a nun. But I need time to change her mind."

"How long?"

"One year. What's your hurry? Do you want to marry her off?"

"Only if she wants to."

"She won't…"

"Are we talking about her or about you?"

Eleonora, who had been standing until then, broke in two and sat down on the other *sgabello* in the room, hiding behind the long table between them. A few tears streamed down her cheeks, and she quickly wiped them away with the back of her hand so they wouldn't show.

"We're talking about her! Of course, she doesn't have to end up like me…"

Then, she couldn't control herself and sobbed. He got to his feet, rounded the table, and forced her to stand up. He embraced her, pressed his lips to her temple, and whispered, troubled, "Forgive me."

CECILIA

Monregalese. A mountainous land, with uninhabited peaks and forests broken, from place to place, by small marble quarries, which the locals knew well. When the Medici family decided to compete with the Vatican's collection of art, the land became gripped by marble fever. Not only Piedmontese, but also Milanese, Genoese, and even Venetians came from all over. Bianco di Garessio, Nero Nuvolato di Miroglio, Viola Piemonte, Bigio di Moncervetto, Seravezza di Moncervetto, and Frabosa marble, it didn't matter what kind of marble, as long as big money paid for the beautifully polished blocks. A whole army of workers — each of whom spoke his own dialect and sat at the same table only with those of a similar standing — toiled from morning till night with their guesswork, the most important thing on the mountain; it had happened too many times that a block of marble, taken out into terrible heat, cut with difficulty, would end up in a sculptor's workshop before cracking under the chisel. A trickle of air would get into the flesh of the stone, and the whole thing would buckle, make long drawn-out sounds, and split, making everyone's work superfluous. They had to make every effort to choose a marble block free of hidden wounds from the beginning. And for this, they needed a stone guide.

As in Girolamo's case, the stone guides were frequently poor children raised near the quarries or orphans. First, his father died in the quarry himself, and shortly afterward, his mother, of poverty and illness. As he had only known marble up to that age, Girolamo turned to the only thing he knew. The same marble that killed his parents. In the summer, he wandered from one end of the quarry to the other. He inherited from an older boy a curved piece of wood, which he slung over his shoulders, and on the ends of which hung two large buckets full of water for the workers. Under their weight, at the end of the day, Girolamo's back muscles became long, aching cords stretched beyond their limits, and his bare heels bled from the bark of the crushed, crumbling earth, trampled by men and their pack animals. But it didn't matter, as everyone in the quarry knew him, fed him from what little they had, and tried to help him as much as they could.

Besides filling his role as a water bearer, when asked, he scaled the larger blocks to help with the ropes, or he remained near the workers: "Girolamo, give me this chisel, or tell Pietro to come over here."

At night, he found a place to sleep, in a cave, where he gathered a small fortune: a blanket, two pairs of socks, an old soldier's cloak, and two wooden bowls, one for water and one for food. He was nothing of a hermit though. In fact, he had loved women and wine all his life, his short life, and started at twelve with both. But he learned something for himself on those summer nights when he hid from the others and huddled in his cave: he learned to listen to the mountain.

In the wintertime, he would go to his grandmother near Mondovì and sleep in a small room in a dark alley with all his cousins, on top of each other, but in the summer, the mountain became his place to play and sleep, and run. Everyone knew he lived in the quarry, but they didn't know where exactly.

There seemed to be no height, no matter how far, that the boy couldn't reach.

In all the nights and days of the five summers he slept in the quarry, Girolamo understood something tacit to others: the sound. The sound of pink marble that reflected the color of the sun differently and had a soft, lacy vibration, the sound of white marble with thin, yellowish-grey edges, and the sound of black shining, which, even if you didn't have it directly in front of you, you could feel everywhere, because it came from the belly of the earth. Where others saw only stone and marble, the boy felt the sound. Girolamo had a talent for finding which stone to cut and could even hear the future statue within it. That's why, in a fairly short time, at the age of sixteen, he became a quarry's guide.

He got up every morning at sunrise and thought about what he had to do. Then, he walked up the mountainside, neither too fast nor too slow, until he heard it. If he felt a light hum underfoot, he would get down on his knees and put his palms together. That's how he'd start: first, he'd feel buzzing under his feet, and then, he would kneel and touch the sound with his palms. Most of the time, he would stand up and tell them: "No, it's too thin for what we need," and he'd move on. Sometimes, he could stop as many as a dozen times in a day. Other times, he would find the block on the first try. He was regarded as the best rock guide in Piedmont, and everyone assumed this was because he slept in caves. However, contrary to popular belief, his aptitude was just innate.

Every two or three years, he would go as far as Florence or further afield if someone specifically asked for him and also paid him to accompany to the workshop the marble, covered with a braid of stems and leaves of reed. When this happened, he would demand a large sum of money so that they would not contact him again. But he generally pretended to be ill and unable to leave. The town had all kinds of different sounds and, above all, it had human voices. Accustomed to the thin murmur of stone, a rustle on the border between stillness and air, Girolamo flinched whenever someone raised their voice at him. The brutal, vulgar sounds that gurgled from inside human throats scratched him, choked him, and clogged his mouth with a kind of cloudy cloth.

At first, after each trip to the city, he would sleep a few nights in the cave on the way back, to cleanse himself. Two years after he got married, he gave it up. His wife didn't like it. She didn't like it either when he spent too much time at the quarry or what people in the village said about him — that he went to other women's houses at night — and she didn't like the smell that accompanied him every time he did. The smell of ground limestone and thistles and sweat.

Girolamo died at forty-two, like his grandfather, like his father. The mountain never leaves you a long leash. All of Girolamo's nights and mornings in his forty-two years had been a supple, elastic umbilical cord all his own, which had let him get drunk, think he had fallen in love a few times, have three children, hear and befriend the rock. Eventually, the mountain ridge teeming with fragmented marble shards, which burrowed under fingernails, claimed its rights and asked the price.

One of the pinkish blocks fell on him and crushed him. A block that had been lurking near him for a long time, and when it broke away downhill, it dragged Girolamo with it. He lived for the two days it took the marble block to reach the city after they brought him down from the mountain. When he cried in agony, Girolamo felt as if the voices of those around him were stabbing his eardrums like knives and tormenting him. At dawn on the third day, death came to him simply, soothingly, calmly. A white space devoid of all sounds.

Girolamo left a wife, two teenage boys, and an eight-year-old daughter, Camilla. None of the boys inherited his talent and climbed the mountain with him. One became a shoemaker, apprenticed to his mother's brother, and another went to Bologna, and nobody heard of him again. Because the girl had been a burden from the beginning, Girolamo's wife decided to send her to a convent at the age of thirteen. She knew that no decent man would marry her daughter and that people would torment her.

When she met Ariadne at the gate, Sister Cecilia was already a nun well past her prime, talking to the statues in the central nave. They all saw her, every morning, as she walked past each marble figure, as she greeted them, lifting her fingertips in the air, "dusting the air," as the novices laughed, behind her. Camilla never turned her head or paid any attention to them, because although she had been born a deaf-mute, someone had inherited Girolamo anyway.

MUSTAFA

Fear reigned from the start. Clammy, choking, dirty. When he went to the palace, Mustafa felt it deep in his gut, even though he had known the Padishah for more than twenty years, and he had never once threatened him. The goldsmith struggled with the thought that a single person's pleasure could determine the destiny of all lives, and he couldn't get used to the smell of power in the shadow of the three Imperial Courts, or seeing the countless executions and heads strung on walls. He had become so afraid because once, in the folly of his youth, he dreamed of the most beautiful diadem in the world.

Fed up with the endless battles on the eastern border, the father of the heir to the throne thought diplomacy the better choice, and he chose a Safavid princess, Havva, one of the daughters of the Shah, as a wife for his eldest son.

To make the wedding ceremony a success, the young Shehzad, educated at Trabzon and passionate about art, announced a competition for all of the empire's jewelers. The most magnificent adornment, or the most exquisite ones, were to enter into the ownership of the imperial dynasty at the request of the proud Persian princess.

Mustafa heard the news in the Covered Bazaar and didn't know what to think. The Seraglio had workshops in the First Courtyard, where more than eighty craftsmen worked: some casted precious metals, some cut and polished the stones, some mounted them, and some made inlays. Apart from the imperial family, all the favorites in the harem, the Grand Vizier's family, the other viziers, and the pashas ordered ornaments here for clothes, furniture, and plates adorned with precious or semi-precious stones, for daggers and swords with hammered handles, for jewelry for wives, odalisques, musicians, dancers, daughters and sons, ministers, and pages. He could have been among the craftsmen here, with pay, as a *zergeran*, but chose to remain in the city. The long line of relatives of the powerful of the day swarming through the palace and the corruption of the Ottoman officials made him weary; besides, he felt everyone's fear. He didn't want to be around their fear because he was sick of his own. If he dared to enter the contest, long sleepless nights, countless drawings, and searches would follow. Whenever a need for exceptional craftsmanship arose, this was the result. If it didn't come out in one breath, he'd grind it until he couldn't get rid of it. On the other hand, the temptation to boast about the Persian princess's wedding wreath tempted him. But this would put his modest person in the way of the imperial family and in the public eye. Quite a danger. The fear's ulcer painfully gnawed at his stomach and intestines and turned his mind into a troubled liquor.

Mustafa not only worked in brass, bronze, gold, and silver but also in other kinds of hard-to-master materials, which other craftsmen shied away from, as they were not worth the effort, while all rich people of Constantinople wore much the same kind of finery. He spent his nights mixing the metals until they were tamed, softened, and took on the shine or, conversely, the dim mystery their master coveted. His desire to avoid foreign eyes and talk led him to covertly pour odd alloys at home; sometimes without giving them names. Bent into soft snakes, the metals obeyed him like a fakir, allowing him to do anything with them: arabesques that caught on dresses' shoulders or in the folds of a wide sleeve, thigh-high girdlers, metal honeycombs that blended into strands. He only encrusted precious stones when compelled to do so by a client's request. But even then, the light trapped for millennia in metals' glow guided him.

When he finished, usually after a few days, rarely a few weeks, he placed them in a wooden box, covered with velvet. The jewels had time to get used to their new life, and Mustafa, to forget the dismay and anxieties he had faced, and to look at them with renewed eyes. He felt as if he were tearing the ornaments from his fingers if some hasty aristocrat came to pick them up before their maker had decided they were ready.

That's why he lied to everyone but Meryem. If a silver-tone chain waistbelt artwork lasted two weeks, he said four. That's what he used to do with necklaces, hairpins, and earrings. When he could keep the jewel that the universe had sent him and that had kept him up nights until unraveling it, he would hand the innocent buyer only a copy, a second, a third copy, a beautiful, dead duplicate, devoid of its first emotion.

Which couldn't happen with the royal tiara. If the prince didn't want to take it, it would be very hard for him to sell it. Few in Constantinople would dare to wear such an ornament. The hardships, the torment to which he subjected himself, made his blood rush, and as the days went by, the billow of his doubts increased.

He attempted, like the other craftsmen, to figure out what Sheikh Safi al-Din's progeny looked like, but had been unsuccessful. It was one of Seraglio's most closely guarded secrets.

As the story went, the princess was svelte and not too tall, with lustrous black tresses that trailed down to her ankles. She walked over the floors, sweeping them with the bottoms of her robes and cloaks without touching them with her feet. The mother of the heir to the throne, the Sultana-Mother Halima, called her future daughter-in-law a witch. Even before the princess's arrival from Isfahan, she had filled all the imperial family's bedrooms with amulets: large blue glass eyes, eternally frozen, above the doors, verses embroidered like huge dead raven wings above the bed, around the windows, and on the walls, and the prince had been ordered by her to wear the entire Koran around his neck, mounted between delicate golden leaves and sealed by a minuscule precious lock, and a round disc of the same metal, with — "mashallah" — Glory to God, written on it.

Shehzad wore them all but still disobeyed his mother because he was in love. Despite the multitude of amulets and charms that made his bedchamber a small museum, he spent his time making gifts for Havva: sheets of the finest Bursa silk, covered daily with petals of purple tulips, her favorite color, sweets from Thessaloniki, carried in a double-walled wooden box for the ice blocks; pomegranates from Kerkyra or dates from Egypt; four Asil foals, born of Al Khamsa mares. He went to great lengths to delight his spouse. In the future, he would be compelled all the time to make peace between the Sultana-Mother Halima and the *birinci kadın* Havva, after the latter bore him a son. Until that point, he relished his break by pursuing quail and deer in the palace gardens and refining his archery mastery near the *cirit*'s grounds. Mustafa had no inkling of this and made no attempt to learn more about Seraglio's secrets or the wedding that was supposed to appease the two empires. His indecisiveness prevailed, and he walked around the house frowning.

"What are you thinking?" asked Meryem.

"I'd like to make another new headband."

"For whom?"

"For the Palace."

"And what's stopping you?"

"Many things, but, if I will do it, once, just once, will you try it?"

"Yes. But why do you want me to try it so badly?"

"That's how you looked when I first saw you."

"In your mind, maybe."

He burst out laughing and looked at her lovingly.

"Yes, in my mind."

For many decades, the jeweler's guild fair had been held on the fringes of the Golden Horn, with roughly five thousand tents built each year. There, for twenty days, you could meet strangers, sell, haggle, meet old friends, make new ones. Everyone rushed around the fair and talked from morning to night, and only the August afternoon's torpor could slow down the bustle. At that moment, the artisans would withdraw to their tents for a break, just to start all over again a few hours later at dusk, when mirrors that appeared to be covered in water made their ornaments enigmatic when illuminated by torchlights and candles. On such a day's evening, when the refreshing sea breeze and the air's sweetness could not tame the scorching heat, Mustafa met her.

Meryem, along with two other girls, came with her master to look for gold and silver threads. In the workshop, they made most of the carpets from wool on a wool warp, or wool on a cotton warp, with knots on two or three threads, but a few times a year, they could receive orders for hanging carpets for the walls or for the prayer rugs of the very high-rank families. For everyday fabrics, for yellows, they used saffron mixed with dried garden chamomile flowers and vine twine, but for silk carpets on silk warps, they used gold which, with the silver added at the end, played with the light spread through the rooms.

It was still terribly hot when the three girls stopped by a well while the market boys scurried around with trays of water and sherbet. Meryem's veil slipped down her back, and he could see her tight hair, arched neck, and frail shoulders. Nothing more. Her hair roots formed scraping curls of their own accord on the arch of her neck, weighted with tiny drops of sweat. Mustafa had longed to press his lips against those curls since the first time he saw her, but he made no attempt to approach the girls.

He waited until they left the fair and then followed the little group, walking slowly behind. That's how he'd found out where she lived, and then easily enough, who she was: a motherless girl, raised by her grandparents together with her sisters. Since the age of eleven, she had worked in the carpet-making workshop of an Armenian, who had a close relationship with her grandfather.

Their story had been straightforward: they were both young, impoverished, and in love. And since Meryem's father hadn't been around for years, Grandpa Harutyunyan said "yes" at the end of that autumn and agreed to let the young family stay with them until they had a house of their own.

A couple of weeks before the wedding, Mustafa bought a muslin *yashmak* hemmed with a Bergama lace border. On the way home, with thoughts of the veil split by knotted and intertwined mahram-like eyelets, Meryem's slender hands, and bright red hair, a tiara popped into his head. Money was tight, and all he could purchase was inexpensive gold, such as that used for prayer carpets. A few days and sleepless nights later, the tiara arched beneath his fingers, and if he lifted it in the air, the metal whispered its name: Meryem, Meryem.

She didn't see it until the morning of the wedding, when she struggled for a while to get the lace edges through the silver clasps. Mustafa let her do so only for the purpose of admiring her, then fastened the fabric to the two braided tails himself. With her hair tight under the *kashbastı*, Meryem resembled the mosaic portraits of the Byzantine empresses, which enriched the walls of basilicas with an uncanny beauty.

But she would wear no tiara and no laced veil. Mustafa tried in vain to change her mind. In their neighborhood, poor girls were not used to wearing finery, even on their wedding day. "What would people say?" she asked in her mind, many times.

The ornament sat sheltered on the rack of good clothes for a while and had disappeared the moment they moved, only to show up at his daughter's funeral. The twelve-year-old girl had struggled for more than a week with fever and headaches that came out of nowhere and then left this world.

For Mustafa, morning never came. In the darkness, he guessed how they washed her, how they wrapped her in a thick shroud that made her look like the mummy of a child pharaoh, how they placed flowers near her fragile wrists, trapped under the cloth. At the ceremony, when they lifted the frail body, he saw the tiara slipping out. He caught it out of the air and adjusted it back into place, as he had once done for the woman who stood behind him, stunned, as if she had died first and then their daughter. "I put the headband there as a sign of her wedding ceremony, so she could have a wedding too." His voice answered her out of the darkness. "That's good, good of you to do so."

ARIADNE

She adored Elena, and they were nearly inseparable under the watchful eye of Sister Cecilia, who let them be. She allowed them to run trotting down the corridors, hide for hours, not say their prayers on time, and disappear into the cellar dug directly into the ground, right next to the greenhouse; a place few people could enter.

Naturally, the Abbess could visit the cellar whenever she pleased, as could Ariadne, who had been granted a key when she began to assist her in picking therapeutic herbs, and then Sister Agnes, a large, grumpy woman. Sister Agnes had the keys to all the rooms, halls, pantries, and the cellar on her belt and resembled a banker who knew all the secrets of the convent rather than Saint Peter.

The day after she offered her the key, Eleonora sent the girl to bring her dried sage leaves and stems to grind in a mortar. Ariadne asked Elena to join her, almost dragging her friend towards the cellar's door.

"Let's go in."

Elena didn't think they should be there, and she looked very pale, as she did every time Ariadne suggested something new, against all rules, like roaming around the convent, sleeping together under the same sheet in summer, and huddling under a quilt in winter, or secretly taking books from the library that they were not permitted to read. Every time Elena accompanied her, Ariadne collected new feelings with the eagerness with which sailors, at the end of their strength, perched on masts, and waited, after four hundred days at sea, to see the land.

The cellar door appeared in front of them. It seemed to Elena that old souls rustled there, returning from time to time to where they had gone.

"Nooo, I'm not coming in."

Ariadne shook her head, making fun of her.

"Yeah, let's go in."

"Ariadne, wait!"

She followed her hesitantly, leaning with her hand against the wall reinforced with stones and wooden beams.

"Catch me, catch me…" She heard the voice somewhere in front of her, closer, then suddenly in the distance.

"Light a candle. Don't you have to look for sage?"

"Not yet… Come here…"

Mother Superior's man-sized amphorae resembled swaddled giant infants sleeping upright in the dry darkness. Ariadne pressed Elena's back against one of them and began to undress her slowly, with small gestures. All around, unsettled by their presence, the wine rose in the vessels through capillaries of air.

ELEONORA

The Crusaders used Santa Maria della Croce monastery as a place for prayer, barracks, and storehouses. By 1200, the settlement already had high fortification walls and more than ninety cells. The preparations for the Holy Land crusades would fill the courtyard with noises, neighs, the smell of horse urine, and manly sweat. On the occasion of one such expedition, they decided to dig a cross-shaped shallow crypt, not an integral part of the monastery's main body but connected to it through a channel. There, a chaotic jumble housed a collection of weaponry, lengthily smoked pork hams, barrels of wine carried in when spring arrived and it was too warm outside, and occasionally, important books and scrolls that demanded prudence.

Several centuries later, when she became abbess, Sister Eleonora inherited an empty cellar. Even though the Catholic Church had long been the region's traditional wine supplier and many families in Liguria were known as "Pittaluga" or "Sciaccaluga," which means, ironically, "he who crushes the grapes," nobody seemed to care for the vineyards of Santa Maria della Croce. Fortunately, the convent had grown wealthy, owing primarily to the aristocrats of Genoa, who sent their daughters here to learn, read, sew, memorize the catechism, and consider marriage, in order to become excellent wives and mothers. All the girls could think about was how they would leave the convent's endless corridors, how they would interact with men, how they would have maids and children. No one dared to tell them how they would have children, and the wonder stifled by viscous virginity floated in the air. In a religion that preached the miraculous birth of the Son of God from a woman touched only by the Holy Spirit, they deftly dodged the questioning. But at night, whispers filled the bedrooms with murmurs, and feet piled on top of each other, stroked to the point of fainting, while long, delicate fingers slipped beneath the bedsheets.

Almost everyone in the convent knew what was going on, but that didn't stop Mother Superior Eleonora from gasping in astonishment when she unlocked the cellar door one spring afternoon. It had been raining for two weeks, and it was still cold outside. Since the noises were absorbed by the soggy ground, they didn't hear her coming. The two girls had taken off their grey woolen cloth uniforms and wore only their thin chemises. Ariadne was atop, swaying softly as they both lay down. Elena had her head tilted back, her eyes closed, and she was breathing raggedly when her friend kissed her neck, murmuring: "my love, my love." Then, Ariadne slipped between Elena's wide thighs, pressing her fingertips against the folded flesh as she sought her out; the caresses wrapped themselves around them, lingering, paused, incomplete, only to begin again.

Next to the two naked bodies, the Abbess's blood brought memories of other lives, as mountain streams drag logs downhill. Eleonora felt a cold breath of air on her spine. She coughed briefly to make her presence felt, and the two girls jumped to their feet. Elena rushed up, trembling, and Ariadne dawdled, with sleepy feline movements. They picked up their dresses from the floor and pulled them over their heads. Eleonora saw the redness on their necks and cheeks, spread like eczema to their ears and the tops of their heads, and deciding not to prolong the punishment, she said in a quiet voice.

"I'll meet you in my library in an hour. You're not allowed to talk to anyone until then."

Turning on the heels, she added over her shoulder:

"Oh… and, Ariadne, after you lock up, please bring me the key."

She gave them an hour — for her, not for them. An hour she spent standing, measuring the room from one end to the other. Scrolls, pots of tinctures, and dried roots piled the table, in the center of the room, and she couldn't locate an empty spot to sit. Finally, she pulled up a chair, took her head in her hands, and began to think.

Instead of leaving, as the years went by, the vivid memories haunted her, unstoppable and harsh. She grew up, together with her two younger sisters, in a dark house, where their mother, almost always ill, would barely get out of bed in the middle of the day, only to lie down again at the first signs of dusk. An old maid who had been her nanny, and a youngster sent from the village to help ran the household. The women's world stretched from the first floor, the girls' bedrooms, the second floor, the maids' rooms, up to the attic. The men's world occupied the ground floor, where the head of the family reigned together with his four helpers.

Don Francesco da Pontremoli worked as a notary public. For about twenty years, their courtyard was filled with individuals who came and went, writing deeds, wills, dowries, and inheritances. Rumor had it that the notary secretly borrowed money as a pawnbroker, but this story had never been proven.

Everyone saw Francesco da Pontremoli as a respectable man with a successful business. So successful that he had to hire two new assistants: Antonio Parodi, the son of a baker from Sampierdarena, who ran a bakery near the Lanterna di Genoa, and Ricardo Montenegro. Ricardo was adopted from the age of two by a childless merchant in Savona; after the Genoese had conquered the small town and destroyed the port, his adoptive father, the cotton, jute, and hemp merchant, had become poor.

The presence of the two new boys in the notary's house marked the point at which the two worlds collided. It began with harmless whispers and glances. Ricardo, very pale, silent, and tall, had in his eyes a glint of passion that only men who become privateers, captains of armies, or saints have. A kind of internal, consuming flame. The combination of Ricardo's solitude and his apparent need for help in fighting his inner demons was what charmed Isabella da Pontremoli, the eldest daughter of don Francesco, and made her fall in love with him. His enigmatic smile was a plus.

Their love — long walks and short, almost violent hugs wherever they could — lasted no more than a summer and a fall. Most of the time, they wandered to Chiavari, along the banks of the Entella, or up to the Santuario di Nostra Signora del Monte, through the thick forest of silver pines, cedars, and oaks in the Bisagno valley. They made love standing, ears pricked on the lookout, strung like two clumsy bows. Usually, Ricardo would arrive at meetings drunk and spend hours telling her how he was going to get rich, and Isabella would watch his ink-stained fingers, listen to him, and dream. That was when she wasn't overcome with fear of being seen. After a few months, she didn't know whether she'd become addicted to the brief, brutal touches, all the twitching and biting and scrambling of bones, or to the unrelenting fear that twisted her life. All of this came to an end by the end of autumn, along with Isabella's pregnancy.

When Ricardo and his daughter arrived in front of don Francesco da Pontremoli and asked for consent, the notary felt for the first time in his life the need to break something. Kitchenware, windows, stained glass, it didn't matter; he longed for the thud of glass broken into a thousand fragments and made into a formless mixture. He didn't give course to his feelings. Sobered, tense, with a ragged voice, he asked them for two weeks to think, then disappeared into the master bedroom, only to emerge in the evening, with the pained expression of a hunted animal and inert eyes.

There are people who know the mysteries of the city, no matter how great these mysteries are. The priest, the doctor, and the notary. They handle all the secrets hidden in beds, in chests, in closets. Signor da Pontremoli thought for a few days. A couple of times, he even spoke to donna Giuseppina, though he didn't give a damn about her opinion, but she had brought him to the brink of madness, night after night, with her stifled sobs. Following the expiration of his self-imposed grace period, he concluded that his credibility would be undermined not only by having a girl with a flawed reputation but also by her marriage to a financially struggling man. And credibility mattered the most. He informed them of his judgment in the same hushed tones he counseled his clients on how to write their wills so that they could not be challenged. Isabella would go to Santa Maria della Croce until she gave birth, and his former employee would disappear forever from their lives.

"I don't want to go," the girl shouted, facing him.

He merely pointed the index finger of his right hand at her belly and said slowly, ignoring Ricardo entirely:

"If you think I'm going to let you destroy your sisters' marriages, if you think I'm going to let you destroy my three decades of work in this city and further destroy your mother's health, you're wrong."

At nineteen, passionately in love and not caring much for her mother, whom she despised and considered a weak creature, or her father's money, Isabella realized how her disgraceful marriage would affect her sisters in a community where everyone knew everything. Her long treks had not gone unnoticed, and neither would the pregnancy. Her sisters' chances of marrying "honorably" were rapidly fading.

"All right," she shouted again to her father — she was the only one to raise her voice, for the two men looked at her, the old one in frozen silence, and the young one in fearful silence — "but only until I give birth."

To her, the response sounded like a condemnation, even if it was yes. Isabella and don Francesco both understood that she wasn't ever going to leave that place, or at least not while her younger sisters and potentially acceptable husbands were alive.

"Ricardo, you're not saying anything?"

The thought of a wife and child terrified the only nineteen, no-income boy-man. He babbled that he wanted to enlist in the Doge's army, and he'd get her out of the convent after the pay allowed him to keep a family. Then, he got lost in the details of his objectives in the army, its organization, and duty assignments, as if Genoa was under threat and he was explaining defense to civilians. Don Francesco da Pontremoli turned his back and looked out the window, and Isabella cried.

She arrived at the convent a few days before Christmas, and the woolen socks and rough blankets didn't keep her very warm. The meager and feeble fire they lit every evening had disappeared by daybreak, when someone ought to have added more wood to the hearth, to keep it going. In the despair of her separation from Ricardo and the fact that she knew nothing more about him — family members no longer spoke to her and acted as if, as soon as the heavy door of the convent had closed, she had died — Isabella lost the child.

She woke up in early February with sharp pains all over her body. The Overseer Sister approached with a candle, saw the stains on her nightgown, and forced her to stand up in the darkness of the bedroom, where over forty girls slept, and go out so that they would not hear her. The nun covered Isabella's lips and drove her like a sack to the end of the corridor, into the small isolation chamber with a mattress strewn on the floor, where the chastised novices ended up. Here, the young woman struggled for two days and nights to give birth; delirious, howling like an animal, and wishing she had died. No one could hear her through the thick walls, and they had left only one sister, two years older than Isabella, to keep watch. The girl had sat beside her on the floor, not even on a corner of the mattress, wiped her heated forehead, dripped water on her lips, and held her wrists as she dug her nails into the flesh in pain. At the end of the second night, she managed to detach the child from her, like a tumor; a soft, bruised, and sad doll, no bigger than a palm. It was a boy.

Even after almost forty years of friendship, Superior Mother Eleonora couldn't understand how Sister Cecilia had so much power that she could help Isabella give birth that morning, when she was only a young girl just entering the convent. At that time, she had no way of suspecting that for years, they had been assigning the deaf sister to sit beside young girls in labor, washing them, helping them nurse their babies, and taking their newborns to bed. That is if they lived. Alive or dead, Sister Cecilia surrounded everyone with her care, even if they were bodies wracked with fever, wracked with grief, or freed of life, laid out on the alabaster table they used in the mortuary chapel. No infection, phlegm, pus, or blood made her sick. She washed even the deepest wounds, dressed even the oldest and most shriven bodies of nuns when they died.

That's how Sister Cecilia began to rule a kingdom in which only she could live. The convent's rules required them to burn all unbaptized stillborn children. The nuns couldn't bury the newborns in consecrated ground, since the Holy Spirit had not descended on them. But Sister Cecilia, in a solitary move of resistance that sometimes took great courage, hid them. Using corn husks, she crafted dolls that she torched while burying furtively the little heathens, in a secret cemetery, at the back of the yard. There, she sowed a seedling for every tombstone. Due to the mild weather, Sister Cecilia's chestnut trees grew very fast, and there ended up being a grove.

Every year, as Christmas approached, Sister Cecilia, with her statues and her little cemetery, was nowhere to be found. But thanks to her, the smell of sweet chestnuts, baked on the cooktop in the kitchen and shared out with everyone, filled the monastery with the distant breath of children who had never breathed.

When she woke up, Isabella asked in signs what she had done with the child, and Sister Cecilia showed her with her arms a swirl going up to the sky. She didn't want to lie to her at any cost, but she also didn't want to tell her about the little graves, so she wouldn't end up praying at her son's grave.

Prior to becoming an Abbess, when she would be solely responsible for the convent's apothecary, Isabella understood why Sister Cecilia refrained from approaching the chestnut trees close to the fence while planting or weeding medicinal herbs. And when she walked close by, she moved gingerly, as if tiptoeing on an invisible keyboard known only to her.

Sister Eleonora's suspicions had been confirmed when the Mother Superior at that time decided to cut the grass and prune the trees in the new orchard. Sister Cecilia sat on her knees for many days and nights, without moving, eating, or drinking water. And the entire time she kneeled in the orchard, praying, the sounds covered the convent. Mollifying, pure, inhuman; a murmur that did not let the sisters have a moment's peace. Soon, they realized they had no escape and surrendered, so the shoots continued to grow, watched over by their protector, Saint Cecilia of the chestnut trees.

Despite all of the strange things that transpired around her, the deaf sister did not harm anyone, and since they needed her so much, they let her draw the limits of her hidden world as she pleased, even though she didn't obey all of the convent's laws. For example, she didn't knock at any door, and this is why Eleonora was not startled to find Cecilia in the center of the room without hearing her arrive. *Had she already found out? Did she know?*

Of course, she knew. Sister Cecilia, the silent soul of the convent, the bridge between the dead and the living, could not have been unaware of the embraced bodies of the two girls, of their love and friendship. Elena and Ariadne, Cecilia, and Eleonora. It wasn't as if what was happening in the centuries-old monastery had never happened before.

"I know what you want. I won't punish them. But what should I do?"

Face to face, two women who had entered the convent a lifetime ago. Eleonora, tall, with grey, badly braided, uncovered hair — she had thrown her monastic veil over the edge of the back of the chair — and Cecilia, chunky, wrapped from head to foot, with her soft, everyday smile.

She took Eleanora's hand and pulled her to the window, showing her something. The Abbess first saw the cemetery of the children who had reached the heaven of angels, and next to them — the apiary. She sighed for a few moments, then nodded.

Eleonora took the cellar's key and ordered Ariadne to tend the beehives while forbidding Elena from sleeping in the bed next to hers. They moved her somewhere near the bedroom door, next to the Overseer Sister. This was the end of the beech wood, full of Pleurotus mushroom mycelia, of the dried apple peels thrown on the floor, of the forest moss, and the barrels of wine. The nymphs in nightgowns, sneaking in the crumbling air of the cellar, reading the chronicles, laughing unabated, hot milk stolen from the kitchen, yellow daffodils in clay jugs, the ink of green walnuts, seeping under fingernails like smoke, the pillow fights, the apple pie, the baked potatoes in wood ash, all had suddenly been replaced by the relentless August sun, the melted wax from the entrails of the beehives, the honey beads hanging haphazardly through the honeycombs, sunflowers, and pollen. Golden, bright, insatiable, bound together with ribbons of wishes and callings, the two girls had grown new bodies in a single summer.

MUSTAFA

In the end, Mustafa decided that the tiara would have fourteen butterflies, the same number as the princess's age, and should look like a hair net. He chose a very pure gold, brought from southern Anatolia, from Diyarbakır, along with precious stones, polished there. He worked each antenna individually under a magnifying glass, and — with pincers — covered the butterflies with a very thin enamel layer, worked in cloisonné. On the misty thickness of the enamel, he had mounted pearls, two small brilliants for the wings, and a ruby for the head. He would also have liked to adorn them with garnets and corundum, highly prized by Persian nobility, but he didn't have that kind of money.

When he finished, the filigree wings fluttered in the air and gave the impression that if the butterflies could just unhook their little legs tangled in the net, they could fly. He squandered the last few ducats on a large emerald, cut into the facets, mounted right in the middle. The golden threads of the diadem encircled the emerald and then broke loose, splitting into strands, descending freely on either side of the head, trailing the greenish glow with them, down to an algae-covered seabed. In the end, he had arranged the unusual, winged ornament on a bed of red velvet, in a box inlaid with mother-of-pearl, covered it with a milk-white cloth, woven by

Meryem at home, and waited for the diadem to settle and its ruckus to die down.

On the day of the contest, the goldsmith sat, like everyone else, in a long queue, not talking much to those around him. He knew those who worked in the First Courtyard, but it seemed like every known craftsman among the *Ehl-i hiref* jewelers was there: mostly Greeks and Jews, but also Bosnians, Georgians, Albanians, Russians, and Persians. They came from all over, attracted by the good wages and the exquisite work. Generally, the Ottoman aristocracy liked large gemstones kept as close as possible to their rough beauty. The direr your circumstances, the more you exhibited your precious gems to the world. Legend has it that, at the time of the construction of the Süleymaniye Mosque, the Shaikh Tahmasp spread the rumor that Suleiman the Magnificent had no more money to pay his army and servants and sent him a chest of jewels as an insult, which infuriated the great Sultan. As a result, he ordered Mimar Sinan, his architect, to crush and mix all the brilliants of the Shah with a mortar in the masonry of a minaret, later named Cevahir — the gem.

The goldsmith's turn came late in the afternoon. He had eaten nothing all day, drank only water, and was slightly dizzy. The back of his neck and shoulders ached from sitting still all day, and from time to time, he would wearily rub his waist to relieve pressure. As he kneeled in front of the throne, he could hear a dry crackling of wooden joints, and he said to himself: *Too many hours standing still in the workshop, Mustafa, too many hours. You'll get all stiff.*

The open jewelry box, resting upon a cushion in front of him, seemed minuscule against the grandeur of the Divan room, rendering the butterflies seemingly insignificant. This was not the fashion in which he would have wanted the diadem unveiled to the world, but he had no choice; in the face of imperial etiquette, no one had a choice. He kept his head to his chest the whole time and could see nothing but men's feet in all sorts of shoes, the boots of janissaries, and cushions on the floor. There wasn't a single woman around.

The empire's heir welcomed Mustafa while the light fell in the distance on a sandalwood screen. He heard a chuckle of surprise. Hidden in the next room, through the partitions of carved wood, Havva saw the open coffer and her wedding gift. The goldsmith received words of admiration, he was enmeshed in thanks, a page vanished with the tiara, he was instructed to stand up, and in less than an hour, all the other craftsmen said their goodbyes. Mustafa almost crawled home, collapsed into bed, and slept two nights and two days in a row.

Over the next years, after the then-young prince had been throned, the meetings remained mostly the same. A messenger would arrive and inform him of the precise day and hour he was expected to be at the Second Gate, where a black eunuch or some agha would be waiting, ready to guide him to the gardens or to the Sultan's private apartment. Apart from rows of flowers, the walls he passed, and the guards, he saw nothing, and apart from the usual polite greetings, spoke to no one.

Instead, he talked to the sovereign for hours, and not about hunting expeditions or the wars that kept the Padishah away from Constantinople for years, because His Highness showed the goldsmith ornaments brought from Tabriz, Venice, or India and inquired about their craftsmanship. Together, they leafed through Byzantine books with satin illustrations and alchemical treatises from Andalusia. They were occasionally disturbed by Shehzad, who had come to see his father, or by Sultana Havva, but they spent the majority of their time alone, sometimes for half a day, between cups of green tea with amaranth, cardamom, and rose petals. Over time, jewelry orders became rarer and stories more frequent, but Mustafa didn't mind that. Since the story with the imperial diadem, his name was known in Constantinople. Musa, he, and Meryem had everything they needed — and if the Padishah had only wanted to talk to him and nothing else, they would still live without lacking anything.

All the greater his surprise when one day, he woke up, and in front of the house, very early in the morning, before morning prayer, were four janissaries and a carriage with the imperial *tuğra*: the Padishah hadn't slept all night, and needed him. This had never happened before, and fear, his old fear, numbed by all the quiet years, used the road to Seraglio and was revived. As the door closed behind him, Mustafa pressed his forehead to the floor, almost breathless.

"Stand up," commanded the voice of one who knew no other way to speak. "What do you know about talismans and amulets?"

Talismans and amulets? Amazement smacked him dry in the face. *Allah Almighty, help me say the right words.*

"What every jeweler in Istanbul knows, Your Highness. Amulets are easy to make. You just need good quality materials. They are for everyone, and charms…"

Mustafa lifted his head a little and rolled his eyes around the room. He didn't understand why he was being asked. The place was full of them.

"…for a talisman to truly offer protection, you need to know the zodiac gemstones, where they can be found, the purpose of each one, and not only that, you need to know when to mount them. The same stone can bring good luck or not. It depends on when it is polished. There are stones that can never be worked together... You need to know the days of the year when it is not beneficial to make a talisman for someone..."

"You know enough, Mustafa, you know enough."

"Your Highness?"

"Have you ever made an immortality charm?"

Immortality? He couldn't believe his ears. He was dreaming, and the Sultan's voice spoke to him in his dream of things he had never thought of. The sun rose over the Golden Horn, and Mustafa fell into a prolonged, bewildered silence. The Padishah took a book from the shelf by the window and handed it to him. Pedanius Disocorides's *De materia medica*. The goldsmith had seen it in Greek, but he was also aware of the Latin and Arabic translations, and as best he could recall, it was just a collection of six hundred plants' descriptions, a few mineral principles' lists, animal remedies, and the recipes' preparation. He had never utilized the treatise, as he had no need to. He possessed neither the skills of a healer, an apothecary, or an alchemist, and he detested the latter. His customers usually wished to have talismans for health, longevity, wealth... but... immortality?

"You can take the talisman from here and make it for me."

The letters of the open book played in Mustafa's head. A saraband that left no doubt. The Padishah did not ask — the Padishah ordered.

"The Grand Vizier will give you money, as much as you need. And the gold, you can take it from here, from the workshops, or you can bring it from wherever you want. You have the complete freedom to choose."

Freedom? He sat back down on his knees and rested his palms on the floor so he wouldn't wobble. He found it very hard to believe that a simple combination of gemstones, however harmonious, could tame death like taming a stallion. He knew that nothing he could say to the richest and most powerful man in the world mattered because that man had already made up his mind. But why him? Why had he chosen him?

Seeming to understand the unspoken question, the Padishah added:

"I don't want anyone to know, Mustafa. Not in the palace, not in the empire. Do you understand?"

His voice went up an octave, suddenly distant and cold. Mustafa gathered all his strength, the last he had left. Bitter, tormenting saliva filled his mouth:

"And what if I don't succeed?"

"May Allah bless us and have mercy upon us, if it is written to succeed, we will succeed. If not... who will know? My honor will remain intact."

The goldsmith understood. When he walked into town, he looked smaller and ten years older. In front of him, the great dome of Ayasofia looked an awful lot like a hair net, filled with butterflies made of gold.

ELENA

They'd never shared that swirl of skirts and petticoats that comes when women run up and down stairs together. They'd never brushed each other's hair, creamed each other's cheekbones, or perfumed each other. All they had together were the rough garments sewed in the convent, the rushed afternoons in the cellar, the touch of the rosary passed from one to the other, warmed by the fingertips, after long prayers uttered in thought. They were both aware of each other's prayers.

It started with a mild fever, followed by coughing; the flames lit up her cheeks. During the last phthisis attack, Elena filled her nightgown with large blood stains, and before long, they moved her from the common dormitory to a small bedroom, and Eleonora was no longer watching them. On the contrary, she encouraged Ariadne to stay with Elena as much as possible, to bring her warm milk in the morning, and to read to her. Typically, the *Lives of the Saints*, but also hefty tomes with enigmatic names. Ariadne concealed them in the sack used to carry the bread for the poor who gathered outside the convent's gate.

In the morning, after Mass, Ariadne would arrive with a chalice of warm milk and the sack for bread slung over one shoulder, and she would compel the sick girl to drink all the milk. After that, she'd then pick a book — she always chose — shake out the dry crumbs between the pages, and start reading aloud. Thus, from the early hours, knights in armor, horses buckling under the weight of tons of iron, hoarse cries of attack, burst into the monastic atmosphere; at the feet of the two girls lay steppes, ponds, and pools of water, and the wounded men fell to the ground, mumbling unintelligible words. As she read, Ariadne changed voices theatrically. She rose on her toes to be taller, or walked on her belly, crawling through the marshes.

After Elena got sick, the summers came together into one season. Of pain. When she couldn't stand, they could only put her in an armchair and carry her to the bee yard. If the sky wasn't filled with the madness of the *sirocco*, they'd leave her in the shade, and Ariadne would read to her. On cool days, Elena would be wrapped in a shawl and doze, fatigued from the coughing spells of so many nights, while Ariadne worked in the apiary.

In the courtyard, you could see even more clearly how different they were. Elena, a ball of air, so transparent that, in the last months before the end, she could barely move without losing her breath, and Ariadne, swirling around her with fiery gestures. The reading, the beehives, the prayers, everything she did was full of passion.

When she didn't like something, you could tell by the lifeless movements, her ashen skin, and her wiped eyes, without the Serratore heiress saying a single word. There was simply nothing anyone could do against her will, and all the years she spent in the convent had not calmed her down, but only pushed her desire not to submit deeper into her being.

It was Ariadne who decided that Elena would stay in the garden every day; and it was also Ariadne who would go to the kitchen and rummage through the pots full of watery thin soups, containing just boiled celery, carrots, green beans, orec-chiette, or macaroni — meat only on Sundays. She would order what the sick girl should eat: chicken soup, soft-boiled eggs, and butter, even if you couldn't find it, and she would also show up with little baskets woven out of wicker, filled with raspberries, which the peasants from the nearby villages sold. It was not known how she got all this, but the sisters had a hunch: Ariadne sneaked out of the convent. Which was true. In Sister Cecilia's wild orchard — where it was easy to hide — Ariadne had hidden some men's clothing wrapped in a cloth. She had bought the clothes before last Christmas, without Tommaso noticing, too tired or too absentminded: a pair of trousers and a tunic she pulled directly over her undershirt, and a head tie, as the peasants in Piedmont wore. Often, after evening prayer, she would change her clothes and, under the canopy of the foliage, sneak through a gap in the fence. She gathered healing herbs, wandering the hills behind the mon-astery, keeping out of sight. Cowslip, burdock, oak, laurel, and willow. Ariadne breathed. Primrose, marigold, hollyhock, juniper, pine. Ariadne breathed.

At twelve and thirteen years old, when they had just become friends and decided to stay together all their lives, to become nuns, to have their hair cut, to have their names and destinies changed, to adore the Immaculate Heart of the Virgin Mary, to take the vow of chastity and to take care of the poor. Neither of them got to do it. Elena, because she died at the end of that summer, and Ariadne because she left.

ARIADNE

After morning Mass, the sisters filed out the side doors, the novices gathered in the study hall, and she hid behind the first confessional next to the altar. The braiding of the confessional walls cast flickering shadows on her face as she knelt before the Son of God. She prayed to the wooden body, to the coarse cloth around His thighs, to the strings, to the nails, but most of all, she prayed to the drops of blood, the size of swallow wings, carved with chisels and painted in shades of red.

"*O Jesus, I believe you are present here in the Blessed Sacrament of the altar. I love you with all my heart and desire that you may rest in my poor, humble, and repentant soul. I know that I am unworthy of such a favor, but I trust in Your goodness.* Let her live, let her live!"

Elena couldn't sleep at all because of the coughing, and every night, Ariadne was nowhere to be found. Calm down, they will catch you, you will get hurt, someone will hurt you, I beg you, don't leave the convent, they will see you. Ariadne was running in the hills: "*Thy love of souls will bring thee also into my heart, that thou mayest abide in me and I in Thee. Most Holy Mother, give me Your Immaculate Heart, to host my divine guest.* Let her live, let her live!"

At first, the anger came and went, and then it turned into rotten water with nowhere to drain. God gave her a mother she had never known, a father who was always away, and took her grandparents. God also brought her to the convent, where she met Elena. Now, Elena was slowly dying, and she walked night after night in the hills or threw herself, by day, at the feet of a crucifix carved out of a cut tree, trying to make Him happy. "*I embrace You, my beloved Savior, and I give myself completely to You. Give me only Your love and make me steadfast, so that I may never forsake You, but always do Your will.* Let her live, let her live!"

Although she had never done it for anyone before, Sister Cecilia allowed Ariadne to sit next to her while she washed Elena. The white body, which Ariadne had never seen fully undressed even when they were huddling in the cellar, was perfect. The blood on Christ's feet, the blood on Elena's nightgowns, the blood by which they befriended each other, had died together with the blood of the wounds in the chivalric tales; her skin took on a greyish nacreous hue; her nails were thin, brittle, the hair darkened.

Ariadne stood frozen, not approaching, nor touching her. She was convinced that if she delayed touching her a little longer, she could delay whatever was about to happen.

After they drew the veil over Elena, Ariadne pressed her lips to her cold forehead, then disappeared; she did not appear again at lunch, or at the evening service, or the next day at the funeral. They wanted to look for the girl, but Mother Superior told them to leave her alone.

She only appeared at the end of the service, when they were preparing to leave for the cemetery, holding a large sheaf of freshly cut branches in her arms and, beckoning the retinue to stop, she covered the body from head to feet with a green shroud. Because of Sister Cecilia's shoots, the coffin wouldn't close, so Ariadne had to lean on the lid with all her weight, and the sap spattered over the walls, the statues, a man's bloody-legged crucifix, and onward to the painted sky of the central dome. When they set off a second time — confined in her new life, Elena was foaming.

MERYEM

Meryem would turn transparent at will. Through her, you could see the tops of the bushes above the fences, the wings of the mills, the batik scarfs, and the turbans, the carboys of water-bearers, the trinket merchants' gunny bags, the caftans' hems, the bridgeheads, as she passed by them. She could sit for hours leaning against a door frame, and no one could suspect she was there. She immersed herself in the walls' stillness, following a habit acquired in childhood, when the universe only gained meaning if it followed a pre-written story. No twists and surprises. Later, especially if it was about her children, she could sense danger with the same instinct that birds use to fly under the wind. Instead of dismaying her with injustice, the deaths of the two little girls strengthened the woman's faith in Allah and drove her even further away from people. Musa came into the world when she was fully prepared to live in a country of one. Her son.

It had been a while since their home had been empty. Like her, Mustafa suffered terribly, especially at Atife's death, but he could no longer bear his wife's constant prayers and glares.

What brought him peace was doing something with his hands, being busy. He worked in the workshop set up in the courtyard until he fell asleep, and sometimes, he wouldn't return into the house; he slept there, on a wooden bed, without sheets, without anything to cover himself with, tired as if after a battle.

The unexpected pregnancy showed everyone that, from the very first days of his precarious fetal life, Musa had the power to turn his parents' world upside down. Because Meryem felt very sick and was vomiting all the time, Mustafa decided to move her loom into their house, to work the carpets here if she wanted. He hired three masons from Fanar and worked side by side with them. Out came a new wing with two workshops, Meryem's on the ground floor with an entrance from the kitchen, his upstairs. He also tore down the old workshop in the courtyard, rebuilt the brick oven, and added a shed for firewood.

The unborn baby spent the first weeks, after being weaned, surrounded by broken Greek, filled with all sorts of Turkish words from the builders, in the sound of rasps and saws, but mostly in the smell of food; Meryem cooked, day after day, for four men. Although she could only drink water and couldn't stand up well because of her dizziness, she managed to prepare pots of soup, trays of shakshuka with rice, lentil kofte, lamb *sarma*, anchovies, and all the boiled, baked, and roasted vegetables of Constantinople from the early hours of the morning. On days when she felt better and kneaded the dough, she also made *dilber dudağı, baklava* with pistachios, *bülbül yuvası* with nuts, *asure,* or just homemade cold yogurt, mixed with sugared fruit. "Efharistó, lady of the house," the Greeks said, and ate it all.

As fate had it, the new wing ended when she was three months pregnant, and nausea and vomiting disappeared like magic. The little tyrant in her belly allowed her some peace for a while, and the woman used the amnesty period to tidy up her workshop, the shelves on which she kept the wool and the old loom; Mustafa kept the beater handtree and changed the treadles. Then, she told her husband to take her bed out into the yard, and things turned upside down; she slept outside and he in their bedroom. Mustafa didn't listen to her. He left the bed in their chamber and made her a brand-new bed, first placed under the bower, then in the workshop downstairs.

In the seventh month of pregnancy, Meryem moved through the rooms like a small mountain. She spent her mornings toiling and her nights sleeping face-up in the garden. The fetus's head faced either Cassiopeia and Perseus if she laid facing the fuchsia and oleander bushes by the fence, or the Big Dipper, Arcturus, and Serpens Caput, if the woman turned away. The drawing of so many skies that were strung night after night made her dream of a carpet for the child, and as she did not know whether it was a boy or a girl, she thought of a sky full of stars.

She hadn't been anywhere for weeks, but for the rare occasion of a woven sky, she decided to go to the Bazaar accompanied by Mustafa. Meryem had to see the wool for herself because not all of it looked the same. The wool on live sheep, from the flocks scattered across the plains of Anatolia, sheared twice a year, shiny and mellow, differed from that of the sheep and rams slaughtered at *Kurban Bayramı* or at the palace's thousand-guest celebrations. The wool of the dead sheep appeared to be mingled with a thin, invisible hemp or flax strand and was a drab, greyish color, making it difficult to spin. When they returned home, after hours of picking, weighing by eye, and asking twenty merchants, she was satisfied. The wool for the unborn being in the family, girl or boy, had not a speck of death in it.

After Mustafa carried her two large brass pots into the courtyard, chopped the wood, and lit the fire, surrounded by little cloth sacks full of powder, Meryem began to dye. She chose the yellow from a mixture of safflower, sweet reseda, onion husks, birch leaves, wicker twigs or yellow clay, and the blue from the woad. First, she ground the leaves in water for a long time, until the colors came out, then boiled them, left them to cool, squeezed the plants, and strained the juice. The green, the Prophet's color, was made from indigo with resin; for the brown, she used mostly walnut husks and leaves; and for the red of the fruit, flowers, leaves of wild apple, thyme, and rose petals or carmine, the colors strengthened with borscht, lye, bluestone, or whey, if she had any.

Though her back hurt and her legs looked like stumps stuck in Mustafa's old slippers, she sat for hours by the cauldron, dipping her wool fleece over and over again, either in boils or in ice-cold water. She would settle down only after all the color in excess was removed and after the yarns were washed in several waters mixed with vinegar and then dried.

Unlike the architects, Meryem didn't draw battle scenes or hunting scenes, the faces of dignitaries, sultans, dervishes and princesses, waterfalls, mountains, plains, seagulls, wild horses, tulips, and egrets before weaving. This is why, always with a pencil in hand before he poured wax casts for necklaces or earrings, Mustafa simply didn't understand how Meryem's round and oval arabesques and medallions came out like that. He'd asked her several times what the spell was, and each time, she'd given him the same answer, "I can see them in my head." The way from head to hand was not her business — it was Allah's business. Allah, the Merciful and Compassionate, who binds all things together, and it was also He, inshallah, who allowed her to make carpets.

Dyeing the wool took some time because Meryem couldn't make up her mind about the sky. She started with orange followed by gold and finished with dark red and blue. During the day, she dried wool that was ready to be spun and laid it on the fences, and at night, she spread it around the house to keep the dew off it. Every evening after *akşam namazı*, Mustafa ate in a kitchen that was either orange, gold, or red and green, and if he somehow got up at night to drink water, he could hardly find his way through the woolly maze. When the time of birth neared, in the center of the carpet sprouted the tree of life, with fruit-like round hearts, and at the end of each twig, a *nazar boncuğu*. A tree with eyes. After so many days leaning with her belly against the loom's wooden frame, the stretch marks on her skin weaved into warp.

Musa came into this world easily. In the cradle made by his father, surrounded by all the auspicious signs woven in the carpet, he sucked, grew, and slept peacefully, which didn't stop his mother from having forebodings and fears. That he wouldn't like her milk, that he would hurt himself, that his gums would hurt, that the djinns would steal his mind.

As time went on, things didn't get any more dangerous for the baby — but as the woman's forebodings never ceased, every year on the boy's birthday, Meryem wove a new carpet.

The stars that you could see in Istanbul in summer with the naked eye were not always the same. The colors changed, and the skin's stretch marks in the loom's texture faded, but the tree with the eye charms hanging in it like wind chimes was there, in the center, getting taller and taller. In her redeeming love, Meryem crafted a precious carpet full of signs of health, wealth, good fortune, which, Allah willing, would pass from her son to her grandchildren and then to his grandchildren. Sometimes immersing herself in walls, and things, and always in the people she loved, Musa's mother held the world tightly on its hinges, weaving.

ELEONORA

Each time, Tommaso brought her, in addition to wine, prayer books with Persian miniatures, Bukhara carpets, parchments, large pieces of quartz from Egypt, silk scrolls, nutmeg and cloves from the Moluccas. Eleonora kept only the unusual and rare gifts for herself. The rest, however precious, was destined to the corruption of the papal establishment. Marble statues, red velvet, Bruges lace, or the finest olive oil traveled to Rome via mysterious routes, but most often, they arrived at the papal nuncio in Genoa or the summer residence of a cardinal.

When she was appointed Abbess, Eleonora tried to make as many alliances as possible, but she soon realized that politics was beyond her. She didn't have enough diplomacy to navigate the world of Vatican men in skirts, and the cardinals and vicars didn't pay much attention to the reclusive, slightly nutty Mother Superior, who was careful enough to send gifts and money.

The few inspections of the Pope's representatives were met by a gaggle of young girls who knew how to embroider, weave, sing divinely — and who read the catechism every day. Besides, the fresh air, the view, and the tasty food did not encourage too much harshness. And their life would go on like this for a long time, as long as the Abbess of Santa Maria della Croce was able to send gifts twice a year, for Christmas and Easter. For that, she needed donations.

One of the most generous donors was, from the beginning, Tommaso, who realized how fiercely Eleonora defended the oasis where God was not threatening, where punishments were mild, and where the Father of Christ was strikingly similar to the old presbyter who conducted their services and lived in the convent, in a little stone house.

He loved the tall woman, who did not inspire carnal desires but knew all the fickle corners of his soul. A vague, tangled suspicion. It was not Christian sin that kept him away or prevented him from confessing the truth, but her presence, astonishing, unheard of. He confined himself to sitting in a sgabello beside her on rare afternoons, savoring the smell of black cherries and smoke from the Nielluccio — a Corsican wine similar to that of Sangiovese grapes — listening to her as she talked about chivalric novels, still plants and herbs laid in the herbariums, or grape varieties.

"Do you always blend Sangiovese with Sagrantino?"

"Only when I have it — Sangiovese is too harsh for me. Now, I don't have it."

"Didn't I send you a Montefalco last year? When I was in Umbria."

"I have finished it, Tommaso. I drink your wine to the last drop; I don't pass them on."

"I never asked you what you do with what I bring you."

"Because you know."

"How's Ariadne?"

"Ready to go, I guess… She has good days and bad days, but she seems to have calmed down. The change will do her good."

"It's a different world… a whole different world. She's only seen the streets of Genoa and the convent up to this age. I hope she doesn't find it too difficult…"

Eleonora pondered for a moment whether to tell him about Ariadne jumping over the fence dressed as a boy, about her nightly walks and everything at Elena's funeral, but decided it was better not to; he had to find out for himself what his daughter was made of.

"I don't think he's going to be in too much trouble, and then she has to leave anyway. Didn't you say you didn't want her to end up like me?"

"Like you?"

"Like me, a prisoner in a convent, among books."

"Ah, that! I didn't mean to make it sound so bad…"

"Nor is it. Look around you, in Genoa, or in any city in the world where you travel. What would I expect? What awaits a woman like me, who has no freedom to do anything, absolutely nothing, that she wants? Whereas here, I'm free. I can really do what I want, within certain limits."

"Yes, but behind walls."

"We all have walls, only mine are visible. Didn't you tell me how hard it was to decide to settle in Constantinople? How suffocated you feel, whenever you have to sit for hours in the antechamber, at all the meetings with the Sultan's dignitaries, the French ambassador, the Venetian *bailo*? How hard do you detest their ploys?"

"Yes, but I sometimes escape on a caravel and go where I want. Nobody holds me back."

"I don't need to leave. I have the caravel here." Eleonora strokes her temple with her finger.

At the corner of her eyes, a yellowish spot was already announcing the liver disease that would kill her in a few years.

"Will you bring me Ariadne again? Will you come again?"

"Of course."

He never returned but continued to send gifts and letters. The first, from his house in Genoa, where he stayed for two months after Ariadne's departure from the convent, until they left for Galata. Then, regularly, several times a year, from all over the world: Muscovy, Feodosia, Licostomo, Caladda, Akka, Gibelet, Famagusta, Lemnos, Malta, Al-Qāhirah, Tabriz, Nishapur, Herat. Their only link: the letters. They were more like a diary, a confession, and Eleonora, with the eyes of a woman in love, saw the world as he saw it. She kept all the pages, but not tied with a ribbon, in a locked drawer. She kept them in the cellar, hidden under a beam.

Shortly after her death, the cardinal appointed a young and ambitious nun from another monastery as Abbess, but not before asking for the important manuscripts and barrels of wine to be sent to him; she could do whatever she wanted with the rest. The new Mother Superior agreed without a second thought, partly because she had no desire to get into a fight with a cardinal and partly because she saw in everything the work of the devil. The new Abbess had also heard about Sister Eleonora, that she died of drink, and the first place that fell victim to the Abbess's desire to cleanse the convent and wipe out sinful traces was the cellar. She threw away everything on the shelves, including the bags of herbs, the pots of potions and tinctures, had the door closed with two large iron bars, and burned the remaining books, but she could not find the thick stack of letters that spoke of impossible journeys and forbidden cities. They traveled through time to become a paste of mold mixed with dust, which dripped onto the floor and disappeared among the stone slabs, taking with them into the earth the worlds of a sixteenth-century Genoese merchant.

KHALIL

He wanted to tell him that it was not good to be around Power. Power is like mercury — it kills slowly.

"You've tried so hard to please the Padishah, Mustafa, you've tried for twenty years. Didn't you ever suspect that at some point, he would ask you for something? It's so unnatural, your connection."

"No… Who knew he thought like that? Will you help me?"

"Of course, I'll help you."

He took Dioscorides' book from his hands and opened it. It was Abdullah ibn al-Fadl's translation.

"I don't know this one. I only know the scrolls of Yahya Ibn al-Batriq. There are several Arabic translations, and they have handwritten notes. Who knows how and when a translator or just a scribe who got bored added the drawing of your talisman for immortality?"

"Am I the victim of a scribe who lived several hundred years before and was bored?"

"No, you're your victim if we're talking about victims, but that's not the case. I'll also look for the original Greek version if I find it, but I'd wager that Dioscorides wrote nothing about immortality. He accompanied the Roman Emperor Nero's army. He was a surgeon. He must have seen enough death, and if he found a cure for it, we would know by now."

"What should I do?"

"Find the stones, and make the talisman according to the drawing in the book. If the Padishah chose the codex with this design, then that's what he wants."

"What if he doesn't like it or says I'm cheating on him? He'll kill me eventually. He said nothing would happen to me, but I feel like he's going to kill me…"

"I'd say just calm down and think about it for a while. How does one prove immortality? If the Padishah dies first, he won't be able to kill you, and if you die first, you won't care. As long as it's just the two of you who know, you're safe. How long did he give you to make his talisman?"

"He didn't mention anything about that. Unless I need gold or other materials. I'm so sorry, now, I'm so sorry…"

Mustafa threw aside the clothes on the bed and a few rolls of paper and tried to sit down. Khalil lived in a single rented room. Clothes and things were thrown on top of each other, in a mess that only the astrologist could manage. He had never married and wanted to own a house; he dressed, talked, and acted like a committed bachelor. After her husband died, his younger sister from Konya came to stay with him for a week and cleaned everything. Shortly after she went back to her children, the mess took over again. The only things that escaped the chaos were the astronomical instruments: quadrants, mechanical calendars, the astrolabe. Wiped, cleaned, and oiled, they sat on the table in the middle of the room.

He opened the tome and waves, waves of oval paintings, no bigger than a tulip petal, swirled under his fingers.

"Why are you sorry?"

"That I stubbornly made the tiara then, that he bought it, that we became friends…"

"I don't know if you two have really become friends, Mustafa…"

"Not like I'm friends with you, but I think he needs me if only to listen to him."

"That I can understand, but then why are you so afraid?"

"Those walls, Khalil. Can you believe it? There's something black there, oppressive. I can't breathe. Even when I walk through the gardens, I can't breathe. There's too much death."

"Dead men don't go anywhere unless they've completed their mission — and when you ascend the throne by killing all the men in your family, what can you expect?"

"But it's imperial dynasty law. What else could he do?"

"Kill all your brothers? To know that all your sons will be killed, except the one who inherits the throne? What law is that? Where in the Koran does it say that? I've spent enough time researching the holy texts. Do you know what it says in Sura Ghaffir about Allah? *That He alone is the Giver of life and the Giver of death, if He decides a thing, He says "Be", and He is.* How does this reconcile with the fratricidal law of the House of Osman? Since when did the Padishah take the place of Allah?"

"Don't talk like this in front of anyone, please. They'll accuse you of treason."

The words sounded corked, like old bells when they crack. Every time he spoke of the empire's rulers, Mustafa seemed to crumple, to fall apart.

"Maybe that's why he wants immortality, Khalil, to stop killing his children."

"You think he's too good. What if, in fact, he just wants to hang on to power as long as possible? Kings, shahs, and padishahs have sought immortality since time immemorial, and all they got was a grandiose tomb and a story that lasted longer, until other kings, shahs, or padishahs came along, and it too faded. All peoples' leaders need this chimera. It helps them get through their hard lives. Much harder than yours or mine, anyway."

"A poor astronomer who pities the Sultan of the world."

"No, just one man pitying another man."

Khalil was right, but sometimes, Mustafa couldn't understand his words. He wanted nothing more in life than to be a good craftsman and, inshallah, to have a good, peaceful life.

"I've known you for so many years and never knew what you really believed in."

"In the nature of things. God left things on Earth in a certain way and created us to live in the nature of things. What is above is below. What is in heaven is in us. I see El Baki — the eternal — everywhere: in mathematics, in the predictable movement of the stars, in the poems of Farid ud-Din Attar. *It takes a man with the heart of a lion to walk this extraordinary path; for the road is long and the sea deep and the journey is made in wonder, sometimes laughing, sometimes crying.* In this I believe, Mustafa. I believe you must live in awe."

"You sure are living in awe. You're closer to the hidden meaning of things than the bed you sleep in every day."

"It should be the only important thing in life. Isn't that what the magi, philosophers, and saints of all religions talk about? Once you find your way and begin your journey, what more could you want? Anyway, I can tell you for sure that by the end of it you don't need talismans, crescents, and crosses. You don't even see them anymore. Your breath is enough. It's the mirror of the world."

"You don't need talismans, the rest of us do — or, well, most of us need all sorts of things to touch or carry with us or pray to. My luck as a jeweler is that it's like this."

"And my luck as an astrologer who makes a living writing horoscopes. Otherwise, we'd both starve to death," the Arab burst out.

"Horoscopes you don't believe in."

"I don't have to believe; they have to believe."

"Don't you ever feel guilty when you write them?"

"Don't you ever feel guilty when you make immortality talismans?"

Whether he would succeed in making the talisman or not, Mustafa knew that his life had changed forever. He parted from Khalil less sad and afraid. In His unending kindness, Allah granted him a companion.

TOMMASO

Tommaso liked muslin, then lace, taffeta, batik, and chiffon best. He was in love with their waterfalls. After so many years of living at sea, next to other men, or between the shapeless veils — stretching from the top of the head to the ground — of the Ottoman women, it filled him with pride that he could dress his daughter in the dresses he dreamed of, design the bell of a skirt or an embroidered bodice.

The day after he brought Ariadne home from the convent, they looked for materials and colors together. For the evening gowns, an emerald green that matched her white skin, and red velvet to highlight her eyes. In a place where blond-haired women usually had light-colored eyes, Ariadne stood out for her dark eyes and the way she fixed everyone with her gaze. Bony-shouldered, too thin and tall to be considered a beautiful woman by the tastes of that time, Ariadne did not go unnoticed, and Tommaso knew it.

Unlike Genoa, for Constantinople, the merchant chose cream and pearl-pink muslin and chiffon for summer dresses, stamen, and cotton for light blue cloaks, and pale-yellow embroidered silk for shawls. In the sweltering heat and dust of the capital of the Sublime Porte, Ariadne had the freedom to move as she pleased, while ensuring that the concealed body shape under the gown remained unguessed. The wives and daughters of the Genoese merchants of Galata did not dress like Muslim women but took care to wear dresses with long sleeves and narrow necklines, and when they left the house, they covered themselves. Not necessarily out of morality — more for safety. He also ordered four straw hats with large brims and ordered his workers to cover them with veils that could be pulled over the face.

Under his brother's sullen supervision, the number of young women working in their workshop increased. Don Matteo Serratore walked past them as if they were made of plaster and hardly spoke to them when he brought dress orders into the workshop or asked for modifications. Unlike the other master, who used to go in and out twenty times a day, always with other drawings scribbled on corners of used paper, where on one side were the ruffles of Ariadne's petticoats, and on the other, long columns of figures from the bookkeeping of other years.

Ever since Tommas returned, the entire house had become imbued with new life. Under the indignant scrutiny of his younger brother, who was infuriated by waste, countless carriages arrived from morning to night and raked the gravel of the courtyard. Bouquets, fish, fine meats, fruits brought from overseas, pastries, and cakes — the festivities began.

Just as he had gone to great lengths to provide a comprehensive dowry to impress the society of Galata, Tommaso had identical intentions for the society of Genoa. Especially for Genoa, as the city-state served as a painful reminder for him. The name Serratore was not too old, and the money made in the East was far too new. Besides, the fact that he married a girl of a *popolare*, even a rich one, did little to help him realize his ambitions.

Apart from the fortunes he earned on each voyage and his position at Galata with "The Merchant Adventurers of England for the Discovery of Lands, Territories, Isles, Dominions, and Seigniories Unknown" company, Ariadne was the ace up his sleeve. Her marriage would finally legitimize their position among the Doria, Fieschi, Spinola, Pallavicino, Grimaldi, Serra, and Balbi, the powerful families of Genoa. In a republic in which the owners of buildings were obliged by decree to host state visits — hence the facades, arcades, inner courtyards, towers and turrets, palaces large and small — the nobility had a say.

Tommaso noticed Matteo's fierceness in rebuking him, but the long years of living among kadis, pashas, ambassadors of the European royal houses, sheiks, and knights changed him. Money was of no value to him unless it was transformed into glitter and luxury, things his tormented-by-gastric-ulcers brother could not understand. "He who does not tread beyond the borders of his city will never understand the one who travels across seas and countries," said Tommaso, and he went about his business, throwing coins left and right.

"Forget Matteo, I'm not spending your money."

"It's family money. It's also my father's money..."

Ariadne was the only one untouched by the turmoil. All those ladies and gentlemen who crowed their salons said nothing to her, and the festive dinners, often ending after midnight, anguished her. She had to wear a corset, entertain strangers — friends of her father's — and sit still for hours. Her cure was always to go for walks in the city.

Only, this time, she went out the gate like all the other people, in broad daylight, no longer jumping the fence to get through who-knows-what grove. She wandered through the town to Mandraccio and even further to the docks where ships left at anchor were unloaded and loaded by an army of human ants, with arms and legs. Wine and wool, spices, corn, olive oil, and furs all passed through the old fortress-walled port. You could sit and watch as if you were at the theatre and not get bored. Captains, pilgrims, Nubians, courtesans, fishermen, merchants, slaves from the Caucasus, gypsies, sailors, and priests on their way to the Americas or Gibelet. While her father spent hours in his offices by the silos, discussing with Sir Horatio Pallavicino — *merchant, financier, and diplomat from England* — the papers of merchandise and diplomatic documents with which Signor Serratore was to appear at the Sublime Porte, she wandered on the stone embankments and enjoyed the salt air, the wind that lifted women's skirts above their ankles, and the smell of wet hawsers.

As in her early years, she spent the nights walking the unlit corridors. The hallway to the cellar and the winter storeroom smelled pungent from the smoked meats and salami hanging from the ceiling on thick metal hooks, unlike the front gallery, full of stacked paper, from the accounting ledgers with their skin-shredded covers on desks damaged by wood-boring beetles. The smell of the corridor that led to the tailor shop changed all the time. The crumbling ooze of rolls of material that unrolled in waves to the floor failed to cover the swarms of faint smells: the soap the workers washed with, the infusion of walnut with chamomile with which they rinsed their hair, or the lavender grains in their garments, hanging in folds and creases. The young girls — women with children who had not come to work here — still dared to hope and dream that their lives would not be like their mother's or their grandmother's.

The upper stairs smelled of walnut and beech ashes and laundry ironed with a coal-fired iron, and as you climbed, you reached the realm of old smells that shared the attic with the belongings of the masters of old.

One gloomy day, when it was drizzling and too cold to go out, armed with a broom, several rags, and a bucket, Ariadne decided to clean the attic. The tools she snatched from the maid and hauled up there with difficulty were flung in a corner with a dry thud in an instant. Among the dolls dressed by Tommaso, a bundle of ostrich feathers, some of her grandmother's dresses crammed into open trunks, her uncle's wooden horse, beads, and spindles, she glimpsed Don Iacopo Serratore's maps. The painted parchments were covered with a thin, beautiful-smelling wax. She looked at them as if seeing them for the first time, picked them up off the floor, and clutched them to her chest. When she opened her arms, shivering, the scrolls slid softly to her feet. She unfolded each one to get a better look, then hung them on the wall.

That same evening at dinner, she announced abruptly:

"In Constantinople, I want you to buy me beehives. At least four."

"And where are we going to put them?"

"Didn't you say we have a house with a big garden? We'll find a place."

"Fine, we'll see."

"I don't want us to see, I want you to promise me."

Sitting close to her at the table, his lips pressed together, tormented by dark dispositions, as he always was when Ariadne was coming up to something, Uncle Matteo watched from the side the determined gestures with which the girl emphasized her words when she didn't want to leave any room for doubt. *My God, she's as strange as her father. Good thing she's going to Constantinople.* For him, the Ottoman capital was a dark place, where the Sultan could cut off anyone's head at any time, where men married countless times and spoke a broken language that made his skin crawl when he heard it at the harbor.

A week or so after the two embarked and he led them to the ship, Matteo breathed a sigh of relief. Alone, with no one left to argue with, he decided that no one must know of his family's madness and locked the attic, with a padlock whose key he soon afterward misplaced. For years, no one asked for it, until, after everyone returned to Genoa, Ariadne's youngest son — named after his father and his grandfather, Moses Tommaso, but they called him Moso — unhappy that the key could not be found, broke the rusty lock.

Hidden under the burden of dust and the pile of Genoese winters, Iacopo Serratore's maps, resembling beautifully colored relics of saints, greeted Moso.

MUSA

Flags and kites. The four-cornered cloth hung crookedly, and the five-year-old boy struggled to catch it on a stick.

"Musa, what are you doing here?"

"A flag."

In the *mahallas*, the city's districts, the older children's kites were always hanging among the branches of the linden and Judas trees, drying in the hot air like transparent giants' nails. Only Musa didn't make kites. He gathered all kinds of pieces of fabric — which Meryem kept in a sack, where she put scraps of wool and other warp threads — and strung them on a rope: red next to red, yellow next to yellow, green next to green. Then, he drew faces on them.

Mustafa asked Meryem one night when they were arguing about him.

"What do you mean when you say Musa is giving faces to the kites?"

"I mean, he makes me sew their eyes and mouths with thread."

"And why are you sewing them?"

"That's how he plays with them. Why not sew them?"

Another time, she tried to find out from him:

"Musa, don't you want a kite?"

The little boy shook his head.

"No, I want a flag."

"Don't you already have enough flags? Let's make you a kite for *Eid al-Fitr* when the festival starts. We can go to watch the janissaries' parade with their trays of baklava, then come home, eat sweets, and fly the kite. What do you think?"

Musa agreed with the idea, and for the three days of the *Shükür Bayramı* holiday, he was caroling in the town with the boys from their alley. Then, in less than a week, he was back to his cotton cloths, scraps of silk, and skeins of colored wool hung haphazardly around the yard. The hot summer air in Marmara made them buzz gently through the bushes, and Meryem kept tripping over the strings.

In fact, the flags were faceless. All he could manage to sew were longer lines, like palm lines, which the boy needed to be able to give them a name and call them out. He made the first three — the Stallion, the Snake, and the Moon — from a kitchen cloth. Then followed Padishah, Ferik, and Vali Ahad, the army's chieftains. Hatun, an adventurous flag, blue and white, hung around with some and others. All the kids in the neighborhood had nameless kites.

By the time Musa was nine years old, the flags' forest spread across the courtyard. Meryem stopped defending him to Mustafa, and it was she who opened the discussion after the child went to bed.

"I don't know what else to do with him. He never asks me for anything but to sew flags. He started making them himself. He gathers string and thin sticks, then ties the flags together. And every day, he changes their order."

"Leave him alone. What's the harm?"

"Nothing to me, but he's not like other kids. What if people laugh at him?"

"Who's laughing?"

"The boys he brings into the yard to see his armies."

"I don't think they laugh, and afterward, no other people really care about him but us."

"Yeah, but he's not like them…"

"I'm not like the others either…"

For reasons other than Meryem, the goldsmith was also worried. He didn't give a penny what people in the neighborhood said, but it seemed to him that Musa's wish to make new flags, even in play, was too dangerous for the times they lived in. Whenever the Sovereign of the Sublime House of Osman, Sultan of Sultans, the Commander of the Faithful, went off to war, the black threads of the horsetails that were mounted in a circle in *tuğ* fluttered in the wind with a mysterious hiss. Behind them, the red flags with the insignia of the double-pointed sword Zülfikar, inscribed *"Lâ fetâ illâ Ali, lâ seyfe illâ Zülfikar,"* "There is no sharper sword than Zülfikar and no hero but Ali." Everyone knew these kinds of flags, but Mustafa had never seen in his life the trapezoids, diamonds, and rectangle shapes with black lines that Musa sorted by their color, "to speak to each other." He kept asking the boy how they spoke to each other and got the same answer: red for war, green for peace, and yellow for truce.

The last time they fought over flags, Musa was eleven or twelve, and some flags were still hanging around the yard, but they were larger and had more insignia. After the boy finished with the scraps of silk, cotton, and wool, he started to use waxed paper and scrolls, materials that Khalil no longer needed; which is why the colored flags often had writing in long-forgotten languages on their other sides: in Byzantine Greek, Syriac Aramaic, and eighth-century Arabic.

"Musa, gather up your kites' ropes in the yard because tomorrow, I'm putting caldron on the wood fire to make quince jam."

"Yes, *anne*..."

"Can't you just pack them up for good?"

"No, I still want to see something."

Mustafa appeared in front of them out of nowhere.

"When are you going to be done with these toys?"

"They're not toys... Imagine, *baba*, flags or sails of the same colors for all the ships. It doesn't matter what fleet you're from, what country, or what language you speak, everyone should understand the same thing... I mean, the same color or sign should be the same for everyone... Do you understand, *baba*?"

The boy's voice sounded low, tormented, indecisive. In Mustafa's mind, thoughts started swirling. *Ships with colored sails? Flags that would mean the same thing for Egyptian feluccas, Portuguese caravels, Spanish galleons — and Ottoman kayaks? What was going on in his mind? And, even if he could make insignia for the flags, who was going to pay any attention to Musa, the goldsmith's boy?*

A few weeks later, after the apricot jam, fig jam, and rose jam had been already boiled, the colorful pieces of cloth, parchment, and paper disappeared from the yard. Musa carefully folded them and placed them in his room in a corner. The talking flags were silent for a while, and Mustafa and Meryem thought they were finally done with them and breathed a sigh of relief.

CECILIA

One night, Eleonora started bleeding out of her mouth, and by morning, she passed away. Sister Cecilia watched over her for more than three weeks after she fell to bed, wiped with a wet cloth her swollen belly as if she were pregnant with twins, and in the last month of pregnancy, slept on the floor beside her bed as in the old days, listened to the feeble babbling.

Pentecost cast a mantle of slow silence over the convent while the burial ceremony faded beneath the falling petals of cherry and plum trees. When the wind blew more flowers away after dusk, and as the lap of the monastic robes brushed the earth whitened by petals on their walk to the chapel, Sister Cecilia vanished.

Sister Agnes from the kitchen noticed first, and then everyone found out because Cecilia stopped coming to Mass. They searched for her for two days, rummaging through the chestnut trees, through the herb garden, through Eleonora's library, where she used to be in the past for long hours, and in the rush of the arrival of the new Abbess, their search soon stopped.

Although she had only seen her in her dreams, the new Mother Superior was afraid of the flying nun and her chestnut tree grove; she did not go near it, but she also did not have the courage to have anyone cut it down. Books could be burned, doors could be bolted, but the thought that a woman could wipe the statues out of the air and know what you meant without hearing you frightened her.

Sister Cecilia left a few hours after Eleonora's funeral, at dawn. She took with her only a rough, rolled blanket, where she laid her head when she rested, and a wooden begging bowl. She decided to walk all the way to the village where she was born. At night, she slept on church steps, wrapped in a blanket, and by day, she walked. She arrived in Mondovì after four days, on a summer evening at the end of June, when the butterfly-weed bushes were just coming into bloom and the air was filled with the smell of cranesbill flowers.

She passed the house from which she left more than fifty years before, without stopping, and climbed into the abandoned quarry where Girolamo had been a stone guide for years. As the men finished carving the blocks, they moved on, to the other side of the mountain, or to another mountain, so the old quarry stood before her, chipped, cracked, with pieces of marble overturned like pieces of a broken wall, with stone wounds all over the mountainside. Sister Cecilia, renamed again with her birth name, Camilla, pressed her forehead to the first deserted block that came up in front of her and stood there, smelling it, caressing it, talking to it, without moving her lips.

Then, when the sun was already halfway up the sky, and the marble steamed up from the heat, she got up and started looking for the cave where her father had slept as a child. She found it easily enough, but after that, she had to go down to the nearest village for water. In the mornings, she fetched water, then wandered among the rocks all day. Far too young to remember Camilla or her family, passing stonemasons were astounded to see a nun hopping through the quarry's massive, upturned funnel. They only knew she was a hermit who spent her nights in the small cave. She didn't shy away from them, but she didn't seek people's company either. She was here for the stones, and she said goodbye to them at length, thoughtfully, unhurriedly. Some still retained the touch of Girolamo's fingers; others were foreign to her.

On the thirty-ninth day, she went down for water for the last time. She hadn't eaten anything for six weeks and was very weak. On her return, she laid on her back on the blanket and waited. Like the people at the convent, the stonemasons who were on their way to work saw that the nun had disappeared, but they suspected that she had left.

By the time some kids, who climbed the mountain to play hide-and-seek, found her, it was already autumn, and Camilla was a small wizened mummy. Some came and lowered the child-like body with a wheelbarrow made to carry tools and buried her in the poor man's graveyard. They didn't know her name, and since no money was found on her, nobody was willing to pay for a stone cross. A priest who arrived in a hurry said a few prayers and nailed a wooden cross to her, made of two branches tied with string. The following spring, the cross collapsed from the rain, and the grave, covered with grass, white sweet-clover, and a few wild vine shoots, was no longer visible.

Then, the flights started. Camilla discovered, to her surprise, that her worldly flights, such as when she soared to the height of the sculptures in the basilica's central nave, became effortless once she was free of her bodily restraints and all the toils of the realm she abandoned. She made her first flight in the sleep of the new Abbess, who woke up, covered in sweat, convinced that she had dreamt of the deaf nun. Camilla didn't linger long; she had shores, plains, country roads, and mountain edges to find; she had fortresses and cities to explore. On the way back to the cave in the quarry where she continued to take shelter, she usually stopped to see what had changed in the monastery and to frighten the Mother Superior. Every Pentecost, all the nuns at Santa Maria della Croce could swear that a swirl of white air passed over the chestnut trees, making them sing.

PART TWO

CONSTANTINOPLE

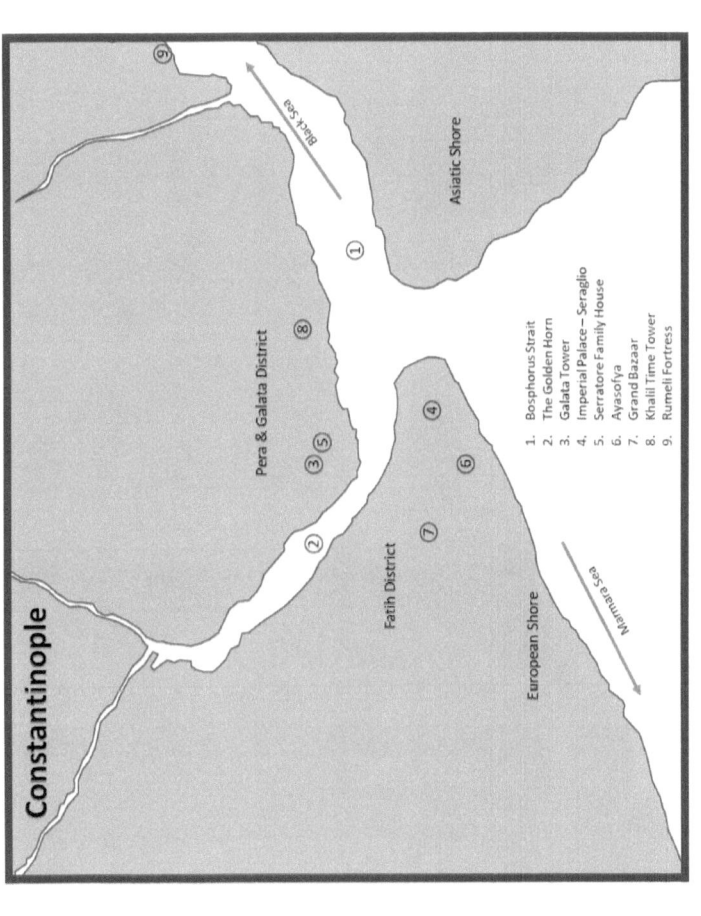

Constantinople

Black Sea

Asiatic Shore

Pera & Galata District

Fatih District

European Shore

Marmara Sea

1. Bosphorus Strait
2. The Golden Horn
3. Galata Tower
4. Imperial Palace – Seraglio
5. Serratore Family House
6. Ayasofya
7. Grand Bazaar
8. Khalil Time Tower
9. Rumeli Fortress

STAVROS

He told them several times that he was going to build an inn at the entrance to Galata — and he did. He found a caravanserai, a dilapidated building with a tavern and a row of dingy rooms, where one had to be far too tired to be able to sleep. Or blind and odorless. In the thirty years since he had bought it, the inn became famous among travelers. Rooms to suit all tastes: the cheapest above the stables, the next category for those more affluent — tradesmen, servants, small shopkeepers, people with families — who arrived at the Palace with demands, and finally, the large rooms on the first floor, reached by a staircase shaded by lime trees and clad in vines, which weren't for everybody. Two large blocks of houses, a hammam, and a couple of shops where one could buy some food, sweets — and if you needed anything else, the Covered Bazaar was not far away.

In the upstairs rooms, heavy curtains kept out the light, soft carpets held back footsteps, and beds with carved canopies wrapped in velvet, witness to untold nights and days, had no memories — and not just of reckless minutes of love, but also of political meetings. Especially of the latter, Stavros tried to keep himself apart, despite the Grand Vizier sending his scouts to watch over him at least once a week. The Greek, always cautious and ready to earn the benevolence of the emirs, pashas, and aghas who stepped into his establishment, trusted very few, and even fewer could he call friends.

The Genoese's house was a few minutes' walk, and Signor Serratore was in the habit of inviting his guests to the inn, where, in front of a sumptuous table, sprinkled with plenty of wine, alliances were made and unmade. Ambassadors from England, Spain, and the Holy Roman Empire spoke of colonies, tobacco, fruits, and vegetables with names never heard of before, galleons full of gold at the bottom of the oceans, new weapons, slaves, and pirates.

Tommaso knew all the foreign dignitaries and many of the Ottoman officials because people would hear that he could procure anything: sable furs from Ivan the Terrible's country, spices from West Africa, *gabardina* from Damascus, paper and silk from China, musk from Tibet, even brocade with gold or silver thread, woven by Genoese enemies — the Venetians. When he was younger, he even traveled as far as China by land. He knew where you could hire Armenian guides — the most prized because they were also bodyguards, he passed through the Zoroastrian cities, slept in Bukhara and Samarkand, and knew the Genoese families that had lived in the Middle Kingdom for hundreds of years. Tommaso Serratore often sent to the Grand Vizier's chancellery rounded bags of *sultanin* or a fur coat, although he did not need such zeal, as he had no real enemies in Constantinople. Most of his acquaintances in Galata and Pera, and even in Seraglio, needed and valued him as a representative of the "Company of Merchant Adventurers to New Lands," later called just the "Muscovy Company."

He had known the Greek who arrived from the Peloponnese from the time Stavros could barely grow a mustache, and the Genoese had helped him with some missives to be exempt from taxes when the inn was still being built. The goodwill of the high-rank officials could be bought, but not with little money, so eventually, Stavros paid his dues. That made them share together the ins and outs of the imperial administration. From sunrise, stocky, short-legged, and with his belly spilling over his belt, Stavros would scramble up the stairs, into courtyards, to the stables, and through the kitchens, until the middle of the night, when he would fall flat onto his bed. And he was honest as one could be in Constantinople. In a city famous for the unpredictable nature of one's fate, where one could go from being a vizier or pasha one day to facing death the next, two foreigners — a refined Genoese and a diligent Greek who worked harder than his own servants — managed to amass wealth.

Assets were written off to the imperial treasury, families were thrown out into the street, and the names of the unfortunate fallen were wiped from the lips of acquaintances too fearful of their own fate to fight for any injustice. Similarly, the Genoese merchant and the Greek innkeeper learned the customs and were doing well. They built their homes here without any mention of returning to their native places or their intentions to do so. For more than a thousand years, Constantinople had been conquering the souls of those who came to find a place and then, having become nobles or beggars, at the pleasure of the deceitful goddess Fortuna or Allah, stayed until death. They got used to the sight of the Golden Horn, the Bosporus, the dust, the crowds, the starry sky above Ayasofya, and the calls of the muezzins, even if they were Christians. They got used to the heavy food, the sweets laden with honey, hazelnuts, and almonds, the covered faces of the women, and above all, they got used to the smell of power that wafted from the place where lived the world's Padishah, the Sultan who ruled a third of the lands marked on the maps of Piri Reis.

Ever since Constantine the Great decided to make Byzantium, founded by the Greeks of Megara, a second Rome, it was the city of greatness and decadence — where even the last soldier from Seraglio could become the apple of the Padishah's eye-breathed power. The smell of power, heavy, stale, greasy, ruled over all of them.

Tommaso came downstairs after meeting a Baghdad merchant and saw Pelagia through the kitchen window. The thin woman, dressed mostly in black, so serious that, though she was a widow and still young, no one dared joke with her, had attracted his attention long ago. She worked as a cook, but when there were lots of guests, she also helped serve.

The Genoese looked after Stavros, and in a few blinks, the Greek appeared beside him, as if from the ground. One of the almost incomprehensible things: Stavros managed to be anywhere in the inn at any time.

"Good afternoon, don Serratore. How can I help you?"

"Don Serratore? Come on, Stavros, don't be so polite. I want to talk to you."

The innkeeper shook his head, and they headed for a side door.

"I want you to sell me Pelagia. I'll buy you another slave. You can go to the slave market and choose any woman, no matter how expensive."

The astonishment on the Greek's face froze their smiles.

"Pelagia is not a slave; she works in the kitchen because she wants to, and she earns a wage."

"No?"

"No, I was friends with her husband. I advised them to come to Constantinople in the first place. When he died, she said she wasn't going back there and asked me to give her a job."

"And do you think she'd want to come to my house? I've brought my daughter, and I need someone I can trust. Ariadne doesn't go anywhere, she doesn't talk to anyone, I don't know what to do with her. What do you think?"

"I say we can ask her."

They called the woman and told her to sit down. Stavros began to praise the Genoese's nobility of soul, the beauty of the house on the hill, and the endowments of the girl she was to serve. Here, he adjusted reality a little bit, for he had not met the girl, but it was clear that he sincerely wanted Pelagia to say yes. It seemed to him that the cook had struck gold; should she give her consent, a good living for a single widow in Constantinople awaited her. He leaned over to her to clarify, mixing Peloponnesian Greek with the Turkish of the street. Tommaso remained silent, glancing at her black headscarf, which she pinned above her head in the manner of Greek women, and from which two dark braided tails jutted out, showing some white strands.

She had a painful, deep furrow between her eyebrows. The woman said neither yes nor no and asked for time to think, and the Genoese believed — from the thin crease of her pursed lips — that she would not come. He didn't understand what was keeping her at the inn, but for sure, with his family, she could have more money, work less, and have a room of her own.

At the beginning of the next week, in the early morning, Tommaso met her at the door. The merchant opened the door himself; Ariadne was asleep. Pelagia asked to go through the whole house, the courtyard, and the cellar, went into the kitchen, and started work. At the end of the same day, behind her, the dishes gleamed, scrubbed with lye and ashes, the floors, washed with lots of water, looked new, and the curtains drawn tight against the windows drowsed, soaked in the wash pail. The room where she was supposed to sleep was somewhere upstairs, but Pelagia refused to go there and squeezed a bed between the kitchen and the winter larder, where they kept fruit, vegetables, and the expensive wine brought from all over the world — sheltered in wide amphorae with red wax stoppers and covered with wet sand.

The Galata mansion underwent numerous changes due to the unwavering determination of her Greek hands. Shelves with clothes washed and ironed without blemish, furniture pulled aside, books dusted off, blankets, quilts, and rugs shaken out, arranged along the walls. From the young Turkish girl whom Pelagia found there on her arrival, and with whom she behaved like an army chieftain, she demanded her money and left as if she had seen the Unholy One. The amazing transformation occurred before Tommaso's startled eyes, without so much as a brush from the woman against Ariadne, who continued to pass by in a daze amidst all the changes. This left the mistress of vegetables, seeds, brooms, utensils, cups, buckets, and honey pots free to do as she pleased. And Pelagia kept cooking.

As for the lonely heiress, who had not taken any maps with her from the attic full of treasures, everything from her past life was far away.

At that moment, the long isthmuses, the city's strips of land that bounded the seas together, the hot gravel alleys over which the shadows had no power, the heavy gates, the ropeless bells hanging empty of air like the holes of skulls, the careless majesty of the imperial capital — all made her dizzy. She missed the convent and Elena very much, and she strongly believed that by coming here, her life was over. As in her first week at Santa Maria della Croce, she couldn't have been more wrong. Her life was just beginning.

KHALIL

The Observatory in Constantinople, an anthill of scholars, teachers, and disciples, was to last only three years. During this time, Turks, Persians, Arabs, Levantines, Andalusians, Mongols, Russians, and even Chinese and Coptic Christians climbed its broad stairs and crossed its doorstep in search of heaven's truths. Khalil Youssef Hamed was one of them.

His grandfather had moved from Damascus to Tarsus, where the Apostle Paul had seen the light of day and Cleopatra had rushed to Mark Antony and death. Tarsus, the city of so many faiths and so many rulers, was in love with legends and words.

Khalil was only in love with numbers. When he was a child, he used to count out loud in the courtyard the stacks of clay pots made by his father, who, no matter how hard he worked, could not fill the mouths of the eight children Allah gave him; so, he put them all to work from a young age. All except Khalil, a strange child. When five years old, on the advice of the imam, the potter took him to the madrasa, although the boy hardly spoke. Khalil didn't seem to bother with paying attention to the others and used words just enough to keep from dying of thirst.

Instead, he could sit for hours, drawing strings of numbers that only he could understand; at first, in the dust, and later on clay tablets offered by his father. They didn't have any paper, and the head of the family, unknowingly, had once again discovered the writing on clay tablets. To keep him quiet, he took the child to his side, put some clay in a small wooden box, and gave him a sharp pointed stick. Until the clay hardened, the little boy drew figures and signs. The tablets dried in the sun the same day and were kept with sanctity, though no one could really read them.

His first teacher, a modest and gentle man, quickly understood Khalil's gift. For every sura of the Koran he learned by heart, the schoolboy was given a book of mathematics to study. Have you finished sura Al-Fathia? Here's Al-Khwarizmi's algebra treatise. Have you finished Sura Al-Baqarah? Here's Omar Khayyam! Finished sura Al-Imran? Leonardo Fibonacci's string of numbers. Yaseen and Ar-Rahman? Here's Al-Battani's trigonometry.

The only bafflement: many of the mathematics books he received were not complete. Old parchments, crumpled in places, with bits missing, didn't help the boy deduce whole equations for himself if he wanted to understand anything. Years later, as a teenager, Khalil was absolutely unable to decipher what he wrote and what the authors had written.

When became a student in Cairo, he and his best friend wrote secret messages to each other with the help of invented signs; then, with an ease that in childhood completed other people's manuscripts, Khalil switched to strings of letters mixed with strings of numbers. He spoke Arabic, Turkish, Persian, Greek, Latin, and Hebrew, understood Spanish and Portuguese fairly well, and wanted to study the languages of the Indies. The languages heard throughout the Sublime Porte Empire, such as Genoese, Lingua Franca, Armenian, and many others, were a piece of cake to him. When he didn't understand something in a certain language, he just created new words; this way, he came to speak about eleven languages, but, similarly to algebra and trigonometry, he invented them. It was difficult to know if the words he heard in his thoughts were spoken by others or discovered in the future, as new countries and peoples appeared on the maps.

Leaving for Cairo was pretty simple. One day, the potter, who did not become rich as years passed, woke up to see the imam and the old schoolteacher in the courtyard. They told him that they wanted to send the boy Khalil to Al-Azhar University; thanks to the *waqf*, the pupil could deepen his studies in mathematics and astronomy, philosophy, and logic, at that time, mixed together under the name of "rational sciences." Hamed, the father, just wanted to know what his share was of his unusual son's journey. Nothing. And everyone breathed a sigh of relief. Most of all, Khalil; it was very clear that he didn't want to drag it out with the *tafsir* and trusted the word "rational."

At the time, Cairo — for a millennium a stop-off for the spice trade between East and West and the road to Mecca for pilgrims — still had a little glory left. The Portuguese ships' routes to Asia were not yet negotiated, and the young Ottoman Empire didn't have time to turn the Egyptian capital into a provincial and depopulated fair.

Khalil's six years at the university were a time of complete happiness. In his world of few needs, he secured a simple livelihood and was free. In addition to his studies, he added calligraphy and literature because he was bored. He had never been interested in women, nor in men. After a few shy attempts with prostitutes around the caravanserais, he easily concluded that restraint was the best choice for him. Too much trouble to get close to a woman, even for a very short time, and if he was forced by their questions to talk about anything other than mathematics, it wore him out. Generally, the young scholar didn't know what he was eating — he fed himself only when he was very hungry — and kept his eyes fixed on the plate or some calculus tables. His clothes were of no particular color — he simply pulled them on every morning — and the thought of starting a family or making a fortune never sprouted, languishing amid so many non-linear equations and the study of Al-Kindi's book on deciphering cryptic messages. It seemed that the decades of a man's life were too few to acquire all the knowledge written before he was born, and nothing else interested him. When he graduated from university, he became a civil servant in Tabriz's local administration, courtesy of the same friend with whom he had once communicated in strings of numbers mixed with letters. He wrote Persian documents in Turkish and Arabic, petitions, and commercial contracts, and relaxed on his days off by typing polyalphabetic ciphers.

Almost a decade later, Khalil decided that the job didn't leave him enough freedom and set off for Constantinople. The Observatory had just opened, and he hoped he could get closer to it. Arriving with four trunks full of books, scrolls, and a few clothes, he was to see that it wasn't that simple. After queuing up with hundreds of other people from all over the empire to petition and acquire signatures from the Padishah's chancellery, he quickly understood that no one needed his knowledge. Magi, alchemists, astrologers, accountants, calligraphers, and cartographers, whether genuine or fabricated overnight, but all lured by the promise of effortless gains, could be encountered on every corner of the sprawling metropolis.

This first attempt to enter the attention of the Imperial Court left such a bitter taste in his mouth that he didn't repeat it, not even when Mustafa pushed him to make connections and seek the vicinity of power, to make it easier for him with all the searches, the stars, the instruments, the books, and the anxieties in his daily life.

Khalil always turned him down, saying he was better off, but he had to find something to live on because he couldn't spend days hunched over like a scribe, copying papers. Salvation came from being an astrologer. It earned him enough money and left him plenty of time to devote to his study. The horoscopes that circulated in those days amused him. When he was at university, students used to play around making celestial charts with the movement of the stars drawn wrong, which they shoved under each other's noses, waiting to see who would figure out first, which planet run out of place. But now, it was different. Now, real people were waiting to be told by him — the one who had no family, no wealth, and no interest in the life of the city — when it was the best time to get married, if they would get rich, or when it was beneficial to start a sea voyage.

Khalil's fate as a soothsayer seemed ironic, but even Pythia in ancient times was an epileptic maiden, or a woman between two ages, with a husband and children, who dressed stridently and wore terrible make-up. None of those women who wandered through the temple at Delphi had probably shot a bow, wielded a sword, or knew what it was like to march at dawn, but that did not prevent them from predicting the Trojan War and the defeat of Leonidas at Thermopylae, among other things. This thought reassured him. After all, even his personal idol, the father of algebra, wrote a history book of politicians' horoscopes; for him, this was enough. If Al-Khwarizmi could do it, he could do it too.

His first client, a rather young and wealthy widow, wanted to know if she would marry again. She stood before him, half her face covered by a veil, her lips pressed together, and Khalil realized that although he had spent more than an hour calculating oppositions and quadratures, she was interested in the answer to only one question. How many marriages she would have. And because he didn't have the heart to tell her that a celestial chart at your birth wasn't meant to show you what to do or how to stay married, he told her a story. For an hour, Khalil spoke without stopping about the movement of the stars and the three Moirae — Klotho, Lachesis, and Atropos — and about human destinies. In the end, the poor woman left convinced that it was up to her to decide her own destiny, so she left the astrologer more money than he asked for.

However, the most stunned by the event was Khalil. He, who never talked much nor recited poems, had overwhelmed an unknown woman with a torrent of words, only to feed a bud of hope in her. He vowed not to do it again, but things repeated themselves with his second client, and the third, and most of those who followed.

People would seek him out, he would quickly make some cursory reckoning, then give them a speech in which his readings from Plato and Rumi were interwoven with the Prophet's exhortations, quotations from Aristotle, the *Bhagavad* Gita, and Avicenna's *Canon of Medicine,* in an overwhelming mixture. Mustafa knew, for he was one of the few people with whom Khalil shared his fears. Or perhaps the only one. After each new client who was treated with mysticism, philosophy, and too little astrology, Khalil vowed to stop — and he couldn't.

"Maybe that's what's important after all. Not your dry numbers, but your words."

"Doesn't it make you laugh, Mustafa? Should I become the greatest storyteller?"

"As long as you don't make horoscopes for important people, I see no danger. I don't think you'd want the Sultan, the viziers, or some pasha to ask you to predict if they're going to win some battle and then cut your head off because it didn't happen. As long as you stick to merchants' fortunes and barren women, you're safe."

"The Padishah doesn't even know I exist."

"Unfortunately, he knows I exist."

"I thought that's what you'd say. The talisman? Any luck finding something?"

"No."

"I looked at Dioscorides' book in Greek and Pliny the Elder's *Natural History*. I also tried to find Theophrastus' manuscript on stones. I know for sure that Dioscorides drew a lot of inspiration from it and that Theophrastus wrote about emeralds, amethysts, onyx, jade, volcanic stones, copper, gold, silver, pearls, and other things, but I can't find the tomes. At the Observatory, it was simple. They were all collected together. Now, they're scattered around Constantinople. Scattered, lost, destroyed. Only Allah knows their fate."

"Didn't you tell me that when you arrived at the university in Cairo, you learned that even the great Saladin destroyed, burned, and threw a whole mountain of scrolls and manuscripts into the Nile? See? History repeats itself."

"He and many others. So do all tyrants, including those of this imperial family. When they entered Cairo, they killed, looted, and burned books... As you can see, no difference."

"You're talking foolishly again; the walls have ears..."

"Why are you so afraid, Mustafa?"

"I have family, Khalil; you know too well. What will they do if I'm gone?"

"Yeah, and I don't have a family…"

"That's not what I meant."

"You go out of your way to please everyone, and I don't care about anyone, right? Am I selfish? I didn't have children, I didn't give the world a great book, I didn't discover a planet, I'm just a translator…"

"And a great friend and an honest man — and a wise man."

"And poor. Just scraping by, anyway."

"Or very rich. First, you're free. Secondly, you can do what-ever you want with your knowledge. You can always travel…"

"Why can't you travel? Go on the *hajj* journey, if you like."

"Now? When I have to make the talisman? They'll think I ran away. And then, who should I leave Meryem with? That reminds me. She's asking you to make Musa's celestial chart."

"Meryem? What's gotten into her? Since when does she believe in stars and astrologers?"

"I don't know… She's always worried about this child. She said she senses something bad is coming… I don't know what to do with her, Khalil. Tell me, what should I do?"

"Give me the date and time of birth. I know the year, and I'll give it to you tomorrow or the day after and try to help you with the talisman. Do you know what I'm thinking? You'll also need Padishah's celestial chart. You are aware that whatever we find, we can't do without it."

"And you know damn well I can't handle that. Whoever knows the day and time of birth of a padishah can calcu-late his date of death. It's treason. It's the best-kept secret in the palace."

"Can't you find out from the Chief Astrologer?"

"From that poisonous snake? I wouldn't dream of going near him…"

"So, what will you do?"

"Anyway, we don't have anything yet. What's the point of taking any risks? Nobody has called me, and I'm not going there on my own initiative."

"As you wish."

"So, no chance for a talisman without knowing the date of birth?"

"Plenty of chances, just as there are chances for you to write poetry and talk to fairies and djinns. Actually, I think you're right. Immortality is a dream. Maybe you don't need me. Maybe you'll dream of the talisman," Khalil mocked him.

"Laugh at me, laugh at me again…"

"Never, Mustafa, I only laugh at myself."

The Bosporus night crouched between them, pricked by a few stars. The Arab stood up and lit a tallow candle, and suddenly all the stars in Khalil's celestial maps twinkled, awakened by the light.

MUSA

When Mustafa sent him with the basket of fresh fish to Serratore's house, the boy said neither yes nor no. He been working for some time for the Genoese, in the port, but had never been to his home. Eventually, he agreed to go, and at that moment, he stood outside the gate of Galata's house, waiting for someone to open it for him. In front of his eyes, the ample arabesque wood carvings, half arches of the doors, two massive bronze handles with the Genoese flag, and a monogram: an S wrapped around a T.

He had known don Serratore for a long time. When he was very young, he had taken his father from the merchant's house several times, helping him carry home the coffers with gems, that the goldsmith ordered and that the merchant brought from distant lands. But there was another house, much smaller, rented in Pera. Before Ariadne's arrival, Tommaso bought a small palace facing the Golden Horn, from whose windows you could see the blue-green water, the old racecourse, the maidans, the squares, the caiques, the seaward gardens of Seraglio.

He knocked on the gate, long and hard, several times, then pushed it in. Somewhere to the right side, a quiet hum. There was no one there, or so it seemed to him until he spotted her out of the corner of his eye. She stood with her back bent over some bees' nests trapped in wicker baskets, stirring at them with a wooden spoon. Curious, the boy rushed towards the baskets in which the honeycombs were muttering, without even getting a chance to greet her.

"Do you have beehives?"

Someone kept bees in the center of Galata. She turned away, not seeming to wonder how a stranger had arrived in their courtyard, and answered slowly, stumbling, struggling to speak in his language.

"Yeah, why are you so surprised? And who are you?"

"Musa," he mumbled. "Mustafa's boy, the goldsmith…"

"Aha! And what's Musa, the son of Mustafa the goldsmith, doing here?"

She imitated the sound of his voice, mocking him. Musa flinched. He was used to the soft talk of girls who didn't raise their heads when men were around. The stranger peered at him through a white net, on which a few bugs perched.

"I brought a basket of fish for don Serratore, from my father."

"Aha! Wait a minute."

She took a few steps away from the beehives, shook her hair, then carefully pushed the net away from her face. The first foreign woman Musa saw up close.

"Follow me to the kitchen!"

"I'm not your servant."

Ariadne turned to him as she picked up a straw hat from a table that then covered her golden-to-heliodon-yellow locks of hair, leaving only her fine chin and round, restless lips visible.

"Follow me to the kitchen, *please*."

Musa took the basket and stayed a few steps behind, so as not to make her feel uncomfortable. The kitchen was full of bronze trays, porcelain jugs, and plates, and under the window were two troughs where thyme, basil, saffron, marjoram, and a few other small-leaved seedlings he had never seen before were sprouting.

"Papa brings them from wherever he travels, sometimes seeds, sometimes shoots or bulbs... and I take care of them. I learned about them a long time ago... healing plants and their purpose... Do you understand?"

"Does he bring them from wherever he travels? By the sea? And they don't die?"

"They don't die. They bring them with the soil. Tell me, what do they bring them on? That's what Genoese men do, right? Trading at sea. They have ships."

She laughed. He felt his cheeks flush. A woman? How dare she laugh at him?

She saw the fury touching his face like a flutter of a butterfly's wing, and before he could leave, she began to speak in *Zeneize,* the lively dialect of the banks of the Polcevera, where consonants sometimes twisted together, sometimes joined together, and vowels rushed to keep up; she mixed everything with the few words she learned in Constantinople. Almost without realizing it, she told him how her mother died giving birth to her, how her father was always away and, even when he wasn't, he mostly sat bent over his files or met his friends, how he had sent her to the convent for six years, and how she came here. And the beehives. And the honey. Mother Abbess Eleonora's voice: "nutmeg, cloves, and black cherry water, to which you add lemon blossom extract, lavender, and wild carnations. Add two tablespoons of honey, then leave in the sun for a few hours. A potion for convulsions, fainting, and blue heart." Words erased, changed, incomplete as in childhood, remembered, postponed for so long that sometimes, they made no sense.

Sheltered by them, she opened her soul to a stranger. Ariadne was sure that he had no idea what she was talking about and that he would probably think she was crazy, but she continued to say out loud everything that was on her mind, without holding back. Musa understood. The passion with which she spoke needed no words — it could be felt in the air — and though he caught only a word here and there, he understood. The door swung against the wall, and Ariadne covered her red cheeks with her palms. Pelagia showed up in the kitchen and began to ask for clarification. What kind of fish, and when had it been caught? Then, she took the basket, put it in the chilly pantry, and headed for the door, inviting him to follow her. Musa found himself in the street, without being able to recover from his state of confusion. What had happened? Where had the blonde girl with dark eyes come from?

That night, he slept only two hours. He tried in vain to quiet the question's torrent. How could he see her again? What could he do to reach her without arousing suspicion? He longed for the stirring magic, the spell that had begun, the unusual feeling that they had seen each other before.

Years later, it turned out that all of Musa's fears at the time been unfounded. Their lives would go on for decades in the same way. Ariadne blended, in all she did, the passion of three generations of Serratore, and he — the son of Meryem and Mustafa, the goldsmith — just listened and understood.

ARIADNE

Constantinople didn't care about anyone. Not even about the Sultan. Sultans followed one after another, clerks, common tradesmen, beggars, and scribes died anonymously, travelers came and went, and the great city went on, through the ages, swallowing them all alike — men and carriages, bridges and dungeons, ditches, gates and peddlers, palaces and cellars.

In her past, the streets of Genoa, lively and full of fountains, cobbled streets, porticos, and wrought-iron garlands, looked much the same; but here, the mahallas obeyed no rules. Greeks in Phanar, Armenians in Samatya, Jews in Balat. Each with prayers, caresses, and cries in their own languages. The sharp towers of the mosques unraveled in the hot air. Creatures of unknowable ages, hidden beneath mountains of cloth, swayed on horses with embroidered velvet shabracks, and the wind sowed wisps of smoke. Living in the belly of a city like a snake stretched across the hills. "Watch your step. All snakes are carnivores," Tommaso had once told her when he had learned of her wanderings outside the monastery. Ariadne could only defend herself by grinding the beads of Elena's rosarium between her fingers. She clung to a past that had somehow faded into the smell of human sweat and horse urine in the streets around her.

She only went out with Pelagia, the guardian of the house. After a couple of months, the woman had moved in completely and no longer slept in the corridor between the kitchen and the pantry, but in her own bedroom. She took from Stavros all her clothes and the three Greek icons: Saint Mary Vrefokratousa, the miracle-working icon, Saint George slaying the dragon, and the third, brought from Mount Athos by her husband, had Jesus Christ perched in the tree of life in the middle, and on the edges hung, like blushing apples, various saints.

Although the icons, crudely painted by some very diligent apprentice, were probably not capable of any miracle, they were her only possession. She had nailed them to the east wall from day one. Underneath them burned a candle with olive oil and string wick, which sometimes gave off a choking smoke. With the Papist girl, she had little to talk about. On one hand, Ariadne didn't know a word of Greek and spoke very poorly the common Turkish of the streets of the empire's capital, and on the other, Pelagia couldn't even say hello in Genoese. They understood each other with signs. If it were really something important, Tommaso would explain. You should learn Turkish, he often said to his daughter, but she refused stubbornly, as if her ignorance of the local language was a protection from the unknown.

When he saw how unhappy she was, the merchant wondered if he had made a mistake in bringing her here. He would have liked to see her eager to get to know the local society of the Genoese, the French, the Portuguese, the Venetians — all the ambassadors he was accustomed to live among; to see Ariadne with their wives and daughters; to introduce her at a dinner party given by the Palace to foreigners. He even bought beehives to ease her longing, but Ariadne no longer cared for them as she did in the convent. At first, the girl was happy to take care of the bees, but as time passed, she ignored them more and more, and in the end, Pelagia, somehow forced by necessity, ended up the one who would clean the hives.

Over time, the woman had mastered her trade so well that she could create nuc boxes for the new families of bees out of twigs weaved with wooden rods, or collect honey to sweeten the fruits for the winter. She gave the honeycombs and sugar crystals to the children at the end of Ramadan, the Christian Passover, and sometimes also at Jewish Passover. Constantinople kept all the celebrations.

Ariadne clandestinely resumed her departures, bringing up memories of the days when she would sneak out by putting on her trousers and tunic and leaping over the convent's fence. In plain sight of all, she went to the market twice a week, with Pelagia leading the way, walking briskly, and Ariadne following closely, concealed by a large straw hat.

Everyone in the neighborhood knew don Serratore, and when the woman and the young Genoese passed by, they bowed, greeting them. Arriving among the counters and stalls, without haste, Pelagia would buy each fruit and vegetable, piece by piece, and Ariadne picked the grapes from Rhodes, the dates from Tunisia, the fresh tomatoes and carrots, holding them in her hands until their smell reminded her of the aniseed, pimento, and rosemary of another time. When the two women had more or less filled the baskets, the merchant would send the goods to don Serratore with a helper, and they would stroll home, where one would bury herself in pots and saucepans, and the other would hang out in the courtyard or read and dream in her room.

At least, this seemed to be the case, and even Pelagia took some time to grasp that, occasionally, Tommaso Serratore's peculiar daughter was nowhere in sight. One day, the young Turkish girl who was previously employed as a servant hastily departed, leaving behind few old clothes, and never came back. The new housekeeper found them, washed them as she washed everything, collected them in a bindle, and stashed them in a corner of the pantry to be taken to the church, but she never got around to doing so. The wrapped clothing seemed to sprout legs, and the woman, consumed by the feverish cleaning and canning of veggies, forgot about them.

But the little package didn't travel very far; it found shelter on the first floor, in one of Ariadne's trunks. Thrilled to discover something that finally made her feel alive, the unsubdued Miss Serratore swiftly appropriated the chemise, the shalwar, and the long dark caftan, patched with coarse brown woolen fabric, to which she added a thick, floor-length veil found among her clothes. A complete disguise so she could wander in peace to the shores of the Golden Horn or through Pera.

Seen through the thick fabric of the veil, which protected her like armor, the city no longer seemed so threatening. What made Ariadne's walks even easier was that Tommaso didn't eat in the morning but stopped for coffee at Stavros' inn, and Pelagia, having been up since dawn, always thought the girl slept late.

One of those mornings when she had set out to roam, she opened the garden gate and found herself face-to-face with Musa. The Serratore's heiress recognized the boy with the fish basket without a shadow of a doubt, and the shabby caftan did not deceive him either. They were both so astounded that not a single sound escaped their lips.

He kept shifting from one leg to the other, then awkwardly put a small tied bag into her arms and broke into a run. With her heart beating in her temples like a gong, Ariadne turned on her heel, crept back, threw her veil on the floor, and untied the strings, revealing a ship, no bigger than a child's arm. Everything was carved and painted to the smallest detail. Every deck, every railing, hull and rigging, sails drawn in pale colors — white clouds in a sky that looked like a young forest. Ariadne remembered the house in Genoa and, dazed, sat down on the bed. She had seen the painted caravel somewhere before. In one of her grandfather's maps.

HAVVA

The wrist. Circles of flesh hung around her arm, filled with fat, giving her body the shape of a sack. She closed her eyes again. It had been quite some time since she had broken up with the heavy bag of fat that held her entire being. She treated it as something that belonged to her but was not *her*. Or she attempted to convince herself that thoughts had nothing to do with the body. She ate without measure on endless nights, convinced that this was the only way she could get through the exhausting days that followed. At least, when she didn't want to get out of bed, torpid, no soul dared enter unless she summoned, because — inshallah — she was *birinci kadin.*

Havva couldn't fall asleep. It had been months since the Sultan hadn't returned from Edirne. Rumors that the Grand Vizier wanted a new military campaign against her brothers, the heirs of the Safavid empire, were everywhere; the Padishah was not there, and the Divan was boiling. She opened her eyes and looked at the ceiling. The pearl and mother-of-pearl inlaid arches descended to the Iznik tiles of the floor, the side porticos were hidden by heavy draperies, the Koran's fragments written with golden letters gleamed on black silk.

She had come from the gardens of Isfahan, where the Damascus roses bloomed from pink to purple, the bridges thinned in the summer steam over the clear water of the

Zayanderud, and the coolness from Mount Sofeh crept into the farthest recesses of the palace. She liked nothing when she arrived here to marry the heir of the world's Padishah. Istanbul seemed crowded, noisy, smelly. Havva had found the people she was surrounded by unrefined — two centuries before, they were still riding like nomads across Anatolia's plains — and too easily corrupted. All the social parvenus of the new empire fed that corruption. They gathered in the old city — only named and masked differently — as if in a crucible, a bottomless funnel.

The proud Safavid princess, the heiress of Cyrus the Great, had been brought up in the tradition of those born to rule. Everyone knew that at some point, she would marry into a state's alliance and that the art of embroidery, dancing, and riding were merely a facade designed to make her agreeable. The real art that Havva mastered was politics: alliances, the swift judgment of situations, and threats intertwined with diplomacy. The girls of the Persian imperial family were brought up to impose their will on everyone. The Shah often said of his children: "I have brought them up as one tames thoroughbred horses in my stables, accustoming them to victory, until they cannot live without it. That way, I know they will never disgrace the dynasty."

With the elegance of the royal courts of Qazvin, Tabriz, and Isfahan in her blood, the princess hated the killing, the slaughter in the Ottoman court. She hated the beheadings, the dismembered bodies, the corpses thrown into the sea. Most of all, she hated the generations-old fratricidal law that allowed any newly installed Padishah to kill his brothers, uncles, his own sons, and their families. Born in a place where Muslims, Zoroastrians, Christians, and Jews prayed at will and traveled freely across the Persian empire, Havva didn't understand the need for such cruelty.

She tried hard to find out how the fratricidal law could be annulled. The Padishah could sign a *firman* or even persuade the *ulema* to give a *fetva*. But she concluded that if the other brothers were left alive, the fate of the heir to the throne, the eldest son of Havva, would be sealed by the rebellions of the janissaries. These soldiers were loyal to either one prince or another, and every time they ended up with increased pay from one, they helped that one win the throne. Even so, Havva couldn't give up. Apart from Shehzad Murad, she had given birth to two other sons, and she loved dearly her youngest, but the Sultana couldn't find a way to save all her sons, and the helplessness overwhelmed her.

She opened her eyes, reached for the silver tray near the bed, and slid a piece of *qottab* — packed with cardamom and chopped nuts — into her mouth. Lately, she had been ordering a tray of sweets to be placed as close as possible to her at bedtime. The conflict between the Persian and Ottoman dynasties was resurfacing, if it had ever ceased, and her role as an intermediary prevented her from sleeping. Instead, Havva ate and read.

She turned for Saadi's volume of poems, but stopped, remembering that Grand Vizier Ahmed Kasim Pasha had asked for an audience. She stood up on the edge of the bed and took another piece of *qottab*. The powdered sugar mixed with saliva and stuck to the roof of her mouth, terribly sweet. She chewed for a long time, her feet dangling off the bed, heavy, almost unrecognizable in the fading light of the cloudy morning, and chose her turns of speech for the Grand Vizier, the most powerful of her enemies, in advance. When she found the most cunning words, she clapped her hands, a sign that she wanted her hair combed and to be dressed. As always, the cakes did her good. She felt ready.

MUSTAFA

After struggling for more than a month to arrange a meeting with the Chief Astrologer, Mustafa was not too surprised when he was left to wait for several hours in front of the Divan's tower until a page arrived and escorted him to the Mosque of the Aghas. The Grand Vizier was expected to bestow upon him an audience here. Everybody knew that the chief of the Palace's astrologers, Abdul Majid, was, in fact, the Grand Vizier's man.

The goldsmith realized that even the meeting's place chosen by the Grand Vizier represented so well what was known of the dignitary's hypocrisy. On one hand, as a sign of great consideration, he had allowed Mustafa to enter the Gate of Happiness, guarded by white eunuchs, a privilege only enjoyed by ambassadors received in the Audience Hall, next to the Gate. On the other hand, he chose a mosque as a meeting place, a sign of humility before Allah. Shaken by the fear that washed over his stomach like lime water, Mustafa wondered what the meaning was of all these signs.

Ahmed Kasim Pasha, a short, fat, middle-aged man, had already arrived and was waiting for him. Fear spread constantly around this man, mostly because of the rumor that he would sell and buy anyone without a second thought, but also because of his greedy eyes, harboring a desire for power, and his thick-lipped mouth. There was nothing majestic or elegant about his stature, but it was true that when he rode behind the Padishah at military parades, he looked taller.

Tired and full of bad foreboding, he received Mustafa coldly. He knew him and knew that Sultana Havva seemed to have taken a liking to him, because she sometimes called the goldsmith to order jewelry for her or for the women of the harem. And the Padishah certainly took a liking to him. The Grand Vizier decided to overcome his indifference. Better to be benevolent and obliging to the privileged craftsman, though in the Seraglio, you could never be obliging enough.

"*Selamün aleyküm,*" the goldsmith bowed.

"*Aleyküm selam,* what brings you here, Mustafa efendi?"

Mustafa hesitated to answer. He couldn't tell him the truth, *Allah korusun*! But he had to say something.

"I was looking for the Chief Astrologer. I need the time of His Highness's birth," he murmured, white as paper.

"No way, Mus-ta-fa!"

He uttered the name, pressing long on the syllables, a poorly concealed threat.

"Who knows the day and hour of a padishah's birth…? May Allah keep His Lightness from harm and grant him a long and rich life…"

The vizier's well wishes for a Sultan who had not come back from Edirne for months, who was rumored to have eaten nothing and never got out of bed, sounded a bit strained.

"But I can tell you that the destiny's number of the great Padishah is nine. He was chosen by Allah to rule over the lands of the East, and over those of the West. The holy light of Islam will shine over them forever."

"*Allahu Ekber*! It will be! Your Lordship, can you at least give me an astral chart of the great Padishah? One that all the astrologers in the Palace have?"

And he continued in his thoughts: *maybe that's how I manage to keep my head on my shoulders.*

"Yes."

Is that all that the goldsmith wants? The vizier considered the fact that he had come all the way to the audience room for nothing. He suspected that maybe Mustafa was conspiring with the Chief Astrologer, that maybe he knew more about Padishah's health than others in the palace, and that perhaps he was the Sultana's spy, but he was wrong. The man trembling slightly in front of him, sitting on his knees, possessed neither the traitor's hunger nor the daring courage of those yearning for fame at any cost.

The dignitary clapped his hands, and a page seemed to appear out of the ground. He whispered something in his ear, and the page hurried out the door behind them. The Grand Vizier left the goldsmith bent on his knees until the agha turned and handed Mustafa a scroll; then, he stood up and went out without greeting anyone. At this time, the goldsmith was neither dangerous nor useful to him.

Left alone, Mustafa untied his wrists, tried two or three wobbly steps to ease his aching bones, and unrolled the scroll: he had not received an astral chart, only printed notes. As suspected, he had been deceived by the vizier. The stars of the altered celestial chart showed nothing but health, wealth, and glorious conquests. Agha was still there, against a wall, waiting for the goldsmith to finish reading.

He thanked him with two short bows and turned away, relieved: the Grand Vizier forgot to ask him why he needed the Padishah's day of birth. Another law of the Seraglio. To stay alive, you had to know its underbelly: its kitchens, gardens, hidden cellars, the armory, *cirit*'s grounds, the hammams. But you had to show that you knew nothing of what went on, especially if it concerned the rooms where fates were made and unmade, where lords were slaughtered in the blink of an eye, or rich countries were broken up into small, easily governable provinces.

When Mustafa managed to show him the annotations, a few hours later, Khalil threw them at him dryly: "You can't do anything with these notes."

"What do you mean?"

"That is, it doesn't help to know the second, fifth, eighth, and eleventh houses, which show self-confidence, favor success, and that time and patience work for the great Padishah, that he is strong like a lion, or that the dominant planets in his chart are Mars, Jupiter, and Uranus. That's all. The transits, the oppositions, the squares? We have no idea. This paper —" He threw it away, and the scroll full of signs floated for a while before hitting the floor. "— doesn't help us with the talisman."

"And what would help us?"

"More, a lot more… There are five planets known to man: Mercury, Venus, Mars, Jupiter, Saturn, and two luminaries: the Moon and the Sun. Each of them has a greater or lesser influence on a person born in a particular year, month, and day. To know how to make a talisman for someone, you need to know the metals associated with the zodiac sign, the gemstones, what time to make it, in what cycle of the Moon, what to inscribe, and when. Besides, that jeweler must handle the metals and stones according to his own day and hour of birth; also, it is important to be in a state of harmony with himself. Only in this way will the charm be beneficial and achieve its purpose. And they have given you nothing. Maybe some things I could judge for myself, but… I think we're where we were in the spring. Good thing the Padishah went to Edirne and didn't call you back."

"But he'll be back, and then I'll be lost…"

"You're not, calm down. Why do I have to tell you a hundred times? We'll get the metals and stones of the zodiac sign, for at least that's what we've found out, and you'll do it without the day or the hour… We'll find something that fits, but I still need time."

Mustafa muttered sullenly, tired of all the terrible news he had gotten, and of his knees aching from sitting with them bent for a long time:

"Did you make Musa's celestial chart? Meryem keeps asking me."

"Yes, but she won't like it. I don't think you will either, and certainly not Meryem. He has the Sun that conjuncts with Venus, which suits his generous nature, as far as I know, predisposition for love at first sight, and early marriage. He will have a fulfilling life, but it won't come by itself. He needs to make some decisions. He needs boldness and luck. But he'll probably get it because he's got the ninth house in Sagittarius: long journeys. He's attracted to foreign countries. He is going somewhere, your boy, Mustafa, and you must leave him, because if he stays here… something bad will happen to him. Don't ask me what, I can't figure it out…"

"You're serious, aren't you?"

"Yes, I know I told you I don't believe in it, but there are some things in these calculations that I feel are true. I can't explain. It's like a message from outside our world. Sometimes, I can decipher it, sometimes I can't, but in Musa's case, I feel — I really feel that there's something there… Your child is very different from others… I mean, I mean, from most… He has something so rare in him…"

"Maybe *you* conceived him when I was away…" Mustafa smiled.

"With Meryem, who can't stand me? I think she'd rather have walled herself in."

"The funny thing is, I think so too, but I can't stop joking about it. She's too far gone down the path of faith, and she's killing me from morning till night with prayers. Allah forbid, you shouldn't be in front of her eyes if you skip one. Anyway, that's it, Meryem is not going to be changed. Do you even know when he'll leave?"

"Soon, pretty soon, I think, a year, two at the most…"

"Now that I'm willingly putting my neck on the line, let's see what I can tell Meryem."

"See? See how hard it is? Stand in my shoes for once and you'll understand. You can either not tell her the truth, just like that, or tell her a story."

Mustafa took his son's celestial map, full of circles drawn in red and black, put it on top of his useless notes, and slowly went home, and Khalil opened on his lap *The Anatomy of the Heavenly Bodies,* in which Bahā' al-Dīn Al-'Amilī had written that the Earth rotates.

Completely absorbed, the Arab read until dawn, and only then, at the border between wakefulness and sleep, he remembered that he had taken Shaykh Baha'al-Din's book from a shelf of Persian books in the *kulliya* library of the Süleymaniye's Mosque. The same shelf where he had spotted, out of the corner of his eye, a treatise on Hindu astrology. He had never come across such a tome before, and it would probably take a lot of time and effort to unravel it, but it was worth at least trying. If not for him, for Mustafa. All of these decided and settled in his soul, Khalil took his mind off worldly cares and drifted off to sleep, truly happy that the Earth was spinning.

MUSA

At night, he dreamed of a three-story galleon coming out of a single tree and smelling the wood's scent. He saw the sawdust, the splinters, the algae, the sunburnt stumps, the thistles carried by the twilight wind to the beach, the dried roots, the sun-scraped strips in the twilight, the long, sanded slats, before the decks and stairs blackened with spit and sweat and blood, and before the stair railings were swept by palms full of corn. In the shipyard, anger and hope and grief and despair were still far away, and the stacked wood looked like a pile of white sheets. He loved the wood that hadn't yet been touched, the immaculate paper, and any surface that could be glided over smoothly with the fingertips. Since his childhood, he saw things that didn't fit into his world, and he felt the need to defend, to tame, to change the whole world into a mosaic of clear glass tiles. No wrinkles, no stains, just a string of stained glass laid on the floor.

"You're stubborn, you're stubborn!" Meryem yelled at him so many times in his troubled adolescence, but he wasn't. He just had a natural need for order. It would have been difficult to explain to anyone how, as he walked the streets behind his mother, carrying her vegetables or lamb, feluccas crossed intersections, heavy carracks appeared in the air from behind mosques, and brigantines hung out under bridges. The fact that only he could see them or that he was not understood by his parents didn't bother him. The boy didn't want his mother and father to see them; he just wanted them to leave him alone, and they didn't.

Mustafa grew tired of the constant shouting during his arguments with Meryem about Musa, so he mustered the courage to request don Serratore to employ his son at the shipyard. He hoped that by doing so, he could avoid the never-ending arguments regarding Musa. The Genoese readily accepted the proposal, but instead of assigning the young apprentice to the ship's carpenters, he placed him in the offices alongside the two Spaniards responsible for calculating the ships' tonnage, mast height, length, and deck width estimates.

The goldsmith told him of Musa's talent and the flags that spoke to each other and had brought him drawings full of symbols. Tommaso studied them and was convinced that the boy was gifted. But, beyond everything, he wanted very much to help Mustafa. The Genoese knew that similar to himself, the goldsmith had a lot of trouble with the only child. Mustafa had received from destiny the boy no one could understand, and Tommaso, the thin, veiled girl who had just now entered through the door.

With a lengthy, shocked expression, her father came out to greet her. Not only had she traveled all the way alone; she, who rarely went out, had put on one of the new outfits, custom-made in Genoa, that she had never worn before. On the bright side, maybe she was finally getting used to her new life.

Ariadne unveiled herself as soon as she stepped in, and her blonde hair glowed.

"I brought you hot pie, just taken out of the oven by Pelagia."

Tommaso lifted the kitchen towel from the basket, revealing not only the hot pieces of pie but also olives, feta cheese, and some dried goat meat sausages.

"Is something wrong? I could have come home for lunch."

"I thought you might want to eat the hot pie, papa."

The sweetness in her voice enveloped Tommaso. He watched her as she walked around the office, leaning over the large boards with drawings of the beams connecting the main deck to the side hull, sketches of the bilge and starboard, asking questions, amiable and calm. From where he stood, he could see the delicate line of her chin across the lacy foam of the Bosporus.

The girl lingered in the room for a moment. Then, she grabbed her veil again, picked up the basket, and flew out the door, waving and smiling. Her mysterious smile really worried Tommaso, for he never knew what was coming next. Musa liked paper in general, but he had fallen in love with a particular piece, a very small patch clasped in his sweaty palm, on which were written two words in Turkish printed in Latin letters. "Tomorrow morning." No time, no place, nothing.

But there was no need: five days before, in front of the gate of don Tommaso Serratore's garden, together with her older sisters — the carracks, galleons, and feluccas — a painted caravel floated in the sky of Constantinople.

ARIADNE

Summer came to an end, and the city belonged to them, and they had no intention of sharing it with anybody. They discovered a location for their tickets in the brick wall enclosing the home, directly close to the garden gate, which became "their" gate.

Both of them wrote their notes as they had started: Turkish words in Latin letters. Ariadne had no knowledge of the Arabic alphabet, but Musa was quite good at reading due to his desire to comprehend the Spanish and Portuguese shipbuilders' and carpenters' manuals purchased by don Serratore. Little by little, he also got used to the syllables of her mother tongue: sweet, velvety, heady Italian.

By faithfully echoing his words — my beloved: *canân,* my beautiful: *dilberim,* I love you: *meftunum sana* — she opened Musa's soul to a cascade of wide honey-colored waves of hibiscus blossoms, late spring afternoons with twilights embracing minarets, mosaics, maidans, bas-reliefs, and coffee shops.

They couldn't meet very often, but when they did, they roamed the *mahallas* at dawn. Accustomed to sneaking out of the convent, Ariadne seemed to have an innate inclination for gliding over the floors, for getting out of the house without being heard. It wasn't the same when she returned and everyone was awake. If she was asked where she had come from, she'd justify herself by mentioning minor events at the morning Mass, which she couldn't even bring herself to attend just to be seen for a moment.

Not far from their street, the Benedictine Basilica had a deserted bell tower in its courtyard. Mehmet II the Conqueror had allowed all the foreigners who remained in Istanbul to practice their faith. The pact, however, included a provision requiring that only the call of the muezzins be heard throughout the empire's capital, with no ringing of the bells. So, they came to rest in their dusty and faded towers in a world devoid of Christian sounds.

Fra Niccolò, a young monk still in his prime, opened a small asylum where he sheltered widows and children, without asking which was their religion. Over the years, Catholic, Venetian, and Genoese orphans, Greek Orthodox, Armenians, Serbs, and even a few children of Ashkenazi Jews found shelter at "Saint Anne's." The priest had been introduced to Signora Serratore when she arrived in Istanbul, but he was far too busy feeding the mouths of God's children to remember which of his parishioners made it to morning Mass and which did not. Ariadne knew this, and the inattentive priest had become her most valuable ally.

On nice days when they saw each other, Musa would come and pick her up, and they would meander the streets. He knew most of the merchants and craftsmen who worked with his father: the Jews around the Çıfıt Gate, the Greeks from Mora and Fanar, the Armenians from Langa, Kumkapı, and Hasköy; he knew their customs, their houses, and their crafts. He could mingle with their crowd, looking like them. Most of the time, the two lovers glided along the walls like hurried ghosts or, when they were lucky, went out on the water using Emrah's caique and escaped the danger of any prying eyes that could wonder what an unaccompanied girl was doing in the crowd. She seemed to be alone because she walked one step behind him.

From the nights he slept in the harbor, Musa knew all the fishermen's settlements along the Bosporus. He knew the ripples of the shore, the coves, the elm trees' groves and thatched roofs, the wooden fences, the vegetable gardens hidden among the bushes and gravel. He knew the thick shade of the docks with their dark woodwork, eaten by mosses, mussels, and a kind of long algae that gathered in reddish islands, swept by cold currents in summer and warm in winter, down to the waters of the Black Sea.

They set off from Tophane-i Amire, the old arsenal, and headed for Arnavutköy and Bebek Bay, past the foam and seagulls, past the Albanian and Greek houses and sleepy empty fishing boats, and then paddled along the shore, hidden by the swathes of Judas trees and dwarf shrubs with sharp, dusty leaves, from behind which they could hear brown-headed nightingales singing.

They weren't touching. Musa couldn't take his eyes off her ankles as the girl lifted her dress to climb into the boat, and he could guess her svelte thighs, slender waist, and bold breasts beneath the coarse fabric. She instead watched his cheekbones, long eyelashes, inherited from Meryem, and the sweaty palms that lingered on the oars as they hid the caique beneath the willows. They were filled with happiness, showing no concern for where they were going or the potential consequences if their secret was discovered. They simply desired to seize every fleeting moment of the early autumn days and savored the emotions they harbored.

The only thing that betrayed Ariadne on her return was her clothes. On days when she actually went to the basilica and sat quietly, twirling Elena's rosary beads between Hail Mary's, the garments hung gracefully on her body. The skirt's folds fell straight, leaning against each other, the wide sleeves didn't wrap feverishly around her wrists, and the bodice didn't constrict her.

On days when she ran with Musa through the streets, in the morning's flavors, or, worse, when they went boating on the Bosporus, all the girl's clothes went crazy. The skirt no longer lay straight and soft as it had been tailored, but always clung to the insides of her thighs, impeding her gait, the hem rose up on all sides, and the lace of the collar went up to her neck and nape, to the roots of the ever-disheveled tresses. So much change in the runaway's hair and clothing could not have gone unnoticed, and it did not. After a few weeks of Ariadne wandering the Bosporus, Pelagia noticed.

KHALIL

His passion began, as most everything else in Khalil's case, with a book, in fact with the seven volumes of Yaqut al-Musta'simi, which he read in one breath, before picking up Sheikh Hamdullah's calligraphy manuals. This was a long time ago, before he joined the Observatory and had more time to read.

At first, he struggled with the curved lines and soft angles, and then got used to them, as if he had learned them as a child. Like the languages he spoke, he couldn't draw boundaries between the signs he imagined and those he learned from his masters. Free from the calendar days, the astrologer floated on the sleepy ice of sheets of paper. Those who had seen his written documents and copied verses could have sworn that he had completed long years of training, mastering the craft of weaving triangles, rhombuses, and accolades. Everybody thought he could acquire a license for the imperial chancellery at any time. The Arab did not listen to them. He chose to keep his skill hidden and live in the solitude of his room, undisturbed.

He couldn't even remember when the mannish desires had stopped bothering him. His skin hung like a woolen fabric on his armpits and legs after so many years spent among sexagesimal calculus and Baghdad School manuscripts, and the hollow chest and sparse hair were so familiar to him. It was like his entire body had become an unpleasant neighbor, but he got used to looking at his blemishes and flaws. Meandering the streets of the poor *mahalla* where he lived, Khalil could think only of finding the truth, of knowing the inner being of things and the foundation of the universe. In his hunger for something so vast, concern for a short-lived body had no place.

At the end of the summer, at Mustafa's request on behalf of don Tommaso, he had agreed to give Ariadne lessons in writing and reading Turkish. The overly flowery horoscopes he had to draw up to live made him feel increasingly guilty, and he was more than happy to cover his meager needs with the payment agreed with Tommaso. It was fairer and easier.

Although he approved immediately, happy with the gift that had come out of the blue, he had asked for a week to think about it, to tell them when, and especially where, the calligraphy lessons could take place. When the respite was over, he sent an epistle to Signor Serratore — also through Mustafa — that he wanted to meet his lordship's daughter every Friday, his day off, in the summer garden of the Observatory.

Everyone said yes. The abandoned garden, with its obscure walkways, entwining and disentwining around the terrace of the summer pavilion, not long ago utilized for discussions concerning Saturn's inclined axis, seemed to be a perfect location.

Ariadne had said yes because she saw in walking the hills of Tophane — where the orchards mingled with the elm trees — new opportunities to meet Musa. On the other hand, Tommaso, unbothered by Ottoman traditions, had no concerns about his daughter spending an hour per week learning calligraphy from an old Arab. First mistake.

Every Friday at noon, Ariadne appeared accompanied by Pelagia. The teacher and the Greek exchanged a few words, and then the woman went off to do her business, and the two, left alone, sat on the grass, holding their walnut boards on their knees. For her little mobile writing table, Khalil had bought a piece of soft leather from Hasköy and had dressed the board so that the paper wouldn't tear if she put too much pressure on her pen. His was just a rough piece of wood, uneven, with knots that didn't bother him. He could write anywhere, on anything: on bare wood, on agate slabs, or on the leather of the coverings. Like the movement of celestial bodies, the Arab harmonized the flow of ink, the glow of *ahar* paper, and the arabesques made by pencils, even with his eyes closed.

Sitting slightly bent over, he first took out the inkwell with fresh ink, the ash, and the rolls of perfectly cut paper, and began to write, while he explained: "The tip of the quill must be the length of the letter *elif*. Don't let the ink flow in waves; make long strokes without pauses. The letters look at you as you look at them. This means a lot because you will truly know how to write not when you understand the letters, but when you feel they understand you."

She listened to him obediently, with her lips slightly parted. Whenever she grew numb and began to stir, her dress would rise above her knees, and she would smooth it with her hand. Khalil would turn his head to one side whenever this happened and couldn't quite grasp the flinch, the slight wobble, the thrill that ran through him. The girl appeared to be a creature from another universe, and he wasn't referring to her unveiled hair or her exposed face: Ariadne breathed differently. The round shoulders under her dresses, the slender collarbones, the straight back, and firm gait announced at every turn: I am free. It was beyond impossible to be around and not feel the invigorating blow of air that accompanied her.

During the first meeting, he tried to disregard the rustle of her clothes and hastily squeezed his eyes shut a few times. That kept his hands from shaking, but it didn't help him much. With the vigor of the line of women who had been her ancestors — the thick-waist, thunder-thighs goddesses of the dawn of mankind — Ariadne subdued him.

In deference to her faith, Khalil made a deliberate choice to abstain from using quotations from the Koran or the name of Allah, a customary convention for any calligraphy apprentice.

He chose Hafez's poems from a copy of the *Divan*, which he almost knew by heart. Second mistake.

In long letters rounded or with the shapes of pointed arcades, braids, and garlands, the Persian's poems revealed themselves, week after week, with the tenderness and patience with which a lover undresses his beloved. The lyrics had never sounded more agonizing to Khalil. He built his own prison of temptations and desires that tormented, as in adolescence, his flesh. He sought out his old prayer mat and tried to pray. Allah, Allah, Allah! His cry went unanswered. His mind was bereft of any sura that could save him. At nights, his fingernails dug into the wood of the floor when he knelt, into the wool of the quilt when he tried to sleep, into the burnt clay of his cups when he tried to drink.

Above his room, above the *mahalla* and the whole city, above the great empire, the starry sky continued its mute rotation. Most of the time, out of desperation, Khalil would take all the drafts, the scribbled or just-touched-by-her sheets, the half-started poems, the fragments of verses, and begin to read them, first in mind, then aloud. Among the smell of the smoke coming from the chimneys, between the creaking of the stairways of the neighboring houses and the dry cough of some late passer-by, poetry was the only thing that calmed him, the same poem that numbed his mind whenever he copied it, suicidally:

> *"He who enriches your cheeks with rosy light,*
> *give me patience and rest.*
> *And He who gave you beautiful and fragrant hair,*
> *out of His mercy with gifts, has blessed me.*
> *And if my hand is empty, I will not complain in vain:*
> *my joy remains, and it is my wealth.*
> *Treasures give to the kings, O Lord, and peace to the poor."*

He arrived at the end of every night pale, with deep, dark circles under his eyes, blood thickened with the mercury of insomnia, waiting to make it to Friday again.

Ariadne paid no heed to the uneasiness she was stirring. She greeted him warmly, with the serenity of a playful, fickle smile.

"May I call you 'Uncle Khalil' instead of Efendi?"

"Of course."

Third mistake. Alone with Uncle Khalil, the girl was back in the house in Genoa, huddled under the table, waiting for Iacopo Serratore to finish another map. The two-headed orange birds, greyhounds, chickens, unicorns, insects bigger than cathedrals and colorful snakes were hers again, only this time, it was no longer fantasy journeys, but big, opulent letters ending in dotted accolades.

Like Iacopo Serratore, Uncle Khalil had the same paleness of hands, the same thin fingers sometimes stained by ink. If she had cast aside his beard, turban, and caftan, Ariadne would have returned to the library, climbed back up into the attic, listened to the summer breeze rustle across the tiles, and sunk into an ocean of gentleness.

When Khalil wasn't paying attention, she used the letters' circles to draw eyes, noses, mouths, and ears; then laughed at the little merry faces. The teacher didn't mind, partly because he was confident that she would understand the secret beauty of Arab calligraphy sooner or later, and partly because he would have something to adore fiercely until the next meeting. He handed her a new sheet and told her to start again.

The magic sheets — just because they had sat on her lap — were more than a poisonous, sweet-tasting liquor without which the astrologer couldn't live. They were more than the stars of the night whose paths he had begun to forget. They were her breath trapped in his lungs, in the basket of his chest, the only place where he could keep it day and night, without anyone suspecting or being able to stop him.

Unaware of the storm she created, the Persian's verses helped Ariadne get even closer to Musa, when she cheerfully showed them to him on the paths they wandered, hidden by wild vines. For the young girl, the roses and the long-dead maidens' hair and the sadness of Hafez's empty cups, overwhelmed with helplessness in the face of the eternity of the poet's solitude, didn't mean anything unless she could change them into the stream of life, into love, into the joy of sharing her feelings with her lover; the same lover who, to Khalil's despair, would appear out of nowhere at the end of every calligraphy class.

"*Selamün aleyküm*, Uncle Khalil."

"*Aleyküm selam*, Musa."

"With your permission, I'll take Miss Serratore home."

The way he said her name, awkwardly, slightly embarrassed, made the noble Kufic symbols disappear, melt like lumps of wax on a hot iron cast stove; the paper sheets were hastily gathered, the veil was pulled over her head, and the eager Ariadne jumped to her feet. Livid, his eyes deep in the back of his head, Uncle Khalil remained to gather the other things while the young people moved away, hidden by the yellow leaves' tapestry. He contemplated multiple times whether to inform the Genoese that he was not accompanying Ariadne home, as they had previously arranged, but Mustafa's son, yet hesitated.

Fate had decided to divide things: on one side Musa, with his charming world, full of talking flags and flying ships, on the other an old Arab, master of unnamed stars, crumbling scrolls, and dead tongues.

The two lovers were long out of his sight when Khalil finished piling in the wooden box the ash jar, the inkwell, the stained pencils, the leather cover for her writing board, and the papers. Overwhelmed, he went down to the dark water of the Istinye Bay, heading to the room where the damp sheets, the oil lamp, the old Ptolemaic mathematic tables, and the same poem by Hafez were waiting for him.

TOMMASO

In 1536, driven mainly by hatred for the Habsburg family, Suleiman the Magnificent signed a treaty with Francis I of France. They then sought to keep it a secret because neither of them was particularly proud of this strange partnership between a Christian power and one that would have taken all Christian powers to their knees if it had been possible. But as a result of the treaty, France had, for a long time, political leverage at the Sublime Porte, and the French in Constantinople were the envy of all the world.

Philippe D'Auréville, a wealthy, middle-aged, childless widower, was one such Frenchman. He had no official position as an ambassador or military attaché; he passed as a well-known merchant who could fill any of the noble courts of Europe with rare objects. Manuscripts, statuettes, or miniatures, Philippe D'Auréville would tell you without fail the period or where they came from, and Padishah's passion for art was no stranger to him. With such fame and acquaintances, Monsieur D'Auréville and Tommaso Serratore were bound to meet very often in the social circles they frequented. If don Serratore needed a mosaic from Magna Graecia, a mechanical Byzantine gold bird that moved its wings and beak, or an Egyptian amulet, Philippe D'Auréville was there. In return, Tommaso Serratore could bring him jade from China, gems from the Indies, or a Bukhara carpet. They were not friends in the true sense of the word, but they trusted each other when it came to money owed or a letter of recommendation; so, somewhat naturally, when Tommaso thought of suitors for his daughter's hand, the viscount was first.

Three weeks had passed since Pelagia spilled the beans. The merchant knew from the little time he spent with his daughter that Ariadne would have to be gently persuaded if he was going to get out of this uncertain situation, so he thought it best to use the opportunity of a party. Nothing seemed more appropriate than to bring her out into the world at a party, in honor of her eighteenth birthday.

Following some thought, he decided to invite only his long-time acquaintances, neither too many nor too few, to avoid drawing attention and to disregard Ottoman officials. The guests of foreigners in Constantinople were usually known to those who poured words into the Grand Vizier's ears; their names, fortunes, and sometimes even the dreams they dreamed, if they inadvertently told them to anyone. Tommaso didn't want concealed spies finding out about his lavish table, strewn with mastic brandy and wine.

He chose the dishes himself: chicken and almond pilaf, roast rabbit with marjoram and coriander, partridges in peach compote, roast turbot in olive oil, and endless trays of sweets, pies, and candied fruit, to which he added a sweet white wine from Rhodes and a red wine from Burgundy that Eleonora liked very much.

As the day of the party approached, he asked Pelagia several times if she needed help. The woman looked at him with a frown. This was the first time since she had lived there that she had had the chance to show her real skill, so she shook her head. No, she didn't need any help with the preparations, just with setting the table a few hours beforehand and, when it was all over, washing the dishes.

In the evening, seated at the head of the table, Tommaso took care to keep his two Genoese friends and the Venetian *bailo* on his right. He didn't share the enmity between Genoa and Venice. He thought the Ottoman Empire was large enough to accommodate everyone, and if the rulers of the two city-states didn't think so, it was their business. For his part, whenever he needed a brocade caftan with silver or gold thread or a cloak hemmed with sable, he would order it from Venice. After all, he was just a middleman. He had never fought a war, held a disdain for politics, and only interacted with statesmen or grandees when absolutely necessary.

The Genoese came with their wives, and the Venetian nobleman was accompanied only by his daughter, three years younger than Ariadne. Fra Niccolo, who had arrived late, clad in his ordinary black cassock, a shadow among the garments and jewelry of the visitors, the silver chandeliers, the china, and the Bohemian crystal cups, added to the number of people seated at Tommaso's right hand.

On the other side, his Serbian friend, a sea captain with whom he sent most of his goods or brought them, then a very rich Armenian bookseller, accompanied by his wife, and Isaac, the trusted man, who kept all his ledgers and the record of his wealth. An impoverished Jew, Isaac had the beard and red hair of the Polish Jews and a noble look that he tried to hide. At the other end of the table, Monsieur D'Auréville, who arrived first, in a carriage bearing the insignia of the King of France on the doors. Having no official position near the High Gate — or at least not one that people knew about — Tommaso wondered for a moment why two angels, guarding the lilies of the House of Valois-Angoulême, appeared on the carriage doors. Finally, he decided to mind his own business and stop asking so many questions, even if they were only in his head.

Big scented candles burned everywhere, spreading a sweet smell and deceptive shadows on the walls. The double-glazed door to the garden was left open to let out the smoke and let in the cool, fragrant night air. In the autumn, the Golden Horn sky flickered over the hills, and the Galata's end of day dipped into the seawater of the bays.

Tommaso brought three women from Stavros' inn for assistance for this evening alone, and Pelagia didn't protest. When the first guests arrived, the housekeeper was still bustling around the kitchen amidst the pans, pots, and steams of food, where the aromas of fish and game in the oven blended with those of vegetables simmering in light sauces. Baked at dawn, trays of desserts laid on the pantry's shelves covered with tea towels.

When D'Auréville appeared, Ariadne had not yet emerged from her bedroom, leaving Tommaso to greet him alone. As a result, the viscount had to present him the enormous bouquet of white tulips and roses, as well as the box containing a tear-shaped necklace set in a white gold mount. It wasn't until the first dish was served and the wine, which had been chilled on ice beforehand, was making the guests feel slightly lightheaded that a teary-eyed Miss Serratore graced them with her presence.

She didn't wear the red velvet gown with its meticulously crafted pearl-filled corset, on which her father had expended great effort, personally overseeing the workers to ensure flawless bead threading and seam integrity. Instead, she chose the light muslin gown, resembling a green mist with subtle blue highlights, that she wore during her first visit to the port offices to meet Musa.

God, she's not cold? She's so headstrong to confront me that she's capable of catching a cold just to not do what I say. Tommaso got up and, without letting her know he was angry, handed her the pendant he had received as a gift from D'Auréville, praising its resemblance to the dress. The Frenchman approached with small steps; he suspected why he was there. As a rich widower and still young, he was wanted as a son-in-law by many Christian fathers in Istanbul, and it was true that among them, Serratore was the worthiest among considerations, but nothing in his behavior betrayed that he knew. All evening, he strove to be gallant to Ariadne, who did not encourage him in the least.

Philippe spoke fluent *Romanesca*, the language of the people from Lazio, and it was obvious that he hadn't picked it up on the streets. This pleased the girl, who didn't have to bother responding to him in the Lingua Franca of Europeans in Constantinople or in the few Turkish words she had learned from Musa and Khalil.

"You speak so well… Where did you learn?"

"I lived for a few years near the Papal Nuncio."

Tommaso was eavesdropping on the conversation. *The papal nuncio? Certainly, this man had a lot of secrets.* Ariadne seemed unimpressed. "Oh, yeah?" — and her attention then drifted to the newest printed edition of Dante's verse — "I haven't seen it, yet." "If you like, I can send it to you." They talked about the height of Michelangelo's dome — "Was it true that it surpassed that of the architect Sinan?" — about the never-ending alterations to the Basilica Papale di San Pietro, and about the statues commissioned by the generous Ferdinando de Medici. Little by little, warmed by the yearning for Genoa and rosy-cheeked by the wine, Ariadne smiled. Not at anyone in particular, but at the night's stains behind the curtains, the silence held captive in the salon's corners, the drapery, and the paintings adorning the walls. When the last guest — also Phillippe D'Auréville — left, Ariadne went upstairs to go to bed, saying farewell to everyone from a distance. A sympathetic witness, the Frenchman bid farewell with the same self-assurance he used to evaluate a rare marble or one of Henlein's early-crafted watches.

Half of the gifts were untouched; in the kitchen, the maids were washing the cups and silver trays. Tommaso blew out all the candles and went out into the courtyard. Darkness united the two continents, across the strait, at that hour, undisturbed by people, boats, or seagulls. Prolonged, humid, stinging — the autumn's chill. He felt it in his shoulders, in his head that throbbed with pain. He had no choice. He had to talk to Ariadne first, then to Mustafa.

ARIADNE

In November, Pelagia prepared the beehives for winter in the garden dressed in crispy mist. She arranged the apples and the quinces in the cupboards in each room, for their scent, and set fire to fallen leaves and dry grass. In place of the dried leafy piles, there remained a few black patches of skinned earth, over which Ariadne kept glancing as she waited for Tommaso to finish filling his clay pipe. At home, the merchant smoked pipe, as he had learned from the Portuguese merchants around the port of Genoa; only, unlike them, he mixed the tobacco threads with aromatic herbs. The subtle savor, spread under the ceilings, reminded them both of Eleonora and another life.

Tommaso took his time. Holding the tamper in one hand and the pipe in the other, he looked as if he wasn't in the room, as if he had left. The air between them shattered into shards. Eventually, gloomily, he started to talk.

"You know I like Musa, as a person, I mean."

"Yeah? As a person… and otherwise, why don't you like him?"

He knew all too well who she had inherited when she was abrupt and cutting. Neither Ariadne nor her father minced words when they had something to say.

"What I like or don't like doesn't mean much now. What matters is that you can't marry him."

"Because he's a Muslim?"

"Yes… and because he's poor…"

"A poor Muslim, what a problem for don Serratore…"

"That's no way to talk to a father. I've spoiled you too much…"

Because Giovanna took her last breath as you took your first, he wanted to continue but stopped himself to avoid bringing up such a painful thought.

"And not just me. Your grandparents and the sisters in the convent spoiled you. Life is not as you think. You were born into a wealth that not many have. Do you want to live here in Constantinople next to a Turk? You have no friends, you don't speak the language, what are you going to do all day? And what will both of you live on? On my fortune?"

"Ah, so that's the question! Isn't that what every parent asks a child who doesn't obey? What will you live on?"

The girl tried to buy time. The truth was that she and the shy Musa hadn't discussed marriage, and she found herself caught off guard. She was terrified of being locked up again, of marrying someone else. A new fear.

"Papa, I don't know what we'll live on, but if you love me, help us leave. Send Musa to university in Genoa, Florence, wherever you want. You've said many times he'll succeed… and I'll go with him… home."

So, she wanted to go back. The tall house, the hills filled with smoke from the burning leaves, the November sky, the garden — all spun around him at once. Tommaso ran his palm over his eyes, to keep his concern from showing.

"You think… he's gonna want to leave here?"

"Yes, Daddy, he will!"

She responded with fervor, without a moment's hesitation, without doubt, jumping on her feet and walking towards Tommaso like an unbridled surge. After Musa and Khalil, it was now Tommaso's turn to witness the procession of women who had subdued men under their thighs that emerged from Ariadne whenever she wished strongly for anything. The father got up from his armchair and put his arms around her shoulders, embracing her. The pipe fell, and the soft ashes scattered into little lights on the floor.

Watching how she rested her forehead on his chest, whispering "please papa, please," Tommaso thought he understood why the timid, good-natured boy, half a head shorter than his daughter and able to remain still for ten hours in front of a pencil sketch, adored her. Musa needed her zest for life, her strong spirit. For the lovers, it was simple: they were free to be together, without asking permission. For Tommaso, other strings were knotted.

"I'll have to think about it… but until I make a decision, you're not seeing him."

Not seeing him anymore? That was impossible.

"But nothing has happened…"

"Even so, it isn't proper. Here you are, not protected by the walls of a convent. Here is a foreign world, often dangerous. Listen to me, it's for your own good."

"Fine, but you don't kick him out, you don't chase him away, you don't hurt him."

"Who do you take me for?"

"And he's not that poor, you know."

"I know, I know his family well; let's just say he's not nearly as rich as you are."

"And he's not so much of a believer either…"

"What do you mean?"

"I mean, he believes that all the prophets say the same thing, that all the holy books are the same, only that they are written in different languages, that Allah is another name given to God, among many other names… and so on… We don't really talk about these things…"

"And he doesn't pray?"

"I don't think so. I haven't seen him. He just said he didn't want anyone forcing him to pray… I don't pray much anymore either, Daddy… My prayers are more of a memory."

She hesitated to disclose whose memory.

That really was something new. Where was Ariadne of Genoa? The adoration of Jesus? What had happened to the sad Virgin Mary, surrounded by white clouds and chubby angels? He didn't like that Ariadne anyway, the one who wanted to become a nun. But to lose her grey robes and her struggle too fast, so eagerly, after falling in love? Then, why did she go to Mass every morning?

"But would he change his faith for you? Would he become a Christian?"

"No, papa, I don't think he'd change it."

The conversation had slipped onto thin ice, and Ariadne didn't feel quite in control, so she hurried to reassure him.

"And neither would I mine. The law allows Muslims to take Christian wives, and the women do not have to accept Islam as their religion."

It is amazing how she managed to find all this out, without talking to anyone and without knowing anyone. Khalil! Sure, it was the Arab!

"Did Khalil tell you?"

"Yes, I asked him."

If Khalil knew, things were more settled than he'd imagined, and they'd probably been going on longer. He wanted to ask if Mustafa also knew.

"And, besides, there are so many Christian girls in the Palace…"

"Have you lost your mind? What are you talking about? Those girls are concubines or slaves, and many have gone over to Islam, which will never happen to you, at least not as long as I live!"

Tommaso felt betrayed. He didn't want to live alone in the house in Galata or go back to Genoa, to argue with Matteo every day. He also didn't want to go to Catarina in China. There wasn't much left for him if Ariadne left. He had worked all his life for her, and now? If only he could move her thoughts away from this marriage, from which nothing good could come...

The girl moved away and sat down, returning to the sulky silence with which she had defended herself since her father had learned from the woman of her love and Bosporus-scented clothes. Behind her sharp black eyes, only one thought: to let Musa know what has happened as soon as possible.

Pelagia came in with a tray of hot tea and went out without anyone seeing her. When she closed the door to the salon, she burst out laughing. Father and daughter looked strikingly alike. Two swords in the same sheath. Who would find it easy to live like this?

PELAGIA

At the first rays of sunlight, she got out of bed, grabbed her evening-prepared pack, and snuck out to the five or six goats. Aside from a stone-walled unplastered house with a corridor and two rooms where they all huddled, a few old vine stumps that produced sour wine, and two rows of olive trees on the outskirts of the village, the goats were all they possessed. Walking the hot lanes to the dusty hills that entered the sea like long tongues, Pelagia took them to graze every day.

She had been wandering for years on the scorching stones in the summers, shaded by rain in the mild winters, looking for tufts, roots, or long strands of grass, when she was caught and raped by some boys from the neighboring village. They had stalked her as she climbed the edge of the hill, hit her on the head with a rock, and she fainted. She woke up many hours later, alone; she stood up and looked at her blood-splattered body, which ached from head to toe. The goats had scattered, and it took her some time to gather them. She trudged, staggering along, without pausing to wash the dried blood clots from her feet. She limped down into the hamlet after gathering all the animals, rubbing her swollen temple, which hurt more than the scratches on her back left by sharp stone.

She opened the gate, led the little flock to the sheep enclosure, and entered the house. The village found out the same day, and no one was to marry her or touch her. Perhaps only some drunkard, some traveler from far away, or some man who was not their kindred would do it. By the time she was an old maid, Nikos had proposed. They were first cousins, and you couldn't say he was a drunkard or of another kin, but he was a traveler. He moved to Constantinople at an early age and held diverse occupations before landing a job as a cook in the establishment owned by Stavros, a fellow Greek countryman.

The exchange of words between the two men didn't last long. Like the whole village, Nikos knew what had happened a decade before, but he didn't care. He'd known her since she was born, older than her by only two years, seen her playing in the yard, soaring, braiding her hair into a single ponytail above her head, going to church. He knew her long hands and firm gait, how she didn't turn her head after anyone, and how she chose her words carefully.

But Nikos had not seen the sadness and the killing loneliness because he was already gone, at the imperial capital. The old man said yes, though he remained alone in the household, not bothering to ask her. Pelagia was used to not being asked, as if her being, after the rape, was no longer hers, and she didn't object to the marriage. But she was mistaken, because the old men of the village had begun to forget the affair, and the young ones had other things on their minds; the only one who bore the God-given burden of whitewashing the family name was her father, who proved himself glad and hasty to conclude the bargain. Pelagia took Nikos as her husband after a single day in the empty village church, without a wedding gown, without a feast, and with only a priest and a deacon by her side. After that, all she had to do was kiss the old man's hand, get into the cart, and leave in less than two hours. She left the land, hoping she would never see anyone born there again.

They spent the wedding night among jute ropes and untanned sheepskins, on a shabby ship that smelled of smoked fish. The captain was afraid of pirates, and they navigated only after sunset, when Nikos, usually drunk and giddy due to the reeling boat, lifted her skirt and climbed on. Pelagia couldn't feel a thing and, as she was to find out in the months and years to come, couldn't have children either, but at least she didn't bleed anymore.

At any hour, Stavros opened the door of the caravanserai to anyone. Sometimes, a lot of people arrived from all corners of the empire, after extinguishing the lanterns in the courtyards, the candles, and oil lamps in the houses, and the torches in the streets. Merchants and scribes, sailors and soldiers, whole families with children, or just a destitute nobleman, unaccompanied, all stepped through the darkness to find shelter, a bowl of soup, the leftovers of a cold pie, a glass of cold milk.

The women who worked at the inn slept upstairs in the servants' rooms at the back of the building. Stavros didn't allow any woman, married or not, to walk at night in the kitchen or around the rooms of the guests so that he would not hear any bad words about his hostelry. Late travelers were greeted only by men, the guards at the main gates, and those who slept in the kitchen at night. Understanding the language of the hot sand dunes, the thick forests, the remote fortresses on the banks of the Danube, the shredded grass under the hooves of Anatolia, and the rains of the Caucasus, they served all clients. As in every inn in the world, Stavros' caravanserai spoke all languages, mixed into one, that of aching bones and stiffened walking joints, of murderous homesickness, of tears and the meandering, deceiving, vast horizon lines.

Over the years, servants and gardeners, cooks and helpers worked day and night at the inn and filled the back rooms with their lives; some left or died, others, like Pelagia, stayed because they had nowhere else to go. At first, the woman lived with her husband in a small room, where only a bed, the dowry chest, and the icons fit. Nevertheless, as the responsibilities of a married woman did not overly strain her, in less than a month, after meticulously cleaning and mending Nikos' garments, she volunteered to aid in the kitchen.

However, Stavros granted her a small stipend, which the woman kept. Her father had the house and the olive trees and the goats and didn't want to know about her anyway, and her brothers had left her long ago, so she didn't have to send money to anyone. Apart from their pay, after a while, satisfied with Nikos and his wife's work, the master of the inn moved them to a bigger room, the biggest and brightest in the backyard.

At first, she didn't dare cook, but soon, sitting next to Nikos, she quickly picked up all sorts of recipes. Anchovies, black horse mackerel, red mullet, blue whiting, freshly cut lamb, leeks, cauliflower, artichokes, cabbage, celery, auberges, green and red peppers, pigeons, quail, beans, cantaloupes, pomegranates, runny honey, molasses from grapes turned under her hands into simit full of sesame or sunflower seeds, *kuzu tandır*, *manaqish* with *za'atar and* olive oil, *pide* with cheese and spinach, *menemen* with fresh tomatoes, countless varieties of baklava, *knafeh* and *lokum*. The roads between fruits and vegetables, fresh or smoked and dried meats, and the kitchen's bowls and flasks, passed through Pelagia's head, giving birth to hidden mountains and valleys. If you asked her, she could bless you on the spot with the secrets of sauce-making, of using spices, simmering broths, and preserving pickles, but her served meals were not just a string of dishes — her cooking held a mysterious geography. Many of the hungry inn's guests hastily or leisurely devoured the wonders born of the woman's hands and then went on their way. Pelagia bore them no grudges — though she rarely heard words of appreciation from anyone — as long as they let her roam freely through the valleys and mountains of fruit, vegetables, and streams of water full of fish known only to her.

When she moved into don Serratore's house, she found herself missing the faces of the travelers, the laughter in the kitchen, Stavros' mumbling when he was scolding a new helper. The Genoese merchant left in the morning, came home in the evening, ate at home once a day, and that wild child, the papist, as she called her in her thoughts, didn't touch the food much.

Wounded in her pride, Pelagia went so far as to ask the girl if she wanted to cook her something of theirs, a dish from her own country, but Ariadne had shaken her head no.

It was only the cooking that never left its place in Pelagia's mind or in her life. From the very beginning, don Serratore ordered her to go to the bazaar twice a week and buy fresh meat, fruit, and vegetables so that she had something to cook with to pass the time. So, almost every day, she remembered the burnt wood filling the oven in her grandparents' backyard when she could barely walk, the clay pots where auberges stuffed with tomatoes and garlic slept, lentil and plum dishes, peppers stuffed with sheep's cheese rubbed with sweet cheese, quinces, spinach pie, raisin-filled Pascua, cinnamon milk, orange, plum, and cherry sherbet, puddings, and doughnuts.

Usually, when she finished, she covered the dishes and walked up the hill to Fra Niccolò's orphanage. Between the two, the Greek Orthodox woman and the Benedictine priest, an unusual friendship was born. He didn't ask Pelagia to be his cook, but she would always show up around noon with food, and everyone would run to greet her. On Sundays, after Mass at St Anne's Basilica, they both blessed — the priest aloud, she without words — plates of thick pieces of *melopita*, honey pie, or *yiaourtopita*. Especially on Sundays, it didn't matter what language you spoke or what prayers you said, it didn't matter how old you were or what you were wearing — the whole orphanage ate Greek dishes.

She soon became known in the *mahalla*, and anyone could tell in advance, based on when she finished climbing the hill, when Father Niccolò's service would end. Sometimes, when they had guests at the orphanage, and the food was finished early, the woman went up the hill a second time the same day with dinner.

Don Serratore didn't mind Pelagia's occupation. His house looked organized, and the coins he gave weekly to her for the orphanage were no big deal, especially when Pelagia managed to feed a large number of souls. "You'll have a place in Heaven for your generosity," the good priest, blushing with joy, thanked Tommaso, whenever he saw him.

After everyone in the orphanage finished their meal, and she had washed the wooden bowls or had the children wash them, Pelagia strolled through the streets of Galata, making her way to her room where, whenever the weather was bad, she knitted. Undergarments, woolen socks, hats, and shawls. She used to buy wool from a Turkish man she knew well and who always wondered at her. "Did you open your own carpet shop, Mistress Pelagia? What are you doing with all that wool?" "Never mind, Ali Efendi, I'll get you a carpet one day," she joked, spending her monthly pay in one go in the Bazaar.

In the presence of Fra Niccolò's children, tending to their bathing, nourishment, or dressing, Pelagia found solace in the only realm untouched by the past. There, apart from the food of her childhood, she remembered nothing.

STAVROS

Words passed through Stavros' inn as if through ears, and many of the town's stories ended here or just rested for a while and moved on. Some crawled through the streets, entered beneath window ledges, under gates, under pier posts, others simply flew, from the old Seraglio on the third hill to the new one, to the Castle of the Seven Towers, or through the boonies of the Covered Bazaar.

Words erased or living words, born of betrayal or love, all founded a place in Stavros' inn. Unlike the rooms upstairs, full of shredded, hidden, sneaking words, in the big hall of the café downstairs, words flew freely among the visitors or under the archways on the edge, resembling empty shells in which a man could stand. Don Serratore ordered such a partition to be prepared for him, for an important meeting. There, Stavros placed with his own hand a couple of pots, two hot sand-filled pans, and coffee cups; around the trays and beside the two low tables, inlaid with mother-of-pearl, on which the hookahs stood, the innkeeper had thrown large cushions covered with embroidered shawls.

The little space had been meticulously readied when the innkeeper beheld the sudden appearance of don Serratore and Mustafa, the jeweler, leaving him utterly taken aback. Mustafa was known for his honesty and character — everyone knew the story of the imperial diadem — but Stavros had expected some high-ranking dignitary, as the Genoese accustomed him to. The Greek opened the curtained door and let them in, asking if they needed anything else. They waved their hands that they didn't, and the innkeeper withdrew with a bow. *I wonder what they had to say to each other that they came all this way?*

Through the minuscule holes in the walls — for which the inn had been nicknamed "The Ear" — Stavros could smell the scent of wood, leaves, resin, and moss coming from the hookahs and see the two men sitting on cushions, leaning towards each other from time to time. They both conveyed a feeling of bitterness, and at one point Tommas, raised his voice:

"She's my only girl, Mustafa. My only child. It's for Ariadne that I've worked so hard to gather so much wealth. What should I do with her, married, here?"

"And my only boy, all I have left, the light of my eyes and his mother's support in old age. Where would he go?"

"But there, he can go to school, he can become a shipowner if he wants, a man of distinction. And Genoa is very different from Istanbul, Mustafa. There, everyone's gone left and right to the Americas, Andalusia, the Levant, Africa, and even China. They go, and they come back. Nobody's going to take a long look at a Muslim, especially if he's rich, like Musa. What about her here? No matter how rich she is, she's still a Christian woman married to a Turk. Let them go, Mustafa, it'll be fine."

The goldsmith stood silent under the white smoke. Meryem had refused to accept the prospect of her son's marriage anyway; but to tell her that Musa would go to live in Genoa, that she would not see her grandchildren for whom she had woven carpets for years, that she would not hold them in her arms, and that they would grow up among strangers, and Christians on top of that, was beyond him. He answered faintly, almost despairingly:

"Why did you bring her all this way, don Serratore? Why didn't you leave her in Genoa to marry into a rich family, and it would have been something else…"

"That's what I intended for her… but when I heard that she wanted to become a nun, I thought that the best thing to do was to take her away from there, to push her away from everything, and bring her to live next to me, to see the world. What can a girl who grew up inside the walls of a convent understand about this world?"

"Even so, she was clever enough at finding a man… I don't understand how these two met…"

"We helped them, Mustafa. I took him to work in the port offices, you sent the fish basket, we, their parents, were God's tools… or Allah's, whatever you want to call it… After all, what exactly do we want to protect them from?"

"From suffering. Their life will be difficult… We want them well."

"Maybe they won't suffer. Do you think we know what's good for them?"

"We are old, don Serratore, and we have seen a lot. Perhaps that's why we are so accustomed to difficulties. Your child remains yours until death. You can't help it. It's the law of nature, and you want to keep him out of harm if you can…"

"I don't know what to say… Do you think we are wiser just because we are older? Maybe we're more used to enduring hardship, not necessarily wiser. Anyway, what's the point of dragging it out now if they're so determined? At least Ariadne will fight me until I let her marry Musa. She'd run off with him, God forbid. What shall I do, lock her up in a convent again?"

…Snatches of words, like butterflies with wings torn off, swirled around the room, disheveled, flakes of ash, and hot beads of sand…

"I say let's not fight it… After all, they didn't break any laws or tarnish anyone's honor, inshallah, and they love each other… and if this departure will help Musa build ships and fulfill his dream, I, as a father, agree. Just, let's delay a little longer, at least three months… Then, we'll see…"

Mustafa needed time to clear Meryem on the subject, and Tommaso, write the marriage contract, buy a house in Spezia — he didn't want the young couple to live with his brother — and find a ship to take them safely to Genoa.

Both hoped, in their heart of hearts, that in these three months, the two would change their minds or that their stubbornness would diminish.

Because Mustafa eventually agreed to his boy leaving, Tommaso consented to a Muslim wedding. Sharia allowed Muslims to marry a Christian woman without her changing her religion, but to be married by a Catholic priest, Musa would first have to be baptized. This would have been too much for Mustafa, who was going to move heaven and earth to reconcile everyone.

They parted in front of the inn, shaking hands and touching their chests, according to the custom of the place — Mustafa already hearing Meryem's shrill sobs in his ears, and Serratore worried sick about how his only daughter would take the three-month postponement.

Stavros called for a maid to take the sandboxes, dirty mugs, and hookahs and open the windows. Through the wooden shutters, which had been pushed aside, the words of Tommaso and Mustafa sneaked out and slid away, amidst needles of ice, *mahalla*'s dust, and wind-tossed thistles.

MUSTAFA

Wax came from Moldova. Not only the melted honey-combs but also the shellac, the earth's moisture, the peat residue with fir resin, mosses, and the dampness of the mushrooms. White, golden, greenish, reddish, as tall as a man's stature, the bulks took the road to the Carpathians, in carts drawn by oxen. Back then, honey traveled to the low barges, split in the sun, asleep at the mouths of the Danube. Plants, animals, and stones — the world of wax swept them all in its path and carried them onward across borders on land and stretches of water to other ports and peoples.

For a few of the wax bars — fewer and fewer — the journey ended in Mustafa's workshop. Earrings, anklets, dagger handles, hairpins: for each of them, the goldsmith poured at least three wax figures. For days, he listened, weighed them in his palms, examined the threads of pollen trapped inside, sniffed the warm, sharp, lively green — the scent captive in the wax of the flowers grown near the beehives. Arches, twists, needles, curves, or circles of gold and silver were first born as a fragmented engraving in the goldsmith's mind. In the next stage, they would reach the clay mixed with sand in which he would wrap the patterns. The reddish dust would get under his fingernails, in the creases of his skin, in his ears, but he would not mind as long as the little wax figures were flawless. Otherwise, he'd have to start over.

Then, he would bake the mold — into which the metal was to be cast — for a long time until the boiling hotness entered the mold's grooves. Gold, silver, pewter, amalgams he had invented with or without names, all understood him. Mustafa knew how and how much to heat them, how to transform them, how to thicken them, when to leave them to cool, how to talk to them. Lately, the only words spoken in the workshop and in the house. After endless arguments, shouting, and crying, Musa had left home again, for the third time, and Meryem had sunken into mute deafness; voiceless, still, wrapped in hatred. Mustafa worked in the workshop all day long to calm himself down.

He put the fine piles down and began to gather his things. Nothing worked. Wax that had been kept too long in the cold air crumbled and had to be cut again; the dirty crucibles loaded the three rings at work with useless metal drips, and the moldings were damaged; a chaotic array of scissors, hammers, pliers, a multitude of wooden wedges, and miniature anvils cluttered the table.

A week before, a carriage had stopped in front of the house's gate, and a page from the Seraglio, together with a janissary, entered the courtyard, asked for Mustafa, and handed Meryem a bag of two hundred ducats. That was all, without any explanation, without anything. Now, that purse lay next to the stone block hewn around the edges, where he cut the threads or thinned the gold leaf. Although six months passed, the Padishah had not forgotten.

He went down to the empty kitchen. Meryem went again to the cemetery near the house, where she used to pray, and Mustafa strolled to the Jewish quarter. The walls' edges hurt him, the air was too strong, and the Bosporus water seemed dark and deceptive. Walking towards Leib Peres' apothecary along the wooden-roofed streets lined with poplars, Judas trees, and chestnut trees, Mustafa did not hear the veiled voices in the courtyards, the sounds of dishes being washed at the fountains, the cry of a child, or the barking of dogs. Tiredness overwhelmed him, and he wanted to turn back several times.

When he finally arrived, the blue-and-white porcelain jars with metal lids, the oddly lettered labels, and the neatly arranged shelves stung his eyes, and he slumped down on the two chairs by the entrance, next to a small table where the Jew placed a water jug and a few small cups.

Leib Peres, a tall, very thin, grizzled man, looking still young, came out to meet him. He dressed in the style of European fashion, donning a pair of dark trousers and a matching jacket that revealed *Kanfot's arba* beneath. If Mustafa had not observed the tassels of the garment and the two mezuzahs, affixed to the right side of the door hinges — two small lead tubes inscribed with the word "El Shaddai" — he would have been unaware of the fact that he was standing in a Jewish apothecary.

"*Shalom aleihem*, Mustafa Efendi, what brings you here?"

"*Aleyküm selam.* I can't sleep… I can't sleep, the worries…"

"I'll make a potion, Mustafa Efendi, it won't take long. Shall I tell Leah to make tea?"

"What kind of tea?"

They both smiled.

"No, I don't want any tea from the *House of Dreams.* I'll have only water."

The Jew rummaged around for a wooden box, picked out a handful of dried poppy seeds, then began to crush them. When only a fine powder remained in the grinder, he carefully poured boiling water over it and then dripped a few drops of honey. When the mixture cooled, he added saffron, castor oil, amber, musk, and nutmeg and handed it to Mustafa to taste.

"I should put in two more glasses of wine, but…"

"No, I'll take it, it's good like this. How much should I drink?"

"Two tablespoons at bedtime, then two more in three hours if needed."

He poured the liquid into a small pot and tied the cork with a thin string, which tangled between his fingers. Mustafa crossed to the other side of the counter and helped him knot the ends.

"I'd like to ask you something. Do you Jews… believe in immortality?"

"I'm a poor apothecary, not a rabbi. How can I answer such a big question?"

"Yeah, but you're a learned man…"

"I have learned to distinguish at a glance young and old plants, fruiting plants and old ones, to dry them, to sift all kinds of powders, to prepare infusions and decoctions. Taught to believe in the God of Israel Almighty, to keep the Sabbath, to perform the Kiddush of the dead in my family… but I, who have so much to do with diseases of soul and body, know that, as it says in the Torah: *because you are dust, to dust you shall return.* You and I are men of the Book, Mustafa Efendi. What good are such questions?"

"Banish the fear of death…"

"Faith banishes the fear of death. But I can understand because I think I know more about fears than the rabbis. All my life, I have helped both those who believe and those who don't, and I have helped them not only with the fear of death but with all kinds of fears. The cure for them…"

He picked up the wooden box of poppy seeds and tapped his fingernail on it slowly.

"Yes, but that's just a numbing, a short sleep, procrastination…"

"Isn't our whole life a delay, a time, longer or shorter, from the moment of birth to the moment of death?"

"I was hoping it was more than that…"

"We all want to believe that. After all, it's up to each human being to figure out the meaning of life. You don't know in advance what will happen. You have to find out for yourself. Sometimes, it's so difficult…"

"But no one has made a treaty with us that it would be easy. Go in good health, Mustafa Efendi, and if you need anything else, you know where to find me."

He took the silver coin held out by the Muslim, led him to the door, and closed the shop. Was that what was bothering the goldsmith? No, it had to be something else. He shrugged and headed for the pavilion in the courtyard, nicknamed the *House of Dreams*. If it was something important, the Jew knew he'd find out sooner or later. In the *House of Dreams*, like in Stavros' inn, the city's secrets were created and dismantled; some under the sign of wine, others under that of opium.

When he built his household in the Balat district, the Jew had chosen a street end. His house was the last, followed by a maidan and some watermelon crop fields. The courtyard pavilion, enclosed by doors and connected to the house by a wooden deck of light beams, was not large, but it was covered from foundation to roof with ivy and roses, making it nearly invisible from the street. Starting about noon and until sunset, local acquaintances could easily find the gate from the maidan and sneak in. After sunset, two Albanians and a Bosnian picked up those who collapsed on the sofas and very gently carried them to the back alley, where a carriage waited for them, or they had to walk. No one could stay overnight, for the well-being of his whole family depended on his good reputation as a merchant and apothecary. Those who crossed his threshold did so because they trusted him, and a good name was often more valuable than money.

The pavilion looked like any cafe in Istanbul, and passers-by might have missed it if they weren't locals. For the latter, opium tea and opium sweets were brought on trays by Leib's two maids and sometimes by his wife, Dvora. Leah, their only daughter, never set foot there. Clients were plentiful and of all kinds. Lonely travelers, horsemen, janissaries, the son of a pasha, storekeepers, physicians, artists rich enough, and few women, single, widows, or married women hiding for a few hours. Draped in veils, they sat in the corner behind cedarwood covered with a velvet drapery, talking only to the maids.

Rich or poor, old, or young, the *House of Dreams* welcomed everyone. Leib Peres ran a legitimate business. Mustafa fully grasped the reason that he told him he knew the cure for all fears. But what the goldsmith didn't know or even suspect was that one of the Jew's most regular guests was Tommaso Serratore.

MUSA

Cruelty — what struck him about her was cruelty. The tight lips, the sharp eyes. He'd heard it too many times:

"I will never, ever come to your wedding, Musa!"

In late autumn, the wind-blown leaves clung to the tops of houses, and the last of the crickets barely crept through the gardens. Meryem cooked a feast, as she did every year on his birthday. Invited: Musa, Ayla, his aunt, his mother's younger sister, two cousins, his father, and a neighbor. She greeted her son on the doorstep.

"You're here now? I thought you weren't coming!"

Anger darkened her fingers and fingernails. She looked fatter, or perhaps shorter. She wore her good dress, but it hung somewhat crookedly, unbecomingly, and one could see that she cried because around her red eyelids, the skin thinned; a large vein twitched occasionally at the corner of her left eye, and her mouth had deepened.

"Stay here!" she hissed, briefly showing him to a seat at the table next to Mustafa, and then hurried to the stove to get some more food.

What else was there to bring? The whole kitchen was full of food. Everything he liked. Was she proving a point? Was she doing it as revenge? Musa didn't know, just like he didn't know where the woman he'd followed around the Covered Bazaar when he was little, carrying her wool rolls, had vanished. They'd stop by the bakers' alley: hot tea, bits of Turkish delight of all colors, rolled in sugar, or halva. Now, she acted as if they were no longer mother and son, leaning on the air between them like a crutch.

As soon as they remained alone, the two men went upstairs to the workshop. The scrolls of patterned parchment, the anvils, the pliers and locks, the shelves, and the gnawed carpet, all well known to Musa, seemed different. They had a different light, or maybe they just lacked light, though the lamp spun large, yellow circles around them.

"How long has she been like this?"

"Since you left. But today was worse."

"And what do you think?"

"What do I think about her?"

"No, about me leaving. You blame me, don't you? I'm the reason she got sick!"

"I don't blame you… I think you have every right to leave or love whomever you want if you live without doing wrong and if you respect the commands of the Prophet, Peace be upon His name, but that's not what you should have said."

"But how was I supposed to tell her?"

"You told her, and that same night, you left… never to return…"

"I couldn't help it, *baba*…"

"What do you mean? That you couldn't have done it any other way?"

"Because if I'd told her otherwise, I wouldn't have left… *Anne* would have made me feel sorry, and I would have stayed, and I can't do that, I really can't. At first, I didn't do anything. Do you remember? You sent me to don Serratore. All that happened came over me, without me searching for anything like this, but after I saw Ariadne... believe me, I prayed myself out of my mind, I made relentless efforts day and night to suppress thoughts of her, however... There was no escaping for me, no eluding all that came afterward."

Musa felt the need to tell him about the turmoil of the nights when he tried to fight off torturous doubts; of Ariadne's body, which burned him for months, though he had not touched her; of the day he had brought her the fish, the day that had sealed their fate; of the vision of a common set of flags and signs for the Mediterranean fleet enabling mutual comprehension regardless of language barriers; of the sprawling cities with towers and cobbled streets where he foresaw his destiny; of beggars and kings he would meet, of adventurers and commoners... His destiny was to leave with the woman he loved for a new world. But in this moment, he just opened his arms, wide in the air, drawing an invisible gate.

"I couldn't have done it any other way... Understand, *baba*?"

"I understand that this is Allah's will. If Allah had not willed, all this would not have happened. And who am I to oppose Allah's will?"

"And why doesn't *anne* say that?

"Well, Musa, you want too much from your poor mother. Her whole life is in this courtyard, on the prayer rug, tending the girls' graves. The border is at the Covered Bazaar. She doesn't even go as far as Constantinople ends. Doesn't want to go; says she doesn't need to. What's to see outside the city? She has everything she needs here. What's the point of meeting people other than her kin? She is afraid of them. They are foreigners, they don't keep our rules, and they don't live their lives as she is used to. How can she see with her mind's eye fleets and oceans, flags, and everything you paint?"

"She can't see them, but she might trust me. Doesn't she know me? Who raised me?"

"See, this is where you don't understand, Musa. She doesn't trust anything. Simply put, she just doesn't get the point of what's going on. She thinks she did something, that Allah punished her when He gave her a son like you, even though she tried so hard all her life to serve Him. She asks me all the time, 'What did I do wrong, Mustafa, what did I do wrong?'"

"She didn't make any mistakes... I just want to pick her up and say, *anne*, let me go, and it'll be okay."

"I say don't do it; you might hurt her more."

"I can't even. She won't talk to me. It's like we live in different countries already."

"I say calm down... at least you... You see, Musa, I, with my goldsmith's mind, don't have much schooling, just enough to read and write, but I realize that you and your mother will never get along. You don't see anything with the same eyes, and you're always trying to convince each other of something... Ever since you were little, you've been arguing with her when she wouldn't leave you alone... Or... what can you do when two people are like the sun and the moon? It's not their fault..."

"And you, *baba*?"

"Me? As usual, in the middle. But you don't have the stomach for it. I'm glad I at least tried to make peace... but I'm tired Musa, of your quarrels, of everything..."

"Did something else happen that I don't know about?"

There was no point in telling him about the talisman. Anyway, Musa was leaving, and he couldn't help with anything. Why burden him?

"No. I've given you my blessing to leave. Go in peace. Too seldom do we have a choice in life. Be glad you have one. May Allah guide your steps and help you achieve your dreams."

"That's just it, *baba*, that if the moments when we can choose are rare, we must not lose them. We must be brave and go forward, don't you think?"

"Courage... it's something that left me a long time ago, and I don't even think I ever had it in a large amount. Anyway, with the only crumbs of it I can find, I'll stand up to Meryem... I'll keep telling her until she understands that even though you were born into our family, you're Allah's creation. We just gladly received His gift. So, who are we to stop you from fulfilling your destiny, if you think that's your destiny?"

Mustafa stood up from his corner and took his son in his arms, then pressed his lips to the boy's forehead: *Who knows when I'll be able to do it again?* He held him tight to his chest.

"You're leaving?"

"Yeah, it's late."

"You don't want to stay the night? In your room?"

"Like this?"

...Like an unwelcome guest, in his bedroom, with his old kite hanging on the wall and the string from the toy ships he had carved himself, to sleep with the bitter taste of moldy spittle in his mouth, in a foreign realm...

"No. I'm just going to say goodbye."

He knocked several times on the suddenly heavy, dark, scratched door.

"*Anne?*"

Silence.

"*Anne*, are you in bed?"

He didn't hear anything. So, he went downstairs and left the house through the kitchen. Trapped inside her life, with her face buried in a pillow, Meryem crumpled onto the bed, sobbing.

HAVVA

She dozed for a while, then sleepily, reached for a piece of cardamom date pie; her fingers slipped into the void. From the bedchamber, trays of *kolompeh*, chickpea cookies with saffron and nut candy, or almond nougat, had been removed at her command. Whenever she lay, naked at the hammam, on the warm marble, waiting to be anointed with oil, she would order her Nubian slaves to cover her as quickly as possible with the white body-wiping sheet, made of the finest Antioch cotton.

The light flowing in droplets soothed her, and baths with lavender oil, rosemary and ginger, geranium, nutmeg, and sea salt whitened and softened the skin on her full arms and two rows of tummies, but she could no longer bear to look at herself or have others see her naked. She was served by girls and women of all ages or races, by fat eunuchs with childish voices, by mutes, by the janissaries who accompanied her carriage, by gardeners and cooks. None of them blind.

She had given birth to six children, four of whom were still alive: three boys and a girl. The dynasty had nothing to fear. However, when the Padishah stopped calling her at night, she was worried. She linked the presence of new favorite women in the harem, more and more of them, to her appearance and tried to lose weight. Furiously. She'd get up in the morning and say: "I'm not eating anything today. I'm just drinking water."

They would bring her water bowls, the rims of which were marked by the whitish sprinkling of ice. To her liking, they would add rose petals or orange peels, fine traces of herbs, bergamot, lemon, jasmine. She held the crystal cups in her hands — the cold burn did her good — sipping each sip slowly, hoping for a miracle.

The first few hours of fasting were easy. Then around noon, she began to feel a claw. At first, a greenish poison in the roof of her mouth. Then, a djinn with a candle burned her stomach from the inside, walking through her body like it was a cave. And the dizziness. All the foods she'd ever eaten or heard about were swirling around in front of her, like a crazy carousel. Food consumed her thoughts from morning till night. Then, yet another day followed, and then another. A continuum of lengthy days fastened together by pointless sips of water. After evening prayer, when she could barely make it to bed, she would request a tray of pilaf without meat, which she would usually consume with her bare hands. She simply couldn't get her mind to stop thinking about eating. With the first mouthfuls, a delicate tingling sensation, a comforting heat, would spread from her feet, through her waist, the crown of her ribcage, to her temples, and the nape of her neck, enveloping her entire being like a triumphant domain. Then, she would fall asleep.

Havva couldn't stop at the first ten or fifteen bites, as she always intended; she ate until she felt she couldn't breathe, until her stomach went numb. In the face of her weakness, she was no longer the Sultana of the world, nor the wife of the Padishah, nor the mother of the Sublime Porte's heir to the throne, but just a heavy body, endlessly bloated with all sorts of dishes. Only with their help could she start every day. When she overindulged, she no longer defended herself from anyone and glided on transparent sled tracks, from cloud to cloud. The birds greeted her with wonder. She floated like Sultan Selim the Mad — who died of wine madness in Dar-us Saadet, the House of Happiness, surrounded by concubines and pages.

After a few months passed, and she had lost a little weight, though not enough in her opinion after all that hard work, she noticed that the Sultan's need to consult her grew, rather than diminished. He confided in her everything that was on his mind, and when he was in the Serai, they met as often as possible, in the gardens or in her apartments.

In opposition, the Sultana's relationship with the Grand Vizier differed; the long-standing feuds resurfaced at every opportunity. Over the years, they sniffed each other, scratched, sought their quarrel, but they all grew old, and the edges of their fight smoothed.

Once the tranquility descended upon her, as the empire laid unquestioningly at her feet, and the serene, dreamless sleep returned, Havva ate again. Although she tried hard to stop the stream of desires that were whipping at her like sharp whips — "I'm not eating anything today, not today" — by the end of each day, she could no longer resist and demanded to be cooked for. After sunset, trays passed from hand to hand from the kitchen to her bedroom, on which steamed, golden with fat: quail and pheasant in pomegranate sauce, salt-crusted fish, roast lamb; and for dessert — roasted chestnuts and quinces, figs and sweet Sabarta apples. Havva kept everyone away from her bedchamber and demanded that nobody would disturb her unless the Padishah called.

In her childhood in the palace of Isfahan, at the iftar table, the whole family of the Shah gathered around the low tables, with *gheimeh, halim, sholeh zard, bamiyeh*, salads, trays with fruits, and countless saffron or rose teas. They ate together and hurried to bed until *sahur*, the pre-dawn breakfast.

When the night shattered over their heads in swarms of stars, Havva would run to her bedroom, where her nanny, Zeynab, waited with hot bread, green nut jam, and tea, and the tales began. The story alternated between pirates killing giant fish in which one could hide a fortress, robbers kidnapping visitors, or just taking their gold bags, wealth buried in the ground, and countless harbors and eternal forests. If someone wronged you, you knew you could always summon the god of fire to put things right. Stuffed by the nanny, swallow by swallow, with her mind wandering to robbers and prisoners, the child fell asleep late — her head in the woman's lap — and never made it to the sunrise meal. Thirty years later, in the dark, the food spoke to the Sultana in many voices. Alone in her bedroom, sweets platters on her lap, Havva listened to them and dreamed.

She got out of bed and asked for the bath to be prepared. It took her hours to be washed, dressed, combed; she told them to hurry. The Sultan waited for her. As her ankles thickened, her breasts sagged, and the apron on her belly almost reached her thighs. She dressed differently, in long tunics of thin chiffon, white as milk froth, over which she drew a caftan: a broad, masculine cloak of silk or dark damask, with gold or silver threads. She finished with a wide belt, fastened with a turquoise and jade clasp for everyday life, or decorated with rubies, diamonds, and pearls for ceremonies. All that remained from her youth were her truly beautiful eyes and hair, and Sultana Havva took care of them. The eyes, carefully contoured by her slaves, appeared long, dark, shining, and in the hair — even on ordinary days, when she didn't receive guests or have to go to the Sultans's chambers — the arabesques born of Mustafa's hands glittered with their vitreous luster through the curls, like water mirrors filled with grass.

She arrived in Edirne the evening beforehand, more than a week after leaving Istanbul. She had the time to think a lot on the journey, to spin things in her head, and she concluded that they couldn't avoid the conflict. *Did she make a mistake somewhere? Could she, as a woman, do more?* Since the Battle of Çaldıran, the border between the two empires had crumbled, and the Treaty of Amasya didn't bring any lasting peace; just bought some time for the two armies.

Since the Sultan hadn't returned from Edirne, the Grand Vizier had been leading the Divan, and he looked for any opportunity to start a new war. And he found it at every turn: whether in the silk trade, or in the fact that Ottoman scouts had revealed a growing number of Persian cannons, or that Turkish subjects of the Safavid Empire were being forced to renounce their faith and become Shiites under threat. Nobody stopped Havva from praying of her own will, but even she, as Sultana, was aware of how little she was valued in the eyes of the imams and cadi. She loathed them for their sole engagement in never-ending discussions of the *hadiths*.

The palace at Edirne, built on an island between two arms of the river, was not as impressive as the one on Istanbul's First Hill, but once you crossed the bridge built by Fatih, the paradise commenced. Verandas and porticoes full of climbing roses, vestibules, bedrooms, siesta rooms, bathrooms with thin windows that quarreled in summer with the too-bright light, gazebos for music, grounds for *cirit*, smooth sandy paths and alleys with fine whitish gravel warmed by the sun. Wild gardens with waving grasses and reeds and seedlings tended by dozens of gardeners, with vine canopies, tulips of all colors, lilacs, saffron and daisies, irises, and jasmine. In autumn, when the hunt began, ducks and wild geese churned over the moors; rabbits, deer, and wild boar, rounded up from the dark foliage at dawn, fell under the guns prepared days before. Far from the deep woods, far from marshes, the Pavilion of the Horizon reigned, with the private apartments of the Padishah family, fresh-water fountains, nightingales in their cages, and peacocks strolling agilely along the marble-stepped terraces. This is where the Sultan spent most of his days, lying on cushions on the highest of the terraces — his bedroom's balcony.

She found him incredibly thin, with gray circles around his eyes. He didn't eat anything. Every day, the food trays went untouched, while he tasted fruits and drank water. Occasionally, he'd take a sip of lentil soup with mint, in which they squeezed a few drops of lemon, but he didn't eat any meat for a long time. Havva weighed everything at a glance: the pallor, the books, and epistles thrown on the floor, the room deserted of life.

The Sultan stood up to greet her. When they were alone, nobody cared about imperial etiquette. She no longer called him Your Majesty, Your Highness, My Brave, Padishah of the World, and he called her simply and naturally: Havva, no Sultana, no title.

Only when she rested her head on his shoulder did she come to feel the frailty of his embrace. Her eyes brimmed with tears.

"Why don't you go back to the Serai in Istanbul? What's wrong with you? What's wrong with you?"

"I don't know. The doctors say I'm fine…"

"Then why are you not coming back?"

"I'm dead inside Havva… I've died somehow… I don't know what's wrong with me. Every morning, I wake up in a black ditch. Ever since I entered this cave, I can't see the sun, even though it's shining high in the sky… And not only the sun. I don't feel… I don't feel anything…"

"And the apparitions?"

"Ah, the visions are red. Come here, let's sit on the terrace for a while. Maybe if you're here, I can see the sky."

"I get scared when you change the subject. The visions haven't left you, have they?"

"No, they're always with me; when I walk, when I read. I see them all: my brothers, my nephews, all those strangled, poisoned. They're drowning in blood or full of blood. Which… considering they've all been strangled, because you can't spill the blood of the House of Osman… it's weird."

He often dreamed of their sons beheaded or covered in blood, yet he felt too remorseful toward Havva to deliberately torment her once more with the idea of the children's death.

"…I can't sleep, I can't eat…"

"I see…"

She took his weak, almost skeletal fingers between her palms, then separated them, caressing gently.

"What can I do?"

"You can't do anything, my Sultana. It's just my troubled mind and the demons in my head."

"Have you talked to the Chief Astrologer? The magicians? With imams, to read from the Koran?"

"I've spoken with them countless times… and done something else. I ordered Mustafa a talisman… for immortality…"

The Sultana turned her head away from the stretched skin on his cheekbones and the blurred look. *What was the point of all this talk of immortality?* She wished she could encourage him, reach out to him, and lift him from his sick sleep.

"There is no immortality, great Padishah. Your Majesty's name will be remembered forever and ever... but our bodies..."

"I know, Havva, but I thought of something. I can't change the fratricidal law; nobody but me wants it. You don't want it either —" She nods briefly at him, approving. "— but I've been thinking... You can prolong your life until your own sons are old, older than you, or even die before you, by Allah's will, and then you wouldn't have to kill them... I no longer want to know that my children will be killed, as my brothers were killed, whom I killed... I no longer want to kill anyone by my own hand or by my command."

Had he lost his mind? With war at the door, with Ahmed Kasim Pasha growing increasingly unruly? He couldn't even think of being at the head of the army? Clearly, her husband had crossed the threshold of sadness, with no return, and had gone on a path of darkness.

"And when does the talisman have to be ready?"

"When I get back, I'll send word to Mustafa... I didn't feel like seeing him or talking to anyone, and I don't want anyone to see me like this."

"When will you be back?"

"That only Allah knows and maybe my doctors, but they won't tell me when the blackness in my head will stop, when I shall feel better. Stop worrying, my dear. Let's eat."

They entered the bedchamber. At her command, the servants brought the dinner, round bowls of rose water for washing, clean hand towels, and then withdrew quietly.

The Sultan struggled to eat, and with each bite, the lump in his throat rose, then fell, painfully, and Havva, for most of the time, shuffled the food between her lips. Despair, a grey, bald, human-faced eagle, stalked them both. Filled with bitterness, the Padishah had delayed too many times his return to the imperial palace, a place he despised. The three gates, the fortifications across the sea, the death embedded in the Serai walls — he hated how everyone waited for him to mount his horse only to ride off to other deaths.

The Sultana, burdened with too many fears as if covered by a shroud, was sewing new anger inside. In that hour, though perhaps against his will, her husband had left her. She felt betrayed. She had to fight alone, facing all future trials without any support.

As they sat, very close to each other, touching shoulders and knees, they were just two old friends dining together.

PELAGIA

Ariadne had no patience. If she had to stay in one place too long, wooden or bone hooks slipped through her fingers, and loose yarn loops forced her to start over, again and again. When she finished, from her hands, there would appear scarves, waistcoats, slender bonnets with withdrawn and twisted eyelets, and Pelagia would have to unravel the circles and knit them again. But the young miss Serratore liked to help her with pouring hot water with soap over the raw wool, rinsing it in salt and vinegar, and spreading it around the yard for drying, especially in winter, when the strands would frost, and she would bring them in from outside like sheaves of twigs torn from colorful trees.

The two women got along wonderfully after Pelagia causally hinted that instead of sneaking around the Bosporus' small boats, it would have been much better for the two loves to meet each other in Serratore's family home every Friday, under her eyes. For the parents, the woman with the stiff dresses and severe face was the best guard they could find, and for the youngsters, a few hours of seeing each other was more than nothing. Turkish lessons with Khalil came to an end.

Once a week, Pelagia would sit at the head of the table with the wooden reels, thin crochets, and the silk unraveled into rays and begin weaving. She would catch the yarn from the spool around her index finger, pass it between her ring and little finger, and at the end of the row, tighten it on the wooden hooks. Once she put her mind to it, she could weave a whole settlement of fluffy bricks: pillowcases, socks, hats, windmills, houses' roofs, chemises, cloaks, gloves, orchards, curtains, streets, cisterns, bridges, walls of wool, cotton, or hemp.

But only on Fridays did she have time to spend hours bent over her knitting. When reels rolled onto the floor, Musa or Ariadne got up and put them back in her lap. Here and there, she could understand the Italian in which the two spoke, but she didn't listen. What could they be saying to each other? What all lovers in this world say. For the first couple of weeks, she was glued to the chair, rigid and numb next to the lace net of the bridal veil, but as the wedding drew closer, aside from some intense words of love and the stealthy touching of hands, not much happened. More and more often, Pelagia left them alone and began cooking for the orphanage while Musa was still around.

The lovers blessed in their minds the relentless hunger of the orphaned children and made sure that whenever Pelagia came out of the kitchen, she did not catch them side by side. They always knew where their Cerberus was, because the light followed the woman around the house. Ever since she had descended to the foot of the mountain at thirteen, her thighs dripping with blood, without crying, without cursing, the light followed her everywhere.

Whenever the due time was running out, Pelagia would appear with her pots covered with kitchen towels. Musa would say goodbye, and they would leave for the chapel together. The woman ahead, and Musa behind, carrying the dishes, and children's clothes, like when he was a boy and would run not to lose his mother in the Grand Bazaar. Fra Niccolò found the pair funny, but he did not ask them what bound them or why they came together to the basilica door every Friday; for him, God had mysterious ways, on which all men walked.

Perhaps it was also God's mysterious ways that made the three months of engagement go smoothly, at least in Serratore's household. Tommaso and Mustafa thought it over in the days after their meeting at Stavros' inn, and their decision was the same: as soon as the wedding finished, the newlyweds were to set sail for Genoa.

No one objected, so, sent to the ship on the morning of the wedding, the large chests were already in the hold. At six o'clock in the evening, the hired *alim* appeared at the gate. Under one arm, he had the Koran, and under the other, a prayer rug rolled like a scroll. The sunset covered the chandeliers, the candlesticks, and the trembling shadows of the five — the bride and groom, the two in-laws, and Pelagia — with a viscous shawl.

Sitting in the corner of the room, Mustafa gazed at Ariadne's tiara. He had chosen only small, even diamonds of a particular brilliance, which he bound together with white gold wires, so thin that you couldn't see them, but you suspected they were there, just as you suspect there are unknown links between the stars in the celestial vault. He refrained from using any other gems, as he wanted to preserve the pristine, luminous, snow-like brilliance of the jewel. For Meryem, he had created the first diadem with love, for Havva with fear, and for Ariadne with endless sadness. Between the three — a life.

The son-in-law, dressed in a white chiffon shirt and a black caftan embroidered with silver thread, entirely matched the ceremonious evening.

Pelagia outdid herself and had woven into each eye of the lace golden spiderwebs: thin strands like those in the bride's hair. Covered in their white foam, Ariadne glowed.

The *alim* laid them down on the prayer mat, read from the Koran, had them sign the marriage contract, took his bag of money, and left, muttering that he would not tell anyone about the wedding, even though no one had asked him to. Meryem, who had pledged not only to avoid the wedding but also to never step onto the pier from which her son was departing, had sent the *nazar boncuk* from his room. Musa slipped it into his pocket alongside the ruby ring his father had given him. That was all he brought from home.

Pelagia cooked as much as she always did on Ariadne's birthday, only the attendants ate almost nothing, and the trays returned to the kitchen almost untouched. After the newlyweds changed into their traveling clothes, they left in silence, together with their fathers, in a single carriage, careful not to touch their knees as they went; on the quayside, they awkwardly said goodbye.

The wind off the Bosporus washed their faces with gusts of water, and in the dark, they looked like marionettes screaming at each other. Mustafa and Tommaso returned to the city in the same carriage, hurried and frozen.

On the upper deck of the ship, Ariadne and Musa searched for each other's palms under their winter coats and laughed, in whispers, about things known only to themselves. An agonizing wait was over. Without borders or straight streets, with its domes covered by night like a cave underwater, Constantinople no longer held any power over them.

All the while, Pelagia gathered the untouched food and the trays of sweets, wrapped them, and put everything in the cold pantry.

When dawn broke, she washed up, picked up the loaded baskets, and hurried out. Fra Niccolò didn't expect her so early.

"Ariadne, don Serratore's daughter, went back to Genoa."

"I know, she got married."

"I want to work here every day."

"I can't pay you."

"Without payment."

"And don Serratore?"

"I'm not leaving his house for good. I'll take care of him too, but there's much less work now. There's no one else in the house, and don Serratore is always away."

"Did you tell him?"

"Yes."

"And what did he say?"

"That if I can keep the house and also come here, I'll do as I please."

Because of the wedding preparations, she had not been there for days, and the dirty dishes, with dried pieces of pita bread and potato peels, laid in a large wooden bucket by the door. The smell of rotten food took her breath away. She placed the baskets she had brought onto the table and got to work. A dozen children, gathered from the streets, would soon wake up.

TOMMASO

He had seen D'Auréville here and there since Ariadne left — a name neither of them had uttered since her departure — but Tommaso needed a private meeting.

On the Bosporus strait, the big ice floes crowded the entrance and glued together. Mountains of ice, forests of ice, overturned castles, transparent, blueish, had caught broken oars, logs, rope ends, sandy straws. Towards the Black Sea, where the restless stretch began, the waves froze strangely. Every drop of salt water died as a clear needle, and the foam was nothing more than a crenelated wall.

If you dared to step onto the streets, you couldn't feel your hands and feet while the biting air scorched your chest. The cold that descended on the capital from the steppes was so much like the one he encountered on his first trip to China. Bursa, Kars, Tabriz, Bukhara, Samarkand, Suzhou, Xi'an. Spindles of hot air under the muzzles of white camels in the Karakum desert, the low voices of Armenian and Turkmen horsemen who took the place of the Sogdian warriors.

By day, the guides rode around the caravan, and by night, they ran from one group to another, tending fires. In the desert, on harsh nights, if you let the fire die, you might wake up sick or not wake up at all. The tall, strong men picked out the tracks of animals, predicted when the wind would fall, haggled with customs officials, and soothed the spirits of travelers. In case of danger, they knew how to draw a sword and quickly bury the dead.

Having passed through the Jade Gate and entered the Kingdom of the Son of Heaven, the then-young widower caught in his nostrils the scent of red sand, sweetened when they stopped with the scents of myrrh, cardamom, sandalwood, aloe, camphor, and opium; he looked thoughtfully for a long time at silkworms, jade, man-height paper scrolls, bought cinnamon, pepper, ginger, cloves, and musk, and learned as an apprentice the spice trade from Catarina. Old days.

In the parlor with walls covered with engravings and kilims, D'Auréville waited for him, buried deep in numbers, with a few slices of sausage, olives, and a carafe of red wine in front of him. On tables, on chairs, directly on the floor, lay fragments of mosaic, ivory, painted Egyptian chests on which Amun, Osiris, and Horus wore the double crown of the pharaohs, Persian saddles with leather pinned in silver. Tommaso struggled his way through them.

"You should get someone to clean up around here."

"I don't let anyone touch these things."

"Why?"

"I keep them until I get bored, and then sell or give them away. I usually sell them."

The Genoese slammed down on the couch. His right leg hurt more than usual. He had suffered an injury while loading purchased silk and muslin onto a ship in the port of Guangzhou.

When it was cold and wet, his knee tormented him.

"What's new, D'Auréville?"

"I don't have the money; I can't find all the money. It's difficult to become a shipowner. Other people have started to build private fleets long before now."

Since the Mediterranean had been cleared of pirates, Portuguese and Spanish fleets were setting sail for the Indies and the Americas, the Dutch were bypassing Africa and establishing new colonies, and the English had made a piracy state policy; all built large fleets, and the hegemony of the Genoese and Venetians had become thin as thread.

"We need to find the money… Maybe we get it before others and get orders from the Ottoman army. We can't build merchant ships, that's okay — we make warships. But let's start somewhere. All the rumors are that they're preparing for war, right?"

"Yes, but not on the water, on land."

"War can always be fought on the water, and even if there are no naval battles, although there are plenty these days, you move troops out on the water, you send them food. An army doesn't live on looting alone, so I don't see how it would do without a strong fleet."

"They have a lot. They haven't been idle so far. It will soon be a century since all the sultans continuously built ships at Tersâne-i Âmire. Actually, what's the matter, Serratore?"

"You know as well as me, D'Auréville, that money doesn't pass through the same hands anymore. It changes hands. Ever since the Spaniards founded Manila, the goods travel across the Pacific and then around Europe on land. You'll see, a whole swarm of new ports will spring up while the Genoese ports are avoided, poorer and poorer every day."

"Yes, but you're more merchant than shipowner. Why do you strive to change that?"

"I feel like it. I think that's where the future is. I'll learn a new business like so many others, and I'll be more a shipowner than a merchant. Who says I'm swearing off the trade?

I just want to make sure Ariadne and her children don't end up poor."

Philippe D'Auréville understood Tommaso's convictions, but he didn't think it was that simple.

"If that's why you came to me, I can tell you right now that you won't get France's money, Serratore. Everyone knows how stubborn my monarch is. He won't listen to any adviser, and the treaty with the Ottoman power he inherited drives him out of his mind if you mention it to him, for there isn't a royal house in Europe that doesn't remind him of the alliance at every opportunity; so, he won't build galleons here in a million years. What if you moved back to Genoa?"

"And leave Constantinople?"

"Yeah, didn't you say you wanted to go back sometime? Your daughter has already left."

"She didn't live here, like me, for over twenty years…"

"Do you want to die here?"

"No, that's clear, no!"

"So?"

"I need more time."

"Nobody says you have to leave tomorrow, Serratore. In fact, what's keeping you? Business? You Genoese have business everywhere."

What's holding me back? Constantinople: the cafés near Mevlevihane Kapı, those in Tahtakale, those in Tophane, which always have a coffee-drinking room at the front and the hidden place in the back; beds covered with dirty mattresses, on which lay, sometimes for nights on end, tramps, sailors, actors, acrobats, poets, and calligraphers, all those who would have sold their houses and their souls to the last coin to the poppy.

"Life's work, D'Auréville, and friends…"

"Nonsense. You're too sentimental. You're getting old, Serratore."

"What can I say? Another age is coming. People are traveling more and more, learning about lands never heard of. An era is dying, and we may die with it."

"Not me!"

D'Auréville jumped to his feet and poured wine into two goblets, handing one to Serratore.

"I was not born, like you Tommaso, in a rich merchant's house. I had to make my way to the Louvre from the slums of Paris."

"And the title? Viscount Philippe D'Auréville?"

"Only the first name is mine. My name is Philippe Bardin. Viscount D'Auréville is a title I bought from a destitute nobleman in Provence, the land where my mother was born. She died; God's mercy be upon her! Buying a title is not unusual in France. Okay, you can't buy a duke's title or claim to be royalty, but viscount, why not? Viscount Philippe D'Auréville sounds nice, doesn't it?"

"And what happened to the real Viscount D'Auréville?"

"He passed away peacefully in his countryside house. He had eighteen hunting dogs. And he fed them all with my money… and that hard-to-heat mansion, which is now mine… You don't know how much money it costs in the winter. I'm thinking of selling it, especially since I'm never there, but who's ever seen a viscount without a mansion?"

"And his children?"

"He didn't have any. The next Viscount D'Auréville is me. People in the village thought I was his bastard son, and that's why he left me everything. Who cares? I don't. The truth is simple: I got nothing from anyone in my life, and the old viscount cost me enough, with his house and his name. So, as you see, Serratore, I can't afford to not survive. Maybe you can."

"To not survive?"

Philippe D'Auréville burst out laughing.

"No, to retire, to go away, finally, to die in peace. I think I'll die on the road, trying to reconcile an increasingly mad and vacillating monarch with a sultan who thinks he owns the world."

"I can't retire, not yet. I'd like to go to China one last time. Then I'll see."

"Let's drink to that." D'Auréville raised his cup and downed it in one breath.

They chatted for another hour or so, grinding the latest gossip and the Sultan's mysterious illness.

They knew the Padishah got out of bed to read or to walk in the garden, and only for very few hours a day. Everyone assumed that he had been poisoned or had been struck down by black magic — and a crowd of astrologers, alchemists, and sorcerers swarmed around him, but no one could unravel the cause.

They parted in the dead of night. Philippe D'Auréville headed for the shore, to catch another late caique to cross the Golden Horn. He intended to spend the night with one of his mistresses — a wealthy Jewess with several houses and shops in the Fatih district, who was said to have an unusual passage to the Palace for lending money to sultana Havva.

Hasan, the hunchbacked Albanian, father of the two guards who worked at Leib Peres' *House of Dreams* during the day, welcomed Tommaso as he did the night before. He asked him to wait a few minutes, for the hookah and the bed to be prepared, and disappeared behind a curtain. The ceilings blackened with smoke, tarnished walls, floorboards full of dried mud, clothes of all kinds thrown on the floor. Men who drank their opium soup or chewed hash couldn't be seen because of the dirty curtains. Here, things had no edges, and people were fringed in steam. Without beauty, without ugliness, poor and rich, young, and old, with dark purple circles under their eyes, dry lips, and gazes deepened into the void, they looked strikingly alike.

Tommaso followed the Albanian, laid down, and thirstily took his first drag. Without undressing, without sitting down; the first smoke poured a warm, thickened ink into his veins.

The brown molasses seized his organs and veins like a realm at war, leaving him no chance of victory or truce. After the second and third smoke, he stretched on the bed, unfastened his tunic's slits and shirt's buttonholes, and, with eyes to the ceiling, waited: the jade-headed, ruby-eyed basilisk, the four-legged, scaly-bodied aspis, the Dog Star glimmering faintly across the salt expanses, Uraeus, the white eagles, the Goddess of Chaos, Mother Hubur, the one who gives birth to all. Instead of the huge flames, from the sky appeared the quiet roofs of Genova and the dolls of his childhood, white-felt dervishes slowly spinning in the air. Wide-eyed, ever young, as death had surprised her, the first doll had Giovanna's translucent face. Behind her, with the head slightly tilted, Eleonora, and then, light as mist, Catarina — the only women he had ever been in love with, though he hadn't slept with either of them. The wine's velvetiness, and the vast flight of opium — stronger than any desire of the flesh — bound him to Eleonora and Catarina for life. The thought of them was his last thought, and he slipped into a sulfurous sleep as the shadows of the dolls on the walls faded with a soft flicker, like burning coals dying in the water.

HAVVA

She dreamed she walked in the shade of portals covered with glazed tiles and ribbons of calligraphy in mosaics. At the ends of rows, where the edges of the minarets bumped against each other, the sinuous wings of butterflies and rebellious arabesques appeared. Sometimes, they sprang from the sleeping, dusty bricks, sometimes from plaster, sand, earth, mist, and sun.

Growing up in her father's throne room, Havva possessed memories of all the caliphs who had ruled the Mediterranean coast stretching from the Red Sea to the Atlantic; memories of Egypt, Persia, Libya, Mauritania, Algeria, Tunis, the Levant, and many other lands that melted under the wax of the ages. But the sand didn't melt; crystallized, gray, enriched with the bones of horses and the bones of men shattered in so many wars, the sand taught her that the only true thing in this world was flow, even when it came to walls or stones. The meanings of flow and many other things unseen by others had first dawned on the princess when her mother — the mad sultana Sayyida, as she was called in the palace of Isfahan — took her on a pilgrimage to Qom.

Sayyida grew accustomed to the harsh desert skies, separated from her only by a tent canvas, and she always stumbled over buildings. No matter how large the mosque or the bedchambers, her eyes searched the horizon but only quenched her hunger for the expanse once a year, when on the way to the tomb of the holy Fatima Masumeh.

As a means of seeking refuge during wartime, the ladies of the Safavid dynasty generously provided large sums of money for the upkeep of the family tombs, and to embellish the mausoleum with fabrics, ornaments, and books. Every year, they collected the gifts at least two months before the pilgrimage, wrapped, counted, and tied them. Once everything was in order, the caravan departed: the soldiers of the Shah ahead, followed by the mother of the Sultan, the other wives, princesses, and other high-ranking women who lived at court, then the servants, whose camels carried spare clothes, cooking pots, foods and carpets, and at the end of the convoy, other soldiers. Thieves would not have dared attack the wives and daughters of the Shah, but enemy tribes were many, and you never knew whose scouts you'd meet on the lengthy journey from Isfahan to Qom.

When traveling, sultana Sayyida spent most of her time on horseback, and she took the opportunity to teach her daughters how to ride, like the soldiers who guarded them. Havva remembered being about four years old when her mother took her, and they rode off, alone, through the sandy salt dunes, commanding everyone — women and men alike — not to follow them. When their thin shadows vanished in the distance, the queen would dismount with the little girl in her arms and let her run barefooted for several hours on the windy wrinkled hills. All around them, limestone stars, shells of petrified clams, motionless chalk lives and dry roots were scribbled throughout the ancient seabed.

At nightfall, as they returned to camp, following the torches, the sand on the mountaintops sang. Things repeated, and on the next pilgrimage, Havva was given a *bakhtiari* colt named Malik — King — as a gift, so that year after year, when they went on pilgrimage, she could run free wherever she wanted, if she didn't stray too far from the caravan.

The dazzling Malik died, and then other equally precious stallions followed, but as time went on, as she grew fatter, Havva no longer rode. She chose the soft cushions of the imperial carriages; the voices of mountains and dunes were left behind — memories, leaves on the water, stars falling from the sky.

She brushed her hand across her eyes, striving to push away memories of a distant past, while her elder son, sitting with his legs folded under him, waited. Despite being so young, it was obvious to all that he had inherited her, as his belly bulged beneath the yellow silk of his tunic. As usual, he wore many jewels and had rings on all his fingers.

Havva looked at him. *Endless vanity. Mehmet, Selim, any of his brothers would have been better sultans than Murad, more masterful, more ambitious, but Allah had decided that he should be the firstborn and would be girded with Osman's sword, and his brothers would be strangled when he ascended the throne.*

And out loud. "You will lead the expedition to Persia, Murad, instead of the Sultan. It has been decided by His Holiness the Padishah and the Divan."

Murad nodded. He had no desire to contradict her. Sultana Havva always knew what was going on in the Serai. She knew the whispers and the rumors; she knew the facts and sometimes even the thoughts. The bulky woman, from whom nothing of her overwhelming before-his-birth beauty could be guessed, had a sixth sense, and Shehzad Murad was afraid of her. He didn't know if she loved him, because she spent most of her time with his sister and younger siblings, but she protected him. Him and the dynasty.

"You and the Grand Vizier will share command. Listen to him. He's been through many military campaigns, and you can learn from him."

"What if he kills me?"

"What a thought, Murad! No one will kill you as long as the Sultan is alive. You're heir to the throne!"

"That's why!"

"The Padishah would not permit it. Anyone who touches you will be stripped of their head on the spot, and it's not just his life, it's his family's, up to the third generation. Besides, if you're going to be enthroned as padishah, you'd better have at least one win of your own. That'll shut everyone up."

The prince had not seen the Sultan for more than half a year since he left for Edirne, but he knew all the rumors.

"How is the great Padishah feeling?"

"Good. His leg wound reopened, and he can't ride, but otherwise, he's fine. He reads the holy texts and rests. He'll be back soon."

"May Allah give him health!"

"So it will be!" Havva allowed him to take his leave, and she leaned back on the cushions.

She often wondered what she would do if the prince was killed and wondered why she felt little at such a troubling thought. Had she grown so accustomed to the Serai's assassinations? For the second time on the same day, the turquoise minarets of the Qom Mosque disturbed the air in her chamber.

Black *chadors*, devoid of voices, touched their foreheads to the floor, meditated with their eyes closed, read fragments of the Koran, or prayed under the high dome. The stillness stretched from one covered head to another, connecting everything into one piece, and the only place alive seemed to be the tomb of a saint who had breathed her last in the eighth century. Around the sarcophagus clad in gold and silver, women of all ages and ranks, equal in the sight of Allah, swirled on endless slabs of gilded mosaic between mirrors, and Havva was spinning together with them. The fervor of the prayers of that time had been lost in vain. Too many births, too many deaths, too many countries to defend. Sultana Havva, daughter of a Shah, wife of a Padishah, and mother of princes, stopped to think that she might go on another pilgrimage to any saint ever. Her paths had changed.

What Murad called his mother's sixth sense was in fact not a sense but a gift she was born with. As she walked through galleries and cellars, bedrooms, and kitchens, along the palace's fountains, and through the gates, the Sultana could hear all the whispers in the walls she was passing by. Living or dead, Christian, or Muslim, man or woman, Havva knew them all by the marks they left on the stone. As soon as their shadows touched her, the walls started to talk to her in a hidden language.

Just like when Sultana Sayyida carried her over the dunes, her daughter could glide through the palace corridors like a flagship through waves of sand. Twice a year, she secretly ordered to be sewn a loose, rough tunic and an ankle-length black hijab, resembling the attire of laundresses. In the darkness of the night, concealed by the servant's clothes, she walked in her sleep, barefoot. That was how she learned of unborn children, forbidden love stories, eunuchs tormented by desires in their dreams, shameful diseases or soldierly wounds festering under gala uniforms, and the imperial officials' wishes to get rich.

Havva knew the Serai, and the Serai recognized her as its mistress. Not the people, the walls. Sheltered by them, the Sultana was strong. All the kings of the Achaemenid, Seleucid, and Parthian empires, all the Fatimids, Sassanids, and many other chieftains in her long line of ancestors had prepared her for this power. And the Sultana enjoyed it.

KHALIL

Prolonged knocks on the door. Mustafa came down the stairs, leaning his hand against the wall.

"What's with you so late?"

"I want to show you something."

"Look, it's snowing. The end of March?"

"Snow of the lambs. It'll melt by morning."

"Light a candle, please, or better, two."

"What are these writings?"

"Today I received them, and I couldn't wait any longer. I want to show them to you. Remember when I told you I found a Hindu astrology book at Süleymaniye?"

"Yes. And you also told me you don't understand much of it, just some drawings."

"True. That's why I wrote to Jagat Qasim. I met him in the Tabriz chancery. When I went to Constantinople, he went to Agra to work as a translator and calligrapher at the Mongol court. He knows Sanskrit, Urdu, Persian, Latin, Arabic, and Greek. When I have questions about manuscripts or books, I consult him. In addition, we play chess through epistles."

"How do you play chess through epistles?"

"He has a chessboard with the game, and I have a chessboard with the same game, and we write to each other our next move."

"But such a letter travels for…"

"Two months. For each move. It doesn't matter. People like him and me have time. What else do we have? Anyway, never mind that I found your talisman. In fact, Jagat found it for you. I know what you have to do, and we don't need the day and time of the Padishah's birth."

He unfolded the paper scrolls on the table, slightly damp around the edges and crumpled.

"Nine rings, Mustafa, linked together: it's called the 'Talisman of Nine Rings.' Apollonius of Tyana is said to have prolonged his life with the help of seven rings taken from an Indian prince. Nine is the number that links the two worlds — the world here and the unseen world — a number we cannot fully know; something always remains hidden. The celestial spheres are nine. The order in which you make the rings and pass them through each other is important."

"And how do I know the rings' order?"

"I'm telling it to you. I need to look at some moon phase charts. I haven't looked yet. I was in a hurry to show you what I got. The gems must be without a single blemish, without a crack, perfectly polished, the purest, like the metals used."

He lifted the notes in front of the oil lamp and realized he couldn't see the shaky letters properly.

"Soon, I'll need a magnifying glass to read. Look what it says here. It always starts with the sun on a Sunday. You have to fast and pray for three days before pouring the metal and mounting the stone. At the end, the seal of the ring is engraved on the inside: the word *immortality*. It is the most powerful thing. If you leave the talisman with only eight rings, even if you engrave the seal on all eight, it will be a talisman for health, prosperity, and long life, but if you add the ninth, with the Stone of Heaven in the middle, it becomes a talisman for immortality."

"Sky Stone? The Blue Diamond? I don't believe it!"

Discovered in India by an Arab merchant from Andalusia, bought with other gems, it had been brought to Europe and sold to a French marquis. In less than two years, the marquis died of a mysterious blood disease, and the Arab merchant lost everything, robbed by his eldest son. The duke who bought the blue diamond was killed in a hunting accident, and the diamond disappeared for a while, only to reappear in 1451 at the court of Basileus Constantine XI. After Constantine's death, the blue diamond went to Halil Pasha who, betrayed by his former Byzantine allies, was executed by Fatih for treason, and all his riches came into the possession of the imperial family. Padishah's grandfather was the last to carry the huge blue diamond with him on the day he died on the battlefield. After his body was buried at Bursa in Muradiye, Sultana-Mother Gülbahar ordered the stone to be embedded in the hilt of a dagger and the dagger to be locked in the Pavilion of the Holy Mantle. Since then, no one has touched it.

"Not that diamond. We need a rock that has fallen from the sky, a meteorite's sliver..."

Meryem appeared in the doorway. Her unfurled hair had turned grey and fell on her back in hemp-white ropes. Mustafa got up and led her out of the room with slow gestures, matching his steps with her shuffling slippers.

"Wait, let me go light her lamp."

He came back, exhausted.

"How long has she been like this?"

"It's like you wouldn't know... What bothers me is not that she keeps forgetting — she forgets the food on the stove — or that she doesn't wash the dishes, but it's the bumping into things, tables, walls; she can't stand up straight. Yesterday, she sat motionless for a whole day in the kitchen, staring blankly. I had to pick her up, wash her, change her clothes, put her to bed. And even though she's lost weight, she's like stone. She's breaking my back."

"And her sisters?"

"They come now and then to cook. I can't ask them for more. They have families of their own."

"It's hard…"

"I'll get used to it. Do I have a choice? So, tell me how to get this rock that falls from the sky."

"Jarat also wrote this. They fall everywhere, every year, but as far as he knows, they are only sold in China. The rich people wear them, on their chest, in a pouch, as amulets."

"I need to talk to don Serratore. Don't know anyone else who has been to China or has connections there. But I'm afraid even if he knows where to get a rock that fell from the sky, it's going to take forever to get it."

"Like my chess game with Jarat. Now that you know how to make the talisman, and you're out of fear, you have time."

"Not true. I need to get on it. As long as the Padishah doesn't send word for me or call me to say he doesn't want it anymore… I have to wrap it up and get it to him."

"I've often thought about you two. I don't think he chose you by accident. I'm curious about what your celestial charts look like. I know yours, and with him, I can figure out what they didn't tell you — what's missing. I'll look them over when I get to *muvakkithane*."

"What are you doing there?"

"I work in the time room. I count the hours for prayers."

"And how are you? Better than when you were writing horoscopes? Better than when you were giving Turkish lessons?"

In Khalil's eyes, the image of Ariadne's flesh burned through. The ankles, the lips, the soft hands. He closed his eyes and squeezed his eyelids shut to banish the pain and thoughts of Turkish lessons.

"Much better, although they don't pay me much. I like it. I'm at peace."

"When have you ever been restless?"

Ariadne's laugh, her fingertips stained with ink, her hair a mess. A torrent of lava that carried down burning trees and bridges and beams and river stones and house walls. Khalil struggled out from under a thick layer of ash to speak.

"It is very late. Go tomorrow and get your gold and hyacinth for the ring of the Sun, so you can start, and write to don Serratore or better, meet him."

"You don't want to stay here tonight? It's late. You can sleep in my workshop on the bench. Musa often slept in there."

"No, I've gotten used to sleeping in my own bed and can't sleep anywhere else."

They opened the door and walked past Meryem, who was shivering in the cold of the stairs.

"Don't accompany me. Stay with her. I know the way."

Khalil stepped outside onto the street. Piercing, silent, merciless, Ariadne continued to prey on his flesh, dividing the world into fragments. The one before he met her, the colorful ribbons of hours spent together, the last of them: her tattered departure. In the only world he was left with, the snow that fell from the sky around him melted at the slightest touch.

PART THREE

XI'AN

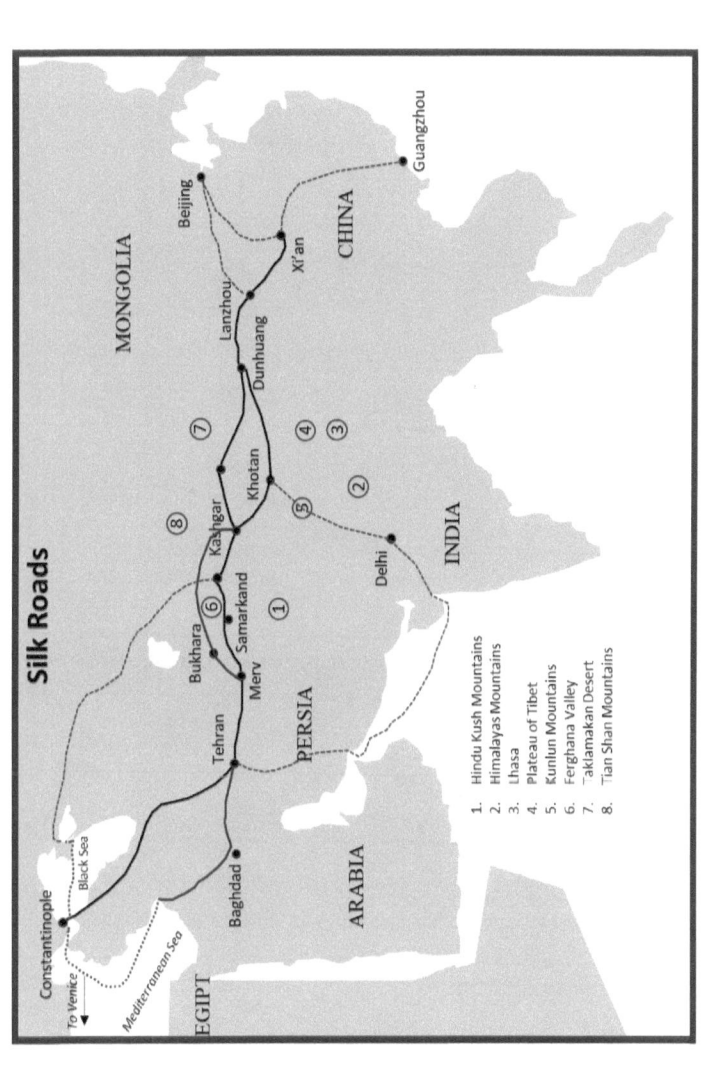

Silk Roads

1. Hindu Kush Mountains
2. Himalayas Mountains
3. Lhasa
4. Plateau of Tibet
5. Kunlun Mountains
6. Ferghana Valley
7. Taklamakan Desert
8. Tian Shan Mountains

MONGOLIA

CHINA

Beijing
Lanzhou
Xi'an
Dunhuang
Guangzhou

Khotan
Kashgar
Samarkand
Bukhara
Merv

Delhi

INDIA

Tehran

PERSIA

Baghdad

ARABIA

Constantinople
To Venice
Black Sea
Mediterranean Sea
EGIPT

YONTEN

He had died twice before. Once, three weeks after his birth, he had stopped breathing and hung in his mother's arms, bruised like a rag doll, and the second time, he had drowned. When the water closed over his head, he entered a white cave where he smelled goat milk and footsteps could be heard. *Did his feet touch the ground? Did he still have feet? Maybe they were someone else's footsteps.* Shadows of all kinds, a whole nation of shadows, passed him by. He would have liked to move forward among them, to go further, to see what lay beyond, but unexpectedly, four arms pulled him tight. They picked up the breathless boy, wide-eyed, and hid him behind the rocks overnight, not before shaking him a few times and pulling him by the wrists. At the ledge, the mountain started downward, jagged with sharp rocks and slippery stones. They had to return the next morning with a donkey and some cloth to wrap him in.

He woke up after dark, and it was freezing cold. The wet clothes on his back had turned to bark, and he shivered. He rose to his feet. He hadn't left the shore of the small blue lake with turquoise edges, lit by an array of stars. Yonten was still there. He stripped off his wet clothes and wrapped himself in long blades of grass, which kept him warm, and from a few patches of moss, he fashioned a cushion, to support his head.

The cold could kill him before morning. He knew what it was like to die, and he wasn't afraid, but there was no one beside him to say the prayers of passage through the *bardo*. What if he got lost?

Despite the grey waves of the ridge wind, Yonten came to see the dawn. The moss's woven cloth of wool, the body's heat, and the dry corner he had found had finally done their job.

The men who came the next morning to take the body to the lamasery saw him coming down the path in front of them and ran away shouting: the living dead, the living dead. That night, Yonten found the stone.

MUSA

The wind, full of hot water, brought from North Africa not only a wandering shepherd's voice in the dusk or the shiver of wet tent canvas but also salt mixed with cloud remnants and small fish or bits of seaweed plucked from the Mediterranean; strong enough to hit the Apennines or disappear into the Ligurian Gulf.

When the Sirocco di Levante blew in Genoa, even his teachers' words had difficulty entering Musa's mind. He hated the tall, stained-glass windows on the first floor of the old monastery, converted into a university. The ground floor of the Commenda di San Giovanni di Pré, without windows, looked more like a warehouse. The Promontorio stone's black gleam on the façade appeared even more overwhelming on stormy days when huge waves crashed against the quays in the harbor.

He lived in a city with sharp streets, windowless towers, painted ceilings, and pebbled terraces. The defensive walls, the Lighthouse, and the old gates, especially the massive Porta Soprana, were so far from Istanbul's hills, with their sunset sky's purple velvet folds and the domes that hung in the air, born of architect Sinan's dreams.

Musa walked home with his ankles buried in sand mixed with mud. The brightly lit windows of the kitchen greeted him warmly.

"What are you doing here alone?"

"Making pesto. I told the maid to leave early, and Uncle Matteo is at the Spinola's."

"Need help?"

In the bowl on the table, the basil leaves washed with rainwater, vivid, like a summer garden, lit up the young woman's face with a golden-green light.

"You can toast the pine seeds. And maybe build the fire in the salon, if you want us to eat there."

"If Pelagia saw how you cooked, she'd be proud of you."

"I don't think so, and I don't think she ever really liked me."

"Maybe not at first, but then… you know how she is. Everybody's mother. I think she tried to be your mother, too. Well, she strived."

"Perhaps it was precisely because she tried too much to be everyone's mother that I didn't feel her close."

"You want everything for yourself, don't you Ariadne? Like you have me."

He grabbed her waist from behind and tried to kiss her neck.

"No, no, let me, I'll spill the oil. And since you brought up that you're mine — I don't feel guilty. That was our destiny, but I do wonder quite often: do you miss it? Constantinople, your parents, I mean…"

"Yes… I never imagined, as I passed by the feluccas and the caiques, by the trees of Judah, by the houses of Greeks, Turks, Armenians, and Jews, without seeing them, that I would come to think so often of them. You know what I miss most of all? The call of the muezzin, the voices. The basilicas' bells are too harsh for me."

"Why don't you pray? Is someone hindering you? I don't think anyone cares. In Genoa, everyone is equal in faith, both in life and in death. Even the cemeteries are mixed. They're not just Catholic."

A month before, on their way to Spezia, they had taken a boat from Vernazza to Monterosso al Mare, and Musa had seen the high buttresses of the cliffs, castles piercing the mountainsides, and a cemetery: a wall of rock in which the dead slept the sleep of eternity on top of each other. Those without life staring at the sea.

"I don't remember everything I've learned by heart, and I should pray towards the east because I don't know where Mecca is. *Anne* wouldn't understand that."

"What do you mean living in a town where you don't know where Mecca is? You can pray with your face to the east, as everyone prays. Did she ever understand you?"

"I don't think so. I was a child who came out of nowhere in her old age, and it tired her out. My flags, my drawings... But at least when I was a kid, she loved me. I don't think she loves me anymore. I'm just an enemy; that's how she behaves."

"Isn't that a bit much to say?"

"*Baba's* right when he says I've brought her world down. My mother's world: nice, tight, clean. The carpet weaving, the backyard, the prayers. Sometimes I think *anne* and I shouldn't have been born in the same place, shouldn't have known each other. Allah, to whom she prays five times a day, decided to give her a son like me. What should I do? I've already accepted my life. There's no point in burdening my soul with such things. It's not in my power to do anything for her. Anyway, I left. I won't go back there. But the thing that gnaws at me most is that a letter takes a month, and if anything happens to them, I can't even find out."

"It doesn't matter that it takes one month. Why don't you start writing them? Maybe it would be easier. You'd have a connection. You'd know if they're in good health or not, or if they're in trouble."

"*Anne* can't read."

"But your father knows. He can read to her. Come on, Musa, don't let me beg you. It'll be fine, you'll see."

In front of the windows, the rain gusted. Soon, the west wind — Garigliano — as the locals called it, would chase the desert thistles from the streets of Genoa, would bring the madness of more storms, sweeping the ships' decks, baffling the breezes along the Corsican coast, ducking under women's skirts, and powdering the white grapes of Cinque Terre with the acidic, mysterious mist of the oceans.

They still lived in Genoa, to the despair of Uncle Matteo who, in the six months since they had arrived, saw how Ariadne spruced everything up with the same zeal that she revised the plans for the house in Spezia multiple times, driving the builders insane. That's why they never finished. In her grandparents' house, the young woman stocked the kitchen with wooden gutters, boxes and crates filled with shoots, and various ropes from which dried roots hung, just as in Constantinople.

In the parlor, where the family, small as it was at that moment, dined, and in their bedchamber, Ariadne strung blue mosaic lamps with elegant thin supports, low cushions, and richly mollified draperies. Seeking to create an atmosphere of warmth and hospitality, she adorned the banisters, stair treads, window frames, and shutters with elegant fabrics, in honor of Musa's native city's lavishness.

Just as he had once stubbornly refused to take part in the uproar of Tommaso's muslin, damask, and lace riots, again, Matteo confined himself to being just a grumpy witness. In an attempt to hasten the newlyweds' move, he wrote several times to his older brother yet didn't receive any reply. Tommaso disregarded him completely, causing Musa and Ariadne to share a hidden laugh as a result.

As on many other evenings when Uncle Matteo was missing, dinner remained untouched. They went up to their room early and looked for each other, with their fingers, with their eyelids closed, with their lips, through the covers' folds, through the cushions and the wrinkles of the sheets, until they had exhausted themselves and fallen asleep with their bodies glued together. Above them, above the old university's halls, beyond Porto Antico and Porto Vecchio, beyond the defensive walls and gates, great gaps of cold air troubled the souls. Tramontana was descending from the Alps.

MUSTAFA

Darkness. A black dog followed Mustafa everywhere and licked his feet, even in broad daylight. He used to hide under the table, eyes closed, and roll across the floor planks to the cellar below when he was little. He could spend hours in the fluffy mist, listening to the dusty strands rustle under the door; as soon as they stuck to the back of his palm, they lit up. But the golden freckles of the time would fall behind. The vine cords of pain wrapped around his joints reminded him of his age and his gaze grew hazy as the evenings drew near, no longer aiding him.

He grabbed a three-armed candlestick and lit the candles. The melted wax, the unnumbered tools on the shelves and on the workbench, the designs for the molds, the scraps of ornaments full of dust, Khalil's notes — rolls of fine paper, marked with lilac ink, scattered everywhere like opened peacock tailfeathers.

The opal ring: when the day ends in the twilight, the opal is the mirror that receives and sends back the faces of the universe. Carefully mount the stone in the silver ring, without unsettling its inner enigma. Choose the lightest of its shades and direct them towards the east. Opal is a stone full of water, influenced by all the phases of the moon, so it can only be perfectly polished when the light of the night star streams through the cracks in the sky.

The amethyst ring: step out from behind your inner wall and give yourself hours of contemplation on lavender grains or violet wine tears, frozen in stone. Their glassy sparkle banishes the fear of the unknown. A ship without a helmsman can wander forever. Amethyst is a map.

Hunger gnawed at him, but going into the kitchen might wake Meryem. A week or so before, he'd found her gasping with all the beddings and wall-hanging rugs, crammed into Musa's bedroom, and had helped her pull the bed near the window, though he didn't understand why she wanted to sleep there. Overall, the change helped the woman since she no longer walked around the house like she was on the edge of a high bridge, staring into the void, and the proximity of Musa's things had calmed her.

Musa had sent two letters by then. One telling of ports with foreign names, the countless rocks of the Mediterranean, shipwrecks, and pirates they heard of but bypassed; the second of Genoese's fortifications, sharp streets, and orange hills, and the new house at La Spezia under construction.

"Meryem, do you want to know how your son is doing? Meryem, Musa wrote, do you want me to read to you?" The boy's name came in large waves, crashing against each other and erasing the letters from the words; her pulse raced harder and faster as she worried about losing what she had written in her mind. Each time, she shook her head no. The world inside herself narrowed, with no room for new memories left. Too much life around — it would hurt her.

Agate ring: make an alloy with quicksilver, then mount the agate on a Thursday, so that the wearer of the talisman may share in earthly glory. Just as the sun and rain give birth to rainbows, agate transforms the low, soft heat within the earth into healing.

The hum of agate carols the nights, and its shimmering streaks of chalcedony divide the sky into swathes.

Emerald ring: pick a Friday and look for the cleanest copper alloy. The goddess Ishtar, encased in emerald stone, will watch you from the height of pure eternity with her calm and powerful eyes. When you work, think of the growing green, of life following after death. And pray. Emerald will transform you in your prayer.

The cold, still stones in the darkness of his soul. Even hot, gold, mercury, silver, copper, lead could not diminish their merciless clutch. Ever since the talisman's work had started, the days flew slowly, driven by fear, by the anxiety of Musa's departure, by the madness of Meryem who walked unaccompanied on her paths between two rooms, muttering old words or singing lullabies in languages she did not speak.

"Do you know Armenian?"

"No."

"Maybe you heard your grandparents?"

"Maybe, I don't remember."

Sapphire ring: sapphire is a blue velvet stone that is set at midnight, when Thursday is over and Friday has not yet begun, in an alloy containing a lot of lead. You need the end and the beginning of things at the same time, for in sapphire shines all the promise of wisdom and knowledge of divinity. If you wear this stone, it will remind you of fate.

A stone fallen from the sky, the talisman of the nine rings, for Mustafa, just a gate that closed and opened at the will of a Padishah. The Palace's silence that had frightened him so much ceased to torment him, extinguished in the whirl of other worries. *What could they do to him? Kill him? Throw him in prison?* He was no longer afraid for his life, but he had no one to leave Meryem with. He was aware that if something bad happened to him, he couldn't rely on her sisters or Khalil.

He had known the Arab for a long time, but he had never seen him like this, immersed in notes and books about stills, about separating rare metals from the ore, about the gold the Egyptians had collected in the desert between the Red Sea and Nubia, and about the great quartz rocks of Sumer. Increasingly, all the anxious polymath's dreams gathered around the stone fallen from the sky, which combined the power of the Sun and the Moon, and the ninth ring, destined — in Khalil's eyes — to bind all the alchemical metals into a single circle. He spent his days at *muvakkithane*, measuring the Earth's orbit, the tilt of its axis, and counting the times for prayers, and his late evenings, often after midnight, he spent burying Mustafa in sheets and tomes.

Obsidian ring: dark and dreamy, obsidian's volcanic glass is a sword that all healers, shamans, and saints yearn for. Don't touch it until you're ready to face your own self. Don't mount it until you have no fear of the unknown. Just as the lone trees are unaware of the orchard, yet the orchard encompasses them all, the dark light of the gem anchors the Supreme Being in the seekers of truth.

Diamond ring: the eighth ring represents the link between the worlds. Formed when time was at its beginning, the diamond links pieces of the sky together with ropes made of bent light. Brilliance... Power... Good and Evil...

He stopped reading and looked around the workshop for a shelf, a rack where he could keep the papers, then changed his mind. He gathered up all the rolls from the floor, crumpled them in his fists and threw them into the dim fire that suddenly rose, lighting up the ceiling. The first eight finished, quiet, sleepy rings glowed in their sockets. Mustafa covered them with a cloth and went to bed. The moment to search for don Tommaso came once more.

YONTEN

The monastery's shadow, gliding slowly behind the mountains. Yonten crouched and gathered his *zhen* around him. He only needed a few more miniatures to finish before he could go eat. The boy picked up the chunks of butter, kneading hard in the frosty air with bruised fingers, and mixed them with the mineral powders. Red, green, orange.

The New Year was approaching, and the large cylinders near the gates would spin restlessly, carrying the pilgrims' prayers. At their lamasery, the highest in Tibet, the monks were usually snowed in for six months, making it difficult for the elderly, sick, and women with children, the most commonly seen worshippers at services, to reach them. Therefore, the lamasery depended solely on meager contributions from poor families in the nearby area, just enough to procure food and a small amount of yak butter. They couldn't afford to adorn the gates with tall sculptures of painted butter like those at the Potala, but this wasn't his job. As long as they let him paint or model, he was happy.

When he was three weeks old, one night, he stopped sucking and burning from head to toe, stopped breathing. In the unusually long time that his mother had clutched him desperately to her breast, Yonten traveled into the *bardo*, met two beings, one dressed in black, the other dressed in white, listened to what they told him, and returned, after seeing his home and the mountains from above.

In his village, things were simple: the older boys would inherit the land and toil on it, while the younger ones would enter the monastery. Having monks in your family bestowed great honor. Their prayers could improve the whole family's karma and help the living and the dead alike. Abiding the unwritten laws of the village, it was entirely foreseeable that Yonten would be destined to become a lama. Not just because he was the youngest, but also because he was *delok*: one who comes back from the dead.

People did not like to approach a *delok* — man or woman — because, returning to this world, they seemed to acquire mysterious powers. Despite the fact that all those who traveled to *bardo* spoke of white light and love, they were largely shunned. One could find them begging at the edge of a hamlet or along the roads. Alone.

The lamasery received him at the age of seven, like any novice. The Abbot and the elders seemed unconcerned about his visions, and they solely demanded him to paint prayer flags that were scattered everywhere or shape little *torma* out of dried butter.

At the beginning of the month, the librarian monk had brought large sheets of yellowish paper and trays with sand to those who drew mandalas. The novices, gathered in threes and fours, had to decide: sand or paper? Unraveling the kaleidoscope of colors in the universe's circles laid out one upon the other, or the napping hidden deities laid in them, proved to be uncomplicated for Yonten. White for spirituality, red for divine breath, yellow for wisdom, blue for infinity, black for mystery. As the mandala progressed, the spirals of the sky gave them a lot of trouble, the hues flowed under their skin, and they would work endlessly, days and nights, without rest.

As the closing prayers approached, the centers of the circles had no dimension. After a supervising monk reviewed and approved the work, the mandala had to be sliced into thin ribbons, beginning to resemble the Chinese volumes in the library. Then, he torched the paper strings into sizzling smoke. On the first day of the following month, they would start again.

Yonten sighed and grabbed the last *torma*. In February, under the roof of the sky, it was so cold that they had to mix butter with wax to make the figurines last longer. In the narrow windows' dim light, the little silhouettes wobbled, rose, reached up to Buddha's nose. Yonten shouted at them to calm down.

Ever since he had entered the *bardo* a second time, the world appeared to him as a phantasm. With one foot in reality and the other foot in the other realm, he couldn't always tell where he really was, much less talk about it; only the drawings helped him make out the boundary between worlds, though he couldn't keep them. The harsh discipline in the monastery forbade attachment. Beauty: only in mind and self. The act of destruction is as important as the act of creation.

The tutors' scrutinizing eyes followed the novices everywhere, so it was a miracle that he had managed to hide a stone that had fallen from the sky. Year after year, after getting another *shemdap*, he would sneakily sew up a small pocket, so as not to part with his meteorite fragment.

In time, the greens of peridot, olivine, and chrysolite, chased away by purple, faded, and its original appearance as an elongated shadow was rounded into a reddish orb. The asteroid's shard acted as his link to *bardo*, to the realm beyond, and was evidence of the ability to be reborn. Again, and again. The rock that had descended from the sky, born in the Universe's dimly lit void, foretold of the worlds above the Earth, around the Earth, and in the Earth's core. It would be easier for Yonten if he could meet someone like him, someone who had crossed the barrier between death and heaven and returned; but he didn't know of any other *delok*.

He heard footsteps in the corridor, hid the stone well, and looked to see who was searching for him at such a late hour. The lamasery's secretary told him that *khenpo* was waiting for him.

He washed his hands thoroughly of butter, rubbing ash and wood ash lye into them, and took off down the cold hallways. He heard as he ran, the voices of everyone at evening prayer, which he had been excused from to finish his work, and the drums. *What does he want from me? I'll stay hungry if I'm late.* After evening prayer, the kitchen, the study rooms, even the library were closed.

Khenchen was just over sixty years old. Small and thin, he stared with a bright face at the boy who had just burst into the room, with butter in his hair and under his nails.

"Sit down, Yonten. Did you eat?" He shook his head: no. The abbot poured some hot butter tea and urged him to prepare his *tsampa*. Yonten shot a glance out of the corner of his eye at the sweets for the feast of *Losar,* laid in piles on a table, and his mouth filled with saliva. He knew he'd get more when he left, as usual when he was around the Abbot. A gentle joy came over him.

"Yonten, how many years have you been in the monastery?"

"Nine years, Nyoshul *Rinpoche*."

"It's time to go."

The boy was stung, sitting with the bowl of hot tea in his hand. The gentle joy snuck up behind him and slipped out from beneath the doors: *Where would I go? What have I done that is making me leave the lamasery?*

"It's time to move to Sera."

"Sera?"

The monastery behind which a hill had blossomed with white flowers after they placed the foundation stone? The University of Sera?

"Yeah, what are you so stunned about? Don't you want to complete your education? Don't you consider yourself ready enough?"

"Thank you, Nyoshul *Rinpoche*," he barely could say.

Instinctively, Yonten touched through his robe's fabric the stone that had fallen from the sky. *Khenchen* pretended not to notice the boy's gesture or know what his pocket contained.

"Don't thank me. You're the one who's proven yourself trustworthy. You're leaving tomorrow at dawn with a caravan of Chinese merchants who want to reach Lhasa before New Year. You're not taking anything, just food for the road. And we'll send word to your family so they know where you are."

He rose, dazed, to his feet and hurried to take the teacher's hand and bring it to his forehead, but the teacher ducked and embraced him.

"Go, Yonten, go. Use your gift for others. Come on, leave me alone, you're unsettling me, and I'm an old man. And if I don't see you around here again, I'll come back in your dreams, and you'll tell me what you've done. But that doesn't mean you can't write to me, does it?"

That's it? That was all? Nine years in the monastery and only a few moments to say goodbye? This was where he'd first arrived, where he'd competed in games with his friends Sonem and Tenzing, where he'd learned how to make butter for figurines, how to mix colors, how to read and write.

At dawn, as the Chinese caravan set off, Yonten curled up on the yak's back and fell asleep, swayed by the low voices of the Han people, his fists clenched on the two ropes that bound the bales of goods and the food baskets. Chomolungma, the Mother Goddess of the Mountains, with huge arms and legs, stone breasts, and thick ankles, was the last thing he saw out of the corner of his eye before he fell into a deep sleep, interrupted only by the unsure gait of the pack animals struggling to climb down the steep steps.

TOMMASO

The hinges creaked for a long time, and the goldsmith appeared in the doorway. They hadn't seen each other for months. Both turned white. Mustafa, of sadness. Tommaso, of bad loneliness and opium.

"With the opium, you have to befriend it, my dear. It's not that simple," Caterina kept preaching to him, on the evenings they smoked together when he lived in her house in Xi'an.

"The opium helps you, but for that, you have to befriend it. He's a two-faced deity — in fact, many-faced. Good faces and bad. A temple where, underground, the opium's demons live, the opium's spirits fly on the roof, and you live between them, trying to hold the world in balance with your prayers. Praying to all of them. Have you ever thought that a world in balance is one in which demons are no stronger than angels?"

"And the angels?"

"They're not stronger than demons. That's the idea of balance, right?"

She laughed with her whole forehead, her lips, her pink gums, and her hair's roots.

"And if you don't make friends with the opium, my dear lady, what happens?"

"Ah, this is much simpler than the angels and demons' story. The opium will kill you!"

She said it with such ease, Catarina the tough and free, surrounded by her jade forest and her jade animals. Green eyes, almond-shaped, huge. Sister of the jade.

Tommaso pushed the memory away with a slight shrug and turned to Mustafa, who had asked him twice:

"You're off to Cathay, if I'm not mistaken, don Tommaso?"

"I'll go, Mustafa Efendi, I'll go. But I don't know when. For now, I want to sell the house here."

"And if it sells, where will you stay?"

"Stavros' inn."

Advancing through the evening twilight, holding a tray of hot tea, Pelagia looked taller. Recently, she had begun to watch Tommaso, to see if he was ill. With sunken eyes, very pale, he justified her fears. The woman frowned.

"What's wrong, Pelagia? Do you want me to take you to China with me? Do you want to go back to Stavros' inn?"

"No, I have enough work to do at Fra Niccolò's."

"See? You work too hard. But even when I sell the house, I'll still pay you, Pelagia, while I'm gone."

For half a year, don Tommaso Serratore had prepared. He went to the harbor and talked to the captains of ships sailing to the Indies and China, bought maps, navigational instruments, and all sorts of gifts.

"I don't need it, don Tommaso. As long as I have these hands, I don't need any other money except the pay for my work."

If the Genoese merchant sold the house and moved out, he had all the time in the world to go down to the cafés laid along the harbor's low shore, with no one to stop him from spending his nights there. He was an adult, not a child in the orphanage, leaving her with no means to help him. However, Pelagia deeply regretted all that had transpired since Ariadne's departure. The woman walked out the door with the empty tray, and Tommaso turned to Mustafa.

"I've seen a rock like this before. When Khalil came to me to tell me that you needed a stone that had fallen from the sky, I remembered seeing one at my friend Catarina's house in Xi'an. If a stone like that can be found, I think she has a way of finding out. I wrote and asked her. She hadn't answered me yet, but I trust her."

"Is she Genoese?"

"Yes. But she was born there. Her family has lived in China for centuries. Her father traded spice. When I met her, early in my twenties, I wanted to build an empire of fabrics: nankeen, selimiye, cambric, madapolam, atlas, brocade, lasting, you name it. I dreamed of being the king of their realm... Now, it's different. But this time, I'm going to the sea. I long to hang on to the rigging at the bow of a ship, to feel the wind, to go down to the harbors, to see unknown nations and countries I've never heard of before — in short, to feel young again, if I can."

"You're not old."

"Not yet, but we're going to be grandparents. Maybe it would be better to..."

He stopped halfway through. Did Mustafa know? They had both received letters. Each from their own child.

"...I know, Musa told me. May they be healthy, they and the baby to come."

Mustafa decided not to add "Allah be praised."

"If Catarina finds the stone, I'll bring it to you. And take this."

He pushed the bag with what was left of the gold sent by the Padishah.

"You shouldn't have brought me gold, Mustafa Efendi. Thank God I at least don't lack wealth. Anyway, we're family, right?"

The glum look and the long shadow of the goldsmith's hands, taking back the bag…

"Yes, we're family," he murmured, and his face covered in mist.

CATARINA

The bells of Zhong Lou Tower rung several times that morning — a sign that a new caravan had arrived from the East — so when she woke up to find the young Genoese man, pale and thin at the gate, Catarina Verga Ducceschi wasn't too surprised. With bluish eyebags, his flesh dwindled from the frost and the hardships he had endured, Tommaso handed her two letters of recommendation: one from the Doge of Genoa and the other from Gian Giacomo Palladio, her uncle.

The flowering magnolias' branches in the courtyard casted short shadows — purple, pink, ruby — across her ample sleeves as she grasped the two envelopes with slender fingers and bent to place them in a drawer without reading them. She would have received him without recommendations.

Close to Song Kul Lake, they had fallen victim to bandits who killed two guards and two Persian merchants who had joined the caravan in Osh. Then, at the foot of Mount Celest, the snow from Pamir and Hindukush came too early, and the yaks' herdsmen had already left when the caravan reached the meeting places.

Therefore, they had to ride camels up the passes. They kept their fires burning all night and sometimes stopped to build fires during the day when their stiff fingers and eyelids thinned from the sharp air that stung too much.

By the time they reached Tash Rabat, with its fortresses, prisons, and warehouses, all made of stone, half of those with whom they left Edirne had died, returned from their journey, or fallen very ill. The latter had to stop in the few Kyrgyz villages they encountered to rest before moving on.

On one side, white skies, high glaciers, air cut into frozen ribbons, steppes, and the pungent smell of dried dung and smoke from yurts; on the other side, tired bodies covered with wounds, sore lips endlessly cracked, frostbitten feet wrapped in rags and furs, and bones welded by so many mountain ranges and deserts. By the time they reached the Dunhuang oasis, Tommaso was so drained of strength that the hiss of silica sand crying night after night on the windy dune ridges didn't frighten him.

Catarina Verga Ducceschi listened to the traveler without interrupting, ordered for a bath of peach and willow leaves boiled with lilac flowers and pearl powder to be prepared, then forced him to drink a hot ginseng soup, and sent her guest to bed.

Tommaso's youth and adventurous spirit, inherited from many generations of Genoese, who had established colonies all over the Black Sea and the Mediterranean, won out even in the Kingdom of Heaven. In less than a week, the merchant wandered the house's hallways, fretting:

"When will I get the approval of the High Commissioner of the Silk? The imperial official in charge of collecting duties and issuing trade permits won't even see me. First, they kept me for four months at the Jade Gate, at the border, and now, no one even tells me how much longer I have to wait."

"Why do you think it's called the Middle Kingdom? For them, this is the center of the world. But the Jade Gate doesn't open for just anyone. That's why they keep all the caravans there, so you can feel the favor they are doing for you. But it's not just politics — in the long months you have to wait, those who are very ill die. So, no one's going to bring different sicknesses into the kingdom."

"Okay, I'm here now. I'm healthy. How much longer do I have to wait?"

"As long as it takes. You've just arrived, and after a few days, you want to go back to Genoa?"

"I don't want to go back to Genoa, I want to go back to Constantinople, to buy a house there. To be a merchant in the Ottoman Empire, which rules a third of the world now, to move freely within its borders. That's the key. With the fall of Constantinople, the Sublime Porte is the future, my lady!"

The green, charcoal-dusted, elongated eyes of the woman born into a millennia-old empire blinked.

"It's not that simple, Tommaso. It's true that the Ottomans have put up customs for years, but it's not just one road. It's a weave of roads. The Portuguese have gone as far as the Moluccas and brought spices without paying any fees. And the Spanish reached the Americas. What can the Ottoman Empire do against their fleets or English or Dutch ships?"

"Then, I'll choose the sea, not the dry land. It doesn't matter now which Silk Road I choose. I'll see then, but I want not only silk, also rare fabrics, shells, perfumes, ornaments. Will you help me?"

"I'll help you, but you have to listen to me."

She bent down and straightened his fingers clumsily holding the thin, dark sticks, and showed him how to grab a few grains of rice. Tommaso had grown accustomed to the inlaid ebony chopsticks, but he found all the food either too spicy or too salty and asked for *minestrone, cima,* and *pansotti* with walnut sauce.

Catarina pointlessly told him about lamb with walnuts wrapped in mulberry leaves and pork cooked with onions, Chinese ash tree, honey and bamboo shoots, duck with white wine and mushrooms.

Pheasant, goose, lamb, golden carp, rabbit, and venison — they all resembled each other. Instead, the flavors of the house were what drove him crazy. Anise, cinnamon, red cardamom, soy, petunias, bamboo shoots, chrysanthemums and, above all, musk.

The musk's scent accompanied Catarina everywhere. A mere touch of the lap of her painted dresses against the furniture, the water pots in the corners, the beddings, and papers, was enough to coat them with a potent aroma.

"You have to forget about public assassinations, fratricide, and violence. Here, privileges are earned with whispers and not displayed, and the favors done to you are always returned, even when it comes to enemies. Here, honor has other faces. It's the empire of Confucius, Tommaso. Only diplomacy will get you where you want to go. And keeping the rules."

"Keeping the rules?"

"Oh, yeah, they have a book on etiquette and ceremonies. They have many books about it. I'll teach you."

Tommaso stood up and came to sit beside her, taking her hands in his. The strange woman, born in Xi'an, who wedded and later divorced a Chinese and was living a life of freedom thanks to the inherited wealth from her father and grandfather, exercised power and influence over him.

"And what is the first rule?"

"The first rule is to never show your emotions."

"And when you're in love, what do you do?"

He touched her palms with burnt fingers. Catarina gently pulled away, poured poppy seed soup cooked with ginger and honey, and handed him one of the cups. Warm steam, tangled dreams, and troubling phantasms wiped the walls for a moment, then melted into emptiness.

I'll teach you that too, Tommaso... sometime...

MERYEM

"Will you tell me a story?"

Meryem leaned down and firstly adjusted Musa's pillow, smoothed the sheet, then tucked the wool blanket more tightly under him.

"Have you been good today?"

"No, but I will be tomorrow. Please, *anne*, just a short one."

Despite the stories consistently centering around a mountain or a forest, the boy's interest never waned. The mountain had to be climbed; the forest had to be crossed. Meryem, however, didn't tell stories about the waterways; the wild rivers and the vastness of the seas made her feel uneasy. But the water was there since all the stories revolved around a realm of treasures and hidden riches lying far away, overseas. And they started with a little boy who knew the snakes' language, the birds' language, and the languages of people from other lands. The boy refused to go to sleep. "And then what happened, *anne*? And after that?" All Musa's childhood stories revolved around distant lands.

Meryem had been feeling better for a week. She stepped out of bed, straightening the sheets as she did in the past. But this time, no story came to mind. The fugitive words leaving her thoughts gave place to handiwork. The braids, the weaves, the knots, and the threads remained with her.

"Mustafa, please fix my loom."

The beater slapped, and the pedals became a wavy clay that shined where her bare soles rested on the wood. Mustafa draped some old quilts over the reed in the now soundless house.

The mute spools disturbed him, and the harsh loom's scaffolding reminded him of death, of piles of broken stone, of the burnt and blackened grass by the roadside.

Meryem pushed aside the kilims and gathered up the bundles of uncombed wool, strung here and there on the floor, and the grey, long, wrapped threads hanging on the shelves like thin rags. She failed to create any sort of order, merely stacking them so that she could move around the workshop easily.

She had a feeling she had something else to do, but she didn't know what. In the kitchen, the dough that had been left to prove overflowed in the full, whitish trough. The woman started to knead, and before long, the flour was strewn all over her. Meryem's arms rose and fell beyond her will, scattering the dough, filling the kitchen with flour arcades. The table, the oven, the windowsill were sticky, full of soft yeast icicles.

When she managed to calm down, she hurried to heat the oil for the lokma. As she washed the sweet sludge, her thoughts flew all over the place, like birds cooped up in a room, bumping into windows. She dumped the dirty water from the pan into the yard, put out the fire, and stood still for a while, unable to remember where she wanted to go.

Weaving a carpet for Musa's birthday had become unnecessary since she no longer saw him. She began to work on a new prayer rug for Mustafa, despite him repeatedly telling her loud and clear that he was comfortable with the worn-out one. The old shredded mat clung to him like an old coat he couldn't part with. Meryem chose the most vivid colors, and wavy wool, delicate to the touch, and as a design, the tall, supple lamp used for the Light sura.

"*Allah is the Light of the heavens and the earth. The example of His light is like a niche within, which is a lamp; the lamp is within glass, glass like a pearly star lit from [the oil of] a blessed olive tree, neither of the east nor of the west, whose oil would almost glow even if untouched by fire. Light upon light. Allah guides to His light whom He wills. And Allah presents examples for the people, and Allah is Knowing of all things.*"

She turned on her heel and walked into the workshop. The red, black, and orange threads of the unfinished carpet stretched almost to the ceiling, like the strings of a colorful harp. She had just finished weaving the *mihrab* niche and the lamp in the center. Around the edges, snatches of carnations, open peonies, and vines.

Mustafa appeared unexpectedly, stirred by the well-known rhythmic noise.

"What are you doing here?"

"Finishing your carpet. It's my last one."

"Don't say that you don't know... And while we're starting to talk about it, I've had a hard time asking you before. Don't you think we should send Musa some rugs from when he was a kid? Old ones. For his children. What do you think?"

The bird flock that was locked in the room slammed against the windows again with a dull thud. She waved her hand in approval, bent over the loom, and the forgotten stories merged with the skipped rows and faded letters of the Light sura.

YONTEN

He used to bring water to Buddha every morning for almost four years when he lived at Sera. He woke up, washed yesterday's bowls, and filled two buckets with fresh water. Once all of the bowls at the statue's feet were filled to the brim, he would light the candles and go fetch hot butter tea for his *tsampa*. Yonten slept in the main dormitory with the other novices, although it was becoming increasingly difficult for him. He wished he could stay the night in the workplace where he worked: a printing shop with two large rooms and windows facing the very old monks' caves, in the mountain, above the monastery. In the beginning, he had started the apprenticeship by carving wooden letters on the printing blocks, but as soon as he mastered the craft of inking, they moved him from books to the second room, the colors' room. The young lama quickly learned to paint prayer flags and meditation illustrations, but he felt overwhelmed every time he started on a new project or, worse, had to recreate an old one. Given the chance, he would have postponed commencing them for hours and embraced meditation, as if retreating from reality.

Yonten was unable to comprehend the reason behind being compelled to memorize the scriptures of detachment, while also being celebrated, recognized as a painter, and asked to paint in other monasteries. For instance, if they needed someone who could paint a *thangka* the size of a wall, they always chose Yonten. Over time, he became convinced that he could accomplish all these tasks solely by touching the sky stone.

His life in the monastery was as simple as it could be. From dawn, prayers, then study classes: *Abhidharma, Prajñā Pāramitā, Madhyamaka, Pramāṇa, Vinaya*. Afternoons, in the printing room. He spent the evenings with his little prayer wheel in his hands, clinging to it like to a mast, and after, he would spin it with eager anticipation, and the whole swarm of sleepy prayers, caught in the metal cylinder's shell, would wake up and take off in the night breeze. Although the monastery's rules allowed very few possessions — his everyday clothes, *chogyu,* the ceremonial robe, prayer wheel, rosary beads, and a bowl for food — Yonten managed to hide — wrapped in a thin silk cloth — the unearthly stone, with the smell of Chomolungma, the eternal mountain, bright lapis lazuli blue, lush moldavite green, and flaming red resembling a burning spear.

It was clear to him that all the colors in the stone were linked to the ones he used in his workshop, but he didn't know how. It was clear that the meteorite sliver was related to the talent he had been born with, but he didn't know how. And he knew that the day he obtained the strength to quit painting, he would be set free. But he had no idea how.

Every Thursday, they painted flags for flying prayers. White for air, red for fire, green for water, yellow for earth. Blue for the heights. East, west, north, south, and center, for the flights.

Yonten readied his long goat hairbrushes, ground the powders, unrolled the silk scrolls, touched the treasure in his pocket, sat quietly in front of the colors, and immersed himself in them.

KHALIL

Amassed on the table: compasses, hourglasses, drawings of terrestrial and celestial globes, azimuthal dials, equinoxes, armillary spheres, and most importantly, the astrolabe. Something inside had broken, and the disks were no longer aligned. The goldsmith told him dryly that this was the last time he would mend it. "I understand," Khalil muttered.

"Fine. I'll see where I can get another one. Can I help you?" Mustafa took out a thin file and began to undo the ring of the dial, gently removing the plates from each other. Accustomed to reading the heavens for so many years, the five engraved sheets came loose from each other in the order of the zodiac signs.

"No. I'll manage. How long have you had it?"

"Yes, it's very old, from about the time I met Taqi al-Din."

"Didn't you meet him in Cairo?"

"I met him for the first time back then, but I knew him better when we spent nights in the Galata Tower, doing different sorts of measurements in the night sky. Anyway, we couldn't have been friends."

"You didn't like him from the start, even though he taught you a lot."

"What made him likable? That he brushed off Hoca Sadeddin? That he'd rush to the Seraglio at the drop of a hat to impress everyone there?"

"Yes, but that's how he managed to build the Observatory."

"And this is how he destroyed it. What did he have to say about a comet foretelling peace and prosperity and the defeat of the Persian empire? And other prophecies? He was deeply aware that this was not the case. For one thing, being a mathematician, he knew more about the stars than I did, and he understood exactly their celestial laws. Why did he mix in with all those charlatans and sleazy servants around the Padishah?"

"Maybe the desire for greatness consumed him, too."

"This is true. Also, he wanted to correct the Ulug Beg's astronomical tables, competing with the universities of Cordoba, Cairo, and Damascus. And many more things. What made his arrogance know no bounds? Now that so much time has passed, and I won't see him again, I can tell you that I still liked something about him: he designed his own instruments. Can you imagine? He was making astronomical tools! And besides, he made clocks."

"Did he?"

"Yes, he was in love with them. We spent hours together measuring inclinations, angles, and angular ascents; in short, everything one wanted to know when drawing celestial clocks."

"Funny, he never showed me one or talked about them."

During his time as Chief Astrologer, Taqi ad-Din had crossed paths with Mustafa at the Seraglio, where everybody knew about Havva's unusual diadem, and sometime after the imperial wedding, he had asked the goldsmith to help him build a small steam turbine, the same one Khalil had been working on, many years after.

"Do you still have any of his watches?"

"No. He took some of them, and others have been scattered after the Observatory closure. I carried everything I could carry here."

They climbed the steps to the first floor of the small time-tower in Tophane, right next to the open platform facing the street, surrounded by instruments, manuscripts, and with all sorts of celestial maps thrown around.

"What's it like here? Is it better to be *muvakkit*?"

"Yes, but I don't have as much quiet study time as I did at the Observatory."

"Why?"

"Because of the school. A whole mix of people come here; everyone says something. Endless talk about measuring the distance between the stars, the Sun and the Moon in the sky, lunar nodes, phases of the Moon, eclipses, and planetary models. I don't have any more patience for this."

"And you are still patient… with what?"

"With your talisman and all the writings about immortality. Now that I've spent so much time looking, I find more and more books. I can't detach myself from them, and I also want to see that meteorite fragment. Living my wretched life of a no-good man, according to some, this is the least I can do: to hold in my hands a piece of meteorite, however small, but to know that it has traveled across the skies since world's creation to reach me."

"And that's not hubris?"

"No, it's a dream."

"But it's not everyone's dream."

"It's an astronomer's dream."

"This is too far for me. I just want this talisman's story to be over. To get away with it. Come and see: the pin holding the plates together broke. I can't fix it today. I'll have to make you a new one. It's late. I should go. I've left Meryem alone too long."

"Wait a minute…"

… He wished to tell him that he had found, by chance, a rare book about the first emperor of China, who had sought immortality; that it was the first time he had held in his hands the long bamboo scrolls painted with letters never seen before; that he did not know who had brought it to Constantinople or who had translated it into Arabic…

… He wished to tell him about slow, perfect, abysmal time cycles, like the one at the birth of the first divine emperor; about the shoots trampled during military expeditions in the land of Chu and Han and Zhao, and Yen and Wei; about the silent blizzard of winter evenings, when hundreds of thousands of laborers with melted bones drew their oil lamps closer and slept for few hours, only to start all over again — the next day and the third, to exhaustion — building the Great Wall of the Kingdom of Heaven; about the salt and tea merchants collecting dues for the tomb that was to be the center of the world, about the underground city laid for an emperor so thirsty for life…

… He wished to tell him about the long autumn nights when in the imperial dormitories, no one had the courage to approach the ailing emperor, and visions continued to multiply, and the Son of Heaven had collapsed to the floor under the shadows; about the anger, the flight, and the despair; about former generals and livid soldiers, an army with which he couldn't conquer death…

… He wished to tell him about the white peonies, reddened in a single hour, as long as it took for the four hundred alchemists to be executed for not discovering the elixirs of eternal life, though they had tirelessly mixed mercury with sulfur, arsenic, and cinnabar with hematite and dust of precious stones…

… He wished to tell him about the increasingly distant searches, about Mount Penglai, where the eight immortals were living, about Zhifu Island, about the yellowish waters of the Bohai Sea, about man-faced fishes, about the stone that fell from the sky, after which the emperor, a prisoner of his own madness, ran for seven years to all corners of the realm…

… He wished to tell him of the wet clothes of those who had sunken in the deep, to find the meteor, of the waters that parted at the emperor's touch, of the wheels caught in the wet sand of the nameless beaches where immortality was found, of the fringes of the imperial canopy, moving in their faint breeze. A kingdom founded to last for ten thousand generations and an emperor doomed to live as long as his kingdom…

… He wished to tell him about the withered roses, hung on the corners of pagodas by weeping women, about the burning in the stomachs of the counselors who carried the body back, about the late snows, about the mercury — the only metal in the world that dissolves the eternity of gold — that came to flow in China's first divine emperor's veins, like the mercury rivers from his own mausoleum…

… He wished to tell him about Qin Shi Huang's descent into an underground imperial city, about the tomb with stairs, lanterns, and a sky encrusted with precious stones. An emperor was never to be left alone, so metal birds hopped from branch to branch, musicians, dancers, and acrobats holding ostrich feathers and lotuses in their hands, hurrying to greet him, while the oceans below sighed, moved by a water clock. The heavy bronze doors had slammed shut, and the last of the convoy, thousands of soldiers of burnt clay, strode in the thin light to the emperor to guard him.

"Why are you so silent, Khalil? Is something wrong?"

"It's nothing. Wait till I get my caftan to lock up here, and I'll come too. It's late. You're right."

TOMMASO

Tommaso Serratore kept shifting from one foot to the other, waiting. Hollow, devoid of furniture and curtains, the rooms suffered in the harsh light. Small, unfinished grooves where the legs of sofas had scraped the floor, the flayed walls behind frames, icons, and mirrors. Everything that had been hidden up until that point was revealed, beyond escape. The servants loaded the last chests for Genoa. Silverware, lithographs, Damascus draperies, embroidered linens, Anatolian carpets, porcelain, all tied with strings by the porters they haggled with in the harbor. Heavy breaths, melted under the trunks' weight, and the empty house's spaces like skull sockets.

For the past two days and nights, he worked side by side with Pelagia at the bales, folding, wrapping furniture in felt and straw. They only finished at dawn, when the woman, weighed down by the bundles swaddled in cloths, also left.

"Are you coming back, don Tommaso?"

"Yeah… Do you think I'm gonna die in China? Death is far from me, Pelagia. I still have much to do."

"I was asking if you're coming back to live here."

"No… I don't think so. Maybe I will come with business, but to get another house here, no."

"So, we won't see each other again?"

"Mistress Pelagia, only God can answer that question. But if we're healthy, why should we stop seeing each other? Constantinople isn't going anywhere and neither is the basilica of Fra Niccolò."

He ordered the woman to take to the orphanage all the clay pots, saucepans, kettles, and baking trays, used tablecloths, old tea towels, and the boiled, baked, sugared, and dried vegetables and fruit that lined the pantries. Finally, the last two trunks, containing his clothes, a few books, two candlesticks, and some bedding, arrived at Stavros' inn.

Philippe D'Auréville appeared in the doorway and leaned on the door frame:

"Forgive me, Serratore, for being late. I'm coming straight from the Seraglio."

"Any news?"

"With this war, there are more and more demands and needs of all kinds."

"Which you, sir, certainly know how to fulfill."

"As do you, sir! As do you. Are you angry?"

"Naturally. You took my house for such a small price..."

"It's a fair price. The plague is getting closer and closer, people are fleeing to smaller towns and villages where they feel safer. Houses don't sell like they used to. Everyone is waiting. And you didn't do me a favor. You haven't had any other bidders, but you can go, now that you're rid of the property. Really, when are you leaving?"

"Soon... I've got more work to do here... Soon..."

"That's what you said four months ago. Are you coming back?"

"You're the second person to ask me this today."

"I wonder why you sold your house just now. It's not really a good time."

"I waited until now… to see Ariadne married… to be rich enough."

"Nobody considers themselves rich enough. Not even the sultans and the kings. If they did, they'd stop being greedy."

"I don't think about people born so high. I'm talking about people like you and me. Shouldn't we, if not stop, at least enjoy what we have?"

"I agree! I'm enjoying my situation, Serratore, with all my heart. Believe me."

"I believe you. Let's go to Stavros and toast some liquor to this and your new home."

"I can't. I have to go back. I just came to get the keys."

"Couldn't you send a servant?"

"I wanted to say goodbye."

"Here are the keys to the cellar, the keys to the rooms, and the keys to the back and front gates."

The whole bundle, which usually hung around Pelagia's waist, rested, quietly, in D'Auréville's hands. On their way out, they passed the sad beehives, with their frames hanging down and their corners eaten by the rain.

"I would like to have some bees in here again. Do you know how I can get them? It looks like they all died or left the place."

"It's not hard to find a servant who knows what to do. You want to keep hives?"

"Why not? It'll remind me of Ariadne, and you, Serratore."

"I just didn't know you wanted to remember us. Or maybe just her?"

The Frenchman gave a broad laugh and a sly glance.

"Well, you don't know a lot about me, Serratore. If I came to her birthday, I had something in mind, didn't I? Anyway, bon voyage to spices and silkworms, and when you come back, look for me. We'll have some wine then." He slammed the carriage door and disappeared around the first corner in a flash, and the Genoese took off on foot. With the afternoon growing late, Leib lit the lamps in his still-open shop. The Jew was dressed, as usual, in his tunic, long and black, which gave him a harsh appearance.

Leib greeted him by putting his right hand to his heart, then to his forehead, then to his heart again, according to Ottoman custom. Tommaso replied in kind.

"We've closed the *House of Dreams*, don Serratore. Because of the pestilence, the deaths are more and more, and I have sent my family away. I am left alone. There is no one to help me serve."

"Already? Is it so dangerous?"

"Not yet, but it will be. I already see how many people are looking for me."

"But there have been waves of plague, and they all stopped sooner or later."

"It won't go out anytime soon. On the fringes, in the *mahallas*, are more and more ill people. You hear of a market where someone's fallen off their feet. Some run, some stay. Women crowd my shop — old Jewish, Armenians, Turkish women. What can I say? They come here and ask me for cures and are overwhelming me with their prayers. What shall I tell them? That I'm powerless? I give them sandalwood and frankincense to smoke around the house, to clean the air, to soak their clothes in hot water and lye… I don't know if it helps, but I've sent my family away from here."

"Where?"

"To my younger brother, in Kermanshah. I just hope the plague doesn't reach Persia. It's quiet there, and the Jews have a good living. I wonder why Leib Peres, the first, my father's father, stopped in Constantinople and didn't go further, if he still took the wandering road… Our lineage is either driven away, or goes willingly, or converts, or returns from exile. They all take their mezuzah from one part of the world to another. Sephardim, Romaniotes, Mizrahi… There's never peace for the children of Moses, don Tommaso."

"Not much peace for anyone…"

All around them: retorts, filters, porcelain jars, mugs, mortars, pestles, scales, weights, crystal cylinders filled with seeds, lizard blood, ox horns, bat wings, dried swallowtails, amber, and musk.

"And what happened to the opium?"

"I sent it by sea to Salonica; I have a warehouse there. I'll sell it to the highest bidder. All in all, I won't bother to share it out to the shops."

"It seems you don't waste your time."

"It is also from the teachings of my family, always on the move, that I draw my inspiration. Smell the danger. After so many centuries of persecution, burned homes, and squandered wealth, you must always be prepared."

"And burnt people, not just houses."

"And people, *Barukh atah Adonai Eloheinu melekh ha'olam, dayan ha-emet* – '*Blessed are you, O Lord, our God, King of the universe, the true judge.*' Everywhere is the same. I can help you though, don Serratore. I'm out of black spice, but I have something else — Anatolian poppy seeds. Let me find them."

Hastily, he vanished through the door, only to reappear within moments, grasping a small pouch in one hand and a pestle in the other.

"I'll add saffron, cloves, marjoram, and a weed, brown grass."

"What brown grass?"

"That's my secret. Takes out the bitterness."

Listening to Tommaso's low voice, Leib opened the bag, and the smell of smoke, salt, and resin wafted throughout the room:

"And you're not planning to join your family?"

"I can't. Who's going to take care of all this?"

"If your life were to end, what use does the fortune hold?"

"It will be no use to me, but I'm leaving it to my daughter, and her children. I have only one daughter. She's kind, well-behaved, does all her duties. I cannot complain, and I hope my brother Nissim will find her a good man if anything happens to me."

"I also have only one daughter. She's in Genoa. She's already married."

"I know, with Mustafa's boy, the goldsmith."

"Is there any rumor an apothecary can miss?"

"I have to, don Tommaso, for my survival in this city... So many people come into my shop... and not all of them my friends."

"I had the impression that Stavros' inn held the role of the 'ear of the town,' but it seems the *Dream House* was not far behind either. Maybe you'll reopen it sometime."

"I hope we can enjoy that day together."

"I hope so too. I'll be gone for a while. It's not because of the plague that I'm leaving. I decided long ago..."

"Have a safe journey and safe return."

When he arrived at Stravros' inn, he ordered boiled water and a jug of wine to be brought to him. He poured a handful of seeds into a small bowl, grasped with his fingertips a few long strands and a few aromatic grains; he stirred them, then sipped the bitter infusion with slow movements. Once it reached the roof of his mouth, the mineral, intense white wine from the island of St. Irina and the poppy tea beguiled each other. A thrust crushed his spine.

With a dry slowness, in the two torches' light, the past rose in boundless waves. Broken memories of lampas, mohair, lace-covered dolls, ribbons, taffeta, and brocades swirled over his head, faltering. Inhabitants of a kingdom that was not to be. With his head in his hands, defeated, he couldn't think of anything he had taken all the way: husband for a few days, father from afar, lover forever gone. His life's meaning slipped through his fingers, and though loneliness did not frighten him, even with it, he could not wholly come to terms.

Once the *House of Dreams* ceased to exist, all that was left were the low plank beds in the harbor teahouses and an unsettling fear.

MERYEM

Allah was no longer there. He had left, and in the vacancy, an abyss swallowed up the braided woolen and silken strings she had woven for Mustafa's caftan, the smell of extinguished candles, the funerals, the silvery swirl of the horizon as she went to look for Musa at the harbor, the blackened wood of caiques, the guarded dreams of her newborn, lest the jinn reach them, the necklaces, the bracelets, the silver lockers of the Greek icon covers Mustafa used to emboss around Christmas, the wild vine under the windows of the carpet workshop where she grew up, the celery, the artichokes, the beetroot, the pumpkin flowers, the peppers, the onions strung on strings, the carpet warp, the living wool, the dead wool, the bridge made of boats over the Golden Horn, the trees of Judas and sycamore trees, the five daily prayers: *Sabah, Öğle, İkindi, Akşam, Yatsı,* the taste of pomegranate juice kept on ice, the Sweet Waters of Europe spring, the fish fried by street vendors over an open fire around the Galata Tower, sheep pilaf with pine seeds and pimento, the grease marks on Musa's fingers, who used to not wait for the food to get cold, the torpor of afternoons, the new leather saddles in the Great Bazaar, the prayers for rain, Aegean olive oil and Thracian sunflower oil, Mustafa clutching her knees in his hands like ovals, porcelain clams, the lutes, the Iftar dinners, the sumptuously decorated saddle blankets for the Padishah horses in the retinue, the cobalt-blue, the turquoise, the violet, the red of the carnations in the carpets, the cherry and plum boughs, the color of the Prophet, the forest of talking flags in the courtyard.

All of them gone, replaced by the sounds. Meryem bumped into things and sang. Daily, when he prepared her for sleep, Mustafa changed her nightgown soiled with urine, cleansed her wrinkled skin with a cloth, covered her with the quilt, and rested beside her. Meryem usually got out of bed around midnight and strolled around in her dream, as if she were walking through the snow.

Mornings would find her curled up, knees to her chest, on the pile of rugs woven for Musa, finger in mouth, eyes wide open. Where formerly, golden milk chrysanthemums bloomed on nightgown breastplates, there were now murky puddles of saliva. She called Mustafa Musa or *büyük baba.* Like Allah, Grandfather Harutyunyan had long departed from her mind, and the childish bones of Yesim and Atife melted beneath the dusty grass of the cemetery.

Meryem didn't eat anymore, and when she moved her lips, a thin sound came out, a swirl of steam in the air, a warm wind.

"How do you know that song?"

"I don't remember."

She had word bits in her head, just bits, single words, a song. A very old Armenian hymn.

"You're like the incense tree,
You are a sweet-tasting fruit,
You bear good fruit,
Mother of God, I have sinned before you"

Did her mother sing it to her? She didn't know her mother. *Maybe her grandmother sang? Great-grandmother?* All the wombs of the women in her family who'd given birth to live and dead babies spoke to each other, in increasingly ancient languages, Aramaic and Syriac, syllables, Chaldean, Phoenician, Babylonian, Sumerian, just sounds, aaaahhhh, iiiii, mmmmmhhhh. Then, Meryem fell silent.

YONTEN

The *Losar* festival was over, and they had begun the new lunar year. The night before, once the monastery gates closed, they had begun to clean up after the thousands of pilgrims. They cleared away the wooden benches and low tables, swept the gravel from the courtyard where they usually held the daily debates, and let the cold February air roughen the long rooms where they studied. Larger and smaller deities dozed in the courtyard under swirls of agarwood smoke. The majority of prayers had already taken flight, and the mantras clinging to the trees of life in the core of the metal cylinders, swooning from so much spinning, enjoyed the silence.

He entered the workshop for the last time. For the last time? At least for a while. He would have to start his ritualic wandering. For three years, he would have to meditate and pray, alone, one with the earth and the sky, having only his robe, his belt, and the bowl for the slices of dried cheese, fruit, butter, grain, and water received from merciful strangers. It had been a long time since he had stopped carrying water to the Buddha statue in the workshop every morning, but he insisted on doing it one more time as a farewell.

The woman wrapped in a thick cloth leaned against a pine tree like a shadow, with her eyes closed and her head tilted to one side. How had she gotten here? Did she sneak into the monastery after they closed the gate? Had she remained since evening mass and hidden herself away?

Yonten put the buckets down and approached her with small steps, so as not to frighten her. The moment he reached her, Catarina opened her eyes. The huge green, surrounded by thin circles of indigo graphite, purplish from pilgrimage's sleepless nights, and many nights before that, made the young monk dizzy. She wore simple clothing — the blanket covering her could be bought on every street corner in Lhasa. Yonten sensed a shared understanding between them. He put his hand to his lips, beckoning her to be quiet, then made another sign: to wait for him. The woman didn't seem to notice anything or have any plans to leave that spot. The lama ran to the workshop, not wanting to waste time because everyone was about to wake up, and someone could chase her out of the monastery, where she was not allowed to stay overnight. He collected off a ledge a little wooden box he'd fashioned from the pieces of the printing blocks, then rushed downstairs, hiding the box, which held five painted prayer flags and a small bag of orange *pulu.*

Catarina remained in the same place. The journey that had stretched over several days tired her terribly, the lack of opium tormented her, the thick cold and the smoke of incense confused all her senses. Last evening remained in her memory like a long string of incantations, covered by the deafening clatter of striking brass plates, the whirling wheels of the dharma, an orange and green and blue sounds carnival, which had made her slip into a hot vigil. After the ceremony, with her last strength, the woman had crawled under a tree to get herself together.

When she opened her eyes a second time, a young lama stood in front of her and held out a little chest of unpolished wood. Once again, the monk covered his lips with his palm. He then walked ahead of her, and unveiled a secret gate in the wall, and showed her a trail that intersected with the road to Sera. Catarina followed him as if in a dream, as she sometimes followed the clouds on her flights from Xi'an.

Yonten returned with the water buckets and, kneeling at the feet of the Buddha's statue, began to rub the brass bowls. After three years of pilgrimage, he could choose to stay in the monastery or climb to the hermitages above Sera. To go out into the world, to teach others, to paint. He was free. The lotus doesn't ask when to bloom, the wind doesn't ask which way to blow. All the illustrations that came out of his hands only traveled through him. The vessel in which water flows is not water.

He had completed the first part of his study and had no further need for the stone that had fallen from above. His gift became love, just as the Nyoshul Rinpoche had predicted over and over again. The purest sound in the universe. In the endless string of chained births and deaths, the one twice turned from *bardo* had changed, after much effort, into a grain of sand.

Yonten washed the last of the dishes, the food bowl, and hung it around his waist, wrapped himself in his robe, and went downstairs. He left through the same concealed passage he had shoved Catarina through just moments earlier. The woman didn't leave, just walked a few steps down the path. Catarina, like any opium lover, seemed to be sleeping on her feet, not relying on anything. Dealing with the states between reality and dream came more naturally to her than dealing with reality itself.

He walked past her and bowed without waking her this time, marveling again at her face and the green eyes that cut the night in two. In the hidden order of things that bind us to one another, the stone from another world was being returned to a being from another world. A closed circle. As he walked, Yonten muttered — *om mani padme hum* — and lost himself in the valley.

Dismayed, Catherine opened the wooden box. Beneath the new prayer flags and the dark red cloth, the piece of meteorite blinked dully, blurring the color of her eyes even more, as when, on a painter's palette, two colors run into each other.

ARIADNE

He couldn't stop himself from following them with his eyes, from listening around corners, from looking inquisitively at them. Until the arrival of his young relatives from Constantinople, the passing years meant little to Matteo Serratore. The courtyard behind the house, with its well-raked gravel, the ledgers kept up to date, the avaricious dinners, and suddenly a whirlwind of fresh life had swept through his quiet living.

Just like when she was just a toddler, Ariadne managed to irritate him with her unexpected gestures, her short orders, the way she took possession of things and people, her new habits that no one had heard of, and the jumbled languages she used when she spoke. Women remained a mystery to him, and despite being surrounded by female workers who looked younger and younger as he grew older, he paid no attention to them, just as he had paid no attention to Tommaso's dolls when they were kids. He saw them and didn't see them.

"Does he like men?" Musa once asked in passing, accustomed to the mores of another capital.

"No, he doesn't like anyone or anything."

Musa didn't pay attention to the women in the workshop either but for entirely different reasons. His innate shyness didn't serve him well in the city surrounded by water, with its sloping roofs, rich porticos, differently tailored clothes, and unusual habits. The Genoese women without veils seemed daring to him, and he avoided furtively gazing at the shadows of their calves as they stepped off from the carriages. The boy blushed when they laughed noisily at his questions, he fell silent when peddlers sneered and twisted their words. In him merged the Seljuks and the Onoğurs, the Khazars and the Mongols' bloodlines, and countless more who had traveled far and wide, subjugating nations and tribes, cities, and villages one after another.

Night after night, caressing her in sleep, he took refuge in Ariadne's arms — the nearest port — and she shielded fiercely. First and foremost, from Uncle Matteo, who did not appear to treat her husband properly, in her opinion; from the merchants of Balbi Street who referred to him as an outlander; from the priests who regarded him with suspicion; and even from the servants to whom the clumsy Musa demanded nothing. Instead, she instructed them to scrub, wash, and change the carpets, to cook dishes other than the ones they were familiar with, to not open doors, and to speak in hushed tones while he worked. Stubbornly, the uncle resisted his niece's wishes, and the voices of those two rose to the ceiling in high-pitched arguments almost daily. Whenever the shouting began, Musa, used to living next to his mother and losing all such struggles to her, would retreat to the bedroom as when he was a child and draw transparent ships, caught in a slow mysterious glide, that he possessed a greater understanding of.

This knowledge, this timeless time of his thoughts, made him have on his face a gentle lone smile, hanging in the corner of his mouth and lighting up his velvety golden-brown eyes, inherited from Mustafa. Musa exhibited generosity toward the lack of comprehension from those around him, yet after a year after their arrival, they all reached their breaking point.

At the wedding, they received, as dowry, a coffer full of Venetian ducats and Genoese lira, then, through various emissaries, Ottoman gold coins, jewels, and gems. Sealed with red wax, accompanied by furniture, silverware, and other things, the last of the missives from Constantinople spread across many pages. In crumbly, unrecognizable handwriting, Tommaso recounted how he had decided to sell his house in Galata, lamented the fact that trade went no longer the way it used to, and advised them not to miss the opportunity to build docks and silos at Spezia. The merchant enclosed a copy of his will, in which he named them the heirs of his entire estate.

Then, other pages. Vague phrases, different inks, a string of unrelated words about voyages East, pirates and helmsmen in the Gulf of Oman, Malacca, sable furs, Cordoba saddles and daggers, Murano glass, and rare wines, that he left under guard at Stavros' inn, and how he went down to the shores of the Golden Horn every day to find a ship. He wrote of having haggled with a Portuguese captain, then a Dutch captain, then an Egyptian captain, none of whom seemed to go where he wanted, for the demand changed all the time. He yearned to travel to Zaiton or the kingdoms of Ache and Johor, Madras, or an enigmatic island in Malay that had yet to be discovered by Europeans but that he knew about from copies of Zheng He's maps he had found in Catarina's home.

Anxious, Ariadne and Musa tried to persuade him to live with them. The answer to each of their demands remained unchanged: he had held onto the dream of traveling to China for an unbearably long period, and there was someone patiently awaiting his arrival. They could manage without him. At the very least, the last assertion was correct.

Despite being immersed in interminable computations and navigation instructions, Musa came to comprehend how things worked, with the help of his wife.

These were days when the African slave trade was on the rise, and gold started to pile up at the courts of Europe; times of a tumultuous competition, blending the smugness of monarchs, the greed of courtiers, and the daring of adventurers. Genoa had seen it all since the armies of the Greek and Roman empires regarded the Mediterranean as a large lake in their backyard; the stubbornness of merchants from father to son had avoided wars — when possible — and had spread on the maps an empire of waters: the Sea of Azov, the Black Sea, the Danube Delta, the Marmara, the Aegean, the Levant, North Africa, Panamá Viejo in the Pacific. Without too much braggadocio or alcove politicking, the stalwart Genoese Republic managed its business with piles of money poured on top of each other and a wish to enlarge its harbor or have another port to serve it.

It came as no surprise when the Doria family, who already possessed an estate in the region, chose the bay of Spezia for the new docks, and the council of the Casa delle Compere e dei Banchi di San Giorgio granted their approval. From there, it was merely a single stride towards the Serratore heir's wish to move to a place devoid of Uncle Matteo's constant surveillance, and Musa's dream of shipbuilding could be fulfilled. They meticulously amassed all the ornate sculptured furniture, luxurious carpets, exquisite Iznik pottery, delicate porcelain, and meticulously packed them into several wooden crates, meticulously fastened with strings, which they endlessly shifted back and forth, as Ariadne struggled to make a decision. She first chose a location for her house behind the church of Santa Maria Assunta, but because plague rumors terrified her, she decided it would be preferable to live outside the city, in Lerici, away from the steep roofs crowding the streets.

Once the winter months had passed, with the wind delicately carving the gravelly shores and the cold extending to the outermost edges of the horizon, they mutually agreed that Lerici was too far for them. However, it would have required yet another amount of time to commence the construction if Musa hadn't inquired whether she wished to give birth in the old house in Genoa. In less than two days, they bought a place in Porto Venere, behind Doria Castle. In that place — the pregnant woman had been entrusted by more than one person — the salty breeze crouched all day beneath the hills full of satiny foliage, and the air was very fresh. Even though she spent the last three months of her pregnancy giving directions to the bricklayers and journeymen, disputing with the architect and the gardener, they didn't finish the work. As a result, she was forced to give birth in a house filled with lime and sand, with no flooring except for two hastily furnished rooms: a bedroom and a kitchen.

The difficult birth lasted a whole night, during which time the midwife wouldn't let Musa get close, and he wandered around, stepping over scraps of wood left over from cutting beams, sawdust, broken brick, and unopened paint jars.

At the break of dawn, when the underwater grottoes of Palmaria Island were dimly illuminated and the shell gatherers were readying their baskets, he saw her. Stunningly white, with a mane of reddish-blonde hair, she looked like no one he knew. Nations that had lived long ago, men and women, with the dust from under their horses' hooves, with their cries, and whispers, and rapes and faith, and faith-denying, and moonlit nights, begat the little being, whom Ariadne clutched to her breast with love.

"You look like a ghost, Musa."

"Can I hold her?"

"Of course, you can."

"Who does she look like?"

"I don't know. My mother died when I was born, and I never saw yours."

"It's true."

Meryem crossed the sky and wiped each window with the bottom of her dress.

"I'd like to name her Meryem, after my mother."

"No."

"Then, Giovanna, like your mother."

"No. We'll name her Elena."

"Elena?"

This name had never crossed Musa's ears before, and the sheer fervor with which it was uttered led him to suspect a concealed truth.

"A friend from the convent. I didn't tell you about her, because she died... a long time ago..."

Between them, the cold air of the Ligurian Sea grew stronger than a palisade. Musa repeated himself, speaking slowly, tightly.

"I wish for us to also call her Meryem." Then, he fell silent — his only power to tame Ariadne's stubbornness.

An hour later, the young mother put Elena Giovanna Meryem to her breast, the midwife left, and Musa withdrew to the kitchen, where he arranged a wooden plank in the corner to sketch intricately-named caravels.

HAVVA

The children came from everywhere. A few were as little as two or three weeks old, with most of them just starting to walk. They crawled through the Hall of Favorites, the bathrooms, the courtyards, leaving blood trails. The *yatagan* swords, penetrating their bodies, exceeded the children's heights, leaving behind intricate designs engraved into the stone slabs by their pointed tips.

Suleiman, Ibrahim, Semsiruhsar, Abdurrahman, Hafsa, Orhan, Mihrimah, Safiye, Isa, Osman, Mahmud, Hasan, Fatma, Gülşah, Davud, Ali, Mehmed, Hatice, Mihriban, Yusuf, Gülbahar, Alemşah, Gevherhan, Cihangir, Nigar, Selim, Malhun, Korkud, Ayşe, Abdullah, Melek crawled around, bleeding. A lively red reigned the rooms and filled them with the scraping of blades on the porous rock of the floors. The sound drove the Sultana out of her mind and woke her from her sleep. On account of the dream, Havva firmly believed that something had happened. Eager to leave as soon as possible, she instructed for the carriage and spare stallions to be made ready for her during the journey to Edirne.

The old capital of the empire greeted it at dawn with the reddish mists rising from the small waves of the Tunca and Marita, the murmuring fountains designed to soothe the madmen tied with ropes at Bayezid's asylum, and the richness of the dome of Selimiye, dressed by oil lamps in silky lights. The servants who came out to meet them didn't know whether the Padishah was still alive, for, at his command, they dared not enter the imperial bedchamber or inform her about his health.

Signor Ambrogino Battifoglio, the Venetian doctor who accompanied him everywhere, had been admitted to his audience only twice in the previous month, despite several pleas. He then prescribed some powerful remedies for his dizziness, but he had no idea if His Lordship took them. The Sultana listened to the doctor and then stopped him with a sign of her hand, no longer concerned by talk of the patient's prolonged sadness, known to all. Wizards and priests, astrologers and healers, doctors, and monks tried everything. Prayers for the Prophet's birthday, cold baths, poppy extract, clay wraps, purgatives, lute music, donkey milk, aromatic oils, lavender, and chamomile compresses. Nothing seemed to banish the melancholy. The Padishah had welcomed a shameless jinn woman into his bed, which sucked his breath, drying him out.

Havva told them she wanted to be alone and entered the imperial bedroom. She stretched out an arm and lifted him. The warm body seemed to have bones filled with air and to have stopped breathing. Heavy curtains in marbled folds covered the windows, obeying the Sultana's hands. She carefully closed the door to the terrace because she needed neither help nor witnesses.

After that, the woman took a paper from the table and wrote first to Prince Murad, who was on a military expedition against the Safavids, then to the Grand Vizier, ambassadors, and foreign envoys. She finished as the silvery March afternoon flowed from Hadrian's walls. She took a few strides because she had been seated at the writing table for a long time and opened the windows again. The illness's heavy smell, rotting fruit and grief, began to fade. The walls cooled down. Havva clapped her hands, called the servants, and ordered that from that moment on, the room would be lit by a single candle.

She commanded that during the day, the curtains of the imperial bed canopy be lowered and the silence be preserved.

She commanded that every morning, soups, teas, and fresh water be brought and left by the bedside.

She commanded that the number of servants who served His Highness be reduced to four and kept only those she knew well.

She commanded that the Padishah's clothes should be washed every day, that the horses and falcons should be tended, and that they should all be ready to leave at all times, but above all, she commanded that in every corner of the halls of the Serai, there should be burners on which incense, myrtle, and sandalwood coals should burn without ceasing. The lace sheets, cushion covers, brocades had to be soaked in rose water.

At last, overweary, and pale, she shut herself and the White Eunuchs Chief in her bedroom to talk about embalming.

As a result of all this, the Sultan was alive for his subjects for seventeen more days. That is how long it took the eldest son to step onto the streets of Constantinople. The entire time, the Sultana did not depart from the palace of Edirne, nor did she ever leave the side of the imperial corpse. Sick-eyed, sleepless, uncertain of the nights' end due to the perpetual gloom in the room, dazed by aromas and white smoke, surrounded by shadows with soft gestures and feeble voices, Havva was slowly unraveling into the depths of the past. She allowed herself to let go of the man who had given her six children only when she heard that Murad had entered Constantinople.

The return journey felt lengthier compared to her arrival in Edirne three weeks earlier; at every crossroads, in every hamlet, people gathered to greet the Protector of the World on their knees, to mourn, to say prayers.

At the Seraglio — a place that the Sultana thought she would never reach — trays of pomegranates, plums, grapes, hazelnut and pistachio cakes, lemonade, and sorbets were prepared as they waited for the arrival of the cortege. Close to the Gate of Happiness, they set up tables, with trays filled with halva and honey doughnuts for chasing away the sorrow of death.

MUSTAFA

"I'm going to buy a shoot, a plum, an apple, maybe a cypress."

"Now?"

"Why not? Don't you know what tradition says? That you have to plant a tree at the grave."

While they prepared the food, the women talked quietly in the kitchen. They came in at dawn, washed her, braided her tails, and now Meryem lay quietly, her face covered with cloth and her eyes closed.

"Yeah, but it doesn't say you have to plant it now before you put the dead in the grave."

"Come on, Khalil, come with me. It's not far from here, the Imam is late, and I don't even think he'll come until the burial of the Padishah is finished."

"That's just it. You can't throw a needle in the city. The stores are closed, and everyone's on the streets."

They had been gathered since morning. On either side of the coffin of the Protector of the Faith, whom Allah took into His mercy, the members of the Divan and the *ulema* were lined up. Following the coffin, only Murad, dressed in a black kaftan, with a modest turban, without diamonds and egret feathers. The *janissaries* and the *spahis* opened and closed the procession. The crowd proceeded to the Süleymaniye Camii, where the funeral prayers were recited. Afterward, with all sins forgiven, His Highness, the dead Padishah, opened the gate of the Garden of Paradise and entered. Until the end of the forty days of mourning, the tomb of the Sovereign had to be visited twice a day by all his sons.

"I won't buy it at the store. I think I'll get a cherry tree though, not a cypress."

"Take what you want, but tomorrow. No, really, Mustafa, what's gotten into you? You didn't plant anything for the girls."

"How do you know?"

"You never talked about it."

"For the girls, I planted hanging roses and daffodils. Do you know how beautiful it smells there when they bloom? But for Meryem, I want to seed a tree — when her soul turns into a bird, she'll have somewhere to sit, and maybe I'll put a little stone bench… for me… to rest in its shade. I think I'll rest more than her because I cannot see Meryem standing still in the other world either: she'll be weaving, praying. She will find something to do. Maybe she'll finally go on a pilgrimage. Not far. On the road between Bodrum and Milas, there's a saint's grave. I don't remember what this saint's name was or if he had a name at all. Anyway, her grandmother told her about him. She kept bugging me to take her there. She kept saying: 'Next year, we'll go on a pilgrimage, but let Musa grow up first.' And after he grew up… she got sick. Let's go get the shoot."

"There's no time. Here comes the imam."

"It's not the imam. It's a hafiz." The small-statured man, with amber eyes, began his prayers, which were not a mechanical recital or a planned phrase, but a continuous and uninterrupted flow. The stream of words didn't cease even after Meryem, wrapped in white strips, was lifted onto her shoulders by her sisters' husbands and two neighbors on the way to the cemetery.

Khalil remained on purpose and shot glances out of the corner of his eye at Mustafa, who walked absent-mindedly, interrupted from his thoughts only by an occasional "*May the great and glorious Allah, who will one day raise us all from the grave, be merciful and gracious to you! May He receive you with mercy and show you the way to salvation, may He enable you to approach His divinity and His prophets, may His forgiveness be with you forever!*"

In less than an hour, the words stopped. Mustafa parted from everyone at the cemetery gate and returned home. He felt embarrassed by their attention and wished to be alone with the emptiness within him. The years of widowhood did not seem threatening to him, just useless.

The morning after the funeral, Mustafa started cleaning. In the downstairs workshop, he gathered up the unfinished carpet with light surah, the wool yarns, and the wicker baskets. Then, he took out the loom. With pursed lips and slumped shoulders, he pulled all her clothes from the closets, washed them, held them in sunlight and moonlight, and brought them in from the courtyard with tear-stained cheeks and glassy hands.

In Musa's room, he spent two days. The first one to wash and dry the covers, bedding, and other fabrics. And the second day for the flags. Meryem had adorned the walls with the boy's creations, akin to a tapestry of colored laundry, but the passage of time had caused the loose ropes to lose their straightness, causing the talking flags to hang askew, halfway between the ceiling and floor.

Mustafa tried to get a ladder, climb up, and adjust the ropes, and he became so fatigued that he had to lie still in the middle of the room for a long time until his heartbeat and dizziness abated.

Then followed the kitchen room, full of dirty pots and plates, left over from the day of the funeral, when he asked everyone to leave and leave everything as it was. He rejected any help with the dishes, which had solely been handled by her hands, making it difficult even for him to approach them. He washed them eventually, as if filled with doubt. Unwittingly, he stepped into a realm where he could erase the memory of her fingers with his own.

The end of the week found him among chisels, sharp files, and pliers. He removed the vise grips, scraped the wax off the tables, cleaned the molds, opened the talisman box, and weighed all eight rings in his palm for a while. Devoid of a stone, the ninth ring waited patiently. Mustafa decided he had no more need for them.

Life, full of grandeur and fears, came to an end. He took them with pliers, one after the other, and beat them, without haste, on his goldsmith's anvil, until there was nothing left but faded, greyish-white, yellowish, mixed sheets, only fit for the furnace urn. Lost, stripped, unlucky gems: opal, amethyst, agate, emerald, sapphire, obsidian also disappeared among the floorboards and clouded the darkness of the floors with their torn velvet sheen.

After finishing on the seventh day, he wrote to Musa that his mother had gone on a journey from Bodrum to Milas to meet a saint.

CATARINA

The Verga Ducceschi family house, built on a hill surrounded by mulberry tree orchards, resembled a small Genoese castle rather than the mansions of Xi'an. In winter, they trimmed and fastened the trees' branches, and fires burned in the orchard to keep the earth from freezing. In spring, a shower of fragile petals filled all the alleys and the inner courtyard. On either side of the entrance, two dragons lounged, facing north. In the house, among the furniture pieces, you came across all kinds of turtles, tigers, dogs, rabbits, and small monkeys. Catarina dusted them herself and occasionally relocated them from one side of the house to the other, following her own exclusive set of rules.

Every year, shortly after the Lantern Festival, Master Bao Fu would pay her a visit, and they spent countless hours in her bedroom, decorated with small tables and shelves bent by the weight of leather-bound books, bamboo rods, and strips of silk painted with letters that resembled the marks left in the wet sand by a flock of cranes. Tommaso was perplexed by how anyone could locate anything in that chaotic jumble, much like he was baffled by the enigmatic movement of the jade zoo.

All the artifacts sprang to life and moved under Catarina's fingers, shocking the Genoese man who thought the Kingdom of Heaven was frozen.

After wasting four months waiting to receive the papers with the emperor's seal, he started all over again with the guilds of silkworm breeders, ropemakers, button makers, serge shearers, and silk yarn weavers. Accompanied by Yang Jianguo, a Mandarin dragoman recommended by Catarina, he ran from morning to night and often received the same answer: "Come tomorrow."

"I don't understand anything in this country. Here, everyone smiles, and when you turn your back, it seems they've forgotten you. Then, when you see them again, they look like they've never seen you before. No one says a clear yes or no. I need a miracle to manage. I think I'll start praying to God to enlighten me on what to do."

"Yours or theirs?"

"Stop laughing at me. To the one with more power."

"Then, I say start with the local God. Actually, with the local Gods."

"Will you guide me?"

"Yes, but I can teach you the customs around here and how to write commercial contracts, which are the emperor's laws. As for God, I'm not the best person for you to talk to, though you know I go to Mass every Sunday at the Spanish mission."

"I know, I was with you, but you didn't look pious at all."

"Neither in the past nor now do I consider myself a believer. My ancestors came to Xi'an so long ago. What do you want me to tell you? It's the city where the Silk Road ends. You can meet all faiths. Each with his own God. Mine's like jade: translucent and matte at the same time. When I was younger, I wanted to convert to Buddhism. I didn't do it in the end, but I talked to several monks and went to remote monasteries."

"Where?"

"In the west of the kingdom, at the beginning of the Lunar New Year. It's the spring festival; lasts seven days. The place fills up with pilgrims. They bring offerings, listen to services. It's a celebration."

"And how did you find it?"

"It was difficult. The road is very long, and it was so cold. The cold in the inns, the cold in the streets, the snow on the mountain tops. When I came back, I thought I'd never get warm again."

"And why didn't you get to pray to Buddha?"

"I don't know… It wasn't meant to be. I think I rather ran out of religion… I got something after the journey though… a strange stone… a stone fallen from the sky."

Catarina walked over to a nightstand, pulled a small drawer, and turned around with a bag made of *pulu*. She opened it. The grey-green light, with orange flames, smelled of musk.

"What's this?"

"A talisman, a stone that fell from the sky during the time of China's first emperor. The one who founded the empire."

"A talisman for what? Good luck, good health?"

"These also, but the legend says of immortality."

"Immortality? Do you believe in immortality?"

"That's a simpler question than the one about God. No, but this stone has an odd quality about it. And I believe the lama who handed it to me was aware of this. But I still don't understand why he chose me. I played the role of a messenger, and I am required to deliver it to someone else? To whom? He didn't say anything when he handed me the box. It came as a complete surprise."

"Then, how do you know it fell from the sky?"

"It was written on the paper I found in the box near a string of prayer flags."

"Have you ever thought of selling it?"

"No, no way. How can I sell it?"

"Then, why not wear it as jewelry?"

"I'm scared. What if it's not for me? What if it's meant for someone else, and it's going to hurt me?"

"Where do these fears come from?"

"Well, my dear Tommaso, if I knew where the fears come from, I wouldn't smoke opium. I have too many fears, and you have too many questions. Wouldn't it be better for us to smoke? It's late at night."

She pulled a carved *nanmu* wood screen from the headboard and revealed to his gaze two thick mattresses covered with cushions, dressed in silk embroidered with wild ducks, peonies, and white chrysanthemums, aligned bamboo rods, porcelain spoons and small ivory-handled cleaning tools.

With her legs crossed under her, she invited him to sit down and began to prepare the tobacco pipes. The oil-bronze lamp cast deceptive shadows and made her long fingers wave. She picked a pea-sized lump of opium paste, held it over the lamp until it swelled, then dropped it into the *wucai*, the opium vessel.

Then, the woman lifted the bowl, held it out to Tommaso, and urged him to move closer to the lamp. The yellow heat dissipated as Catarina watched her apprentice meticulously, leaning on one elbow against the large enameled serpentine chest full of mysterious tools. Attention to the smallest detail was the quality even her ex-husband — *"Woe to him who marries a bold and strong woman"* as is written in *Yi Jing* — highly prized in her.

"Did you learn to smoke from the Han people?"

"Are you starting with the questions again?"

"I won't ask you anything else, but I can't stop thinking about how amazing you are. I think you're the freest woman I've ever met. You're divorced, you have your own house, you talk to everyone as an equal, you manage your wealth, you're rich."

"People who live by listening to their souls should not amaze others. In my judgment, it's the most natural thing in the world."

"It's natural, but so few do it…"

"Also, very few try. And to answer your question: no, I did not learn to smoke from Han people at all. Many of them don't know what tobacco is, and those who have seen Portuguese sailors in ports smoking *madak* think it's a barbaric custom. I, as you can see, got used to tobacco mixed with opium quite quickly. I like it."

"Have you met Portuguese sailors? I don't believe it!"

"There was merely one person, a Portuguese captain, who happened to be a dear friend of my father. The old men both died, and now his son and I, who is also a sea captain, are continuing their business. Nothing that breaks any rules or virtues around here. It is true that what you see on deck are crates of pepper, nutmeg, saffron, cloves, ginger, Kain-du cassia, ginseng, cardamom, and other spices. About opium and tobacco, not many know. It's better that way."

"Maybe *madak* is your true religion."

"And now it's yours, too."

"Ah, it is not the same thing. I'm not saying I don't know what religion I have anymore. I'm pretty sure I'm Catholic, though."

"What can I say? A Catholic from Genoa, who wants to buy a house in Constantinople and has been living in the Land of the Son of Heaven for almost a year. You're a follower of a nomadic God, Tommaso."

"And you, of a lonely God, madam!"

They lived together for almost a year, and Tommaso never saw her naked. In the first few weeks after his arrival, he had tried to sleep with her, but like the shopkeepers in the alleys of Xi'an, Catarina said neither no nor yes. She only asked him first to smoke an opium pipe together. Their game. The twists of desire replaced by deception. Dreams rose and fell like tides. At the end of each night, enveloped in opium, their motionless bodies lay untouched. After a couple of weeks, the man with the ink-filled veins lost his desire.

Pursuing a myriad of opium journeys that spawned from the depths of China's nights, from that point on, every time in his life that he descended into the depths of bronze mirrors, regardless of his location or age, the final barrier between him and oblivion would be Catarina's eyes, two colossal shells with verdant flesh, unveiling the ceiling.

HAVVA

The inauguration procession for the new Padishah began early in the morning. People were chanting "Praise be to Allah!" from every window, as the lord of the empire reached the front of their houses. Murad — clad in armor, on a black Persian stallion with rich, embroidered silk saddle blanket cloths — looked out somewhere above the rooftops, above the minarets, above the seven hills of his capital. In the rear were the Grand Vizier, all the viziers, and emirs, then Havva's carriage, drawn by four Nogai steeds, draped on all sides with curtains to the ground.

Arsenal officers wore imperial banners composed of gold thread and silk. Black eunuchs, white eunuchs, and five hundred janissaries of the Palace Guard followed them. Towards the retinue tail, the cortege thickened: pageboys, lute players, musicians beating on drums or blowing their breath into wind instruments, acrobats with lighted torches, guilds rattling their tools, bakers, tinners, potters, tailors, masons, carpenters — even the Fishermen's Chief, who had cleansed himself thoroughly and rubbed his hands and hair with mint leaves and chestnut oil for the occasion.

When the procession finally reached the Imperial Gate, the crowds briefly dispersed. As evening fell, the reception followed into the Pavilion on the Shore; courtiers, ambassadors full of gifts, wishes of long life, health, and greatness of empire, in Turkish, Elin, Syriac, Hebrew, Italian, Serbian, Albanian, Spanish, Egyptian, English, Turkmen, and many other languages. The entire time, Ottoman galleys from Kız Kulesi and Sarayburnu fired countless cannon salvos. The astrologers had all agreed that the crowning's evening heralded future triumphs, so the banquet for eight thousand people was to end with a fireworks display, the likes of which had never been seen before.

The hours hardly ticked by for the mother of the most powerful man in the world. Her back hurt, and her adornments pressed against her; at one point, she made a subdued sign that she wished to retire to her chambers, and the eunuchs followed her. Havva made her way to the harem under the arches, and not a sound came from the Palace.

It wasn't the first time this had happened, since she had felt the same when they laid Padishah's body facing Mecca and the Imam uttered, "Come Munkar and Nakir, come, here is a true believer! He is waiting for you to come!" On that day, when they closed the new shiny green mausoleum in the garden of Ayasofya, after the ceremony, she had entered the cathedral-mosque. With the folds of her dress rounded by the mosaic of the dome, in the sad distance, the Virgin Mary, covered in black velvet embroidered with the golden letters of verses from the Koran, looked like a widow. The basilica walls fell silent and turned their backs on the Sultana as she advanced towards the mihrab on the soft, inert floor, like dough that had been left in the pantry for days and had gone bad. Allah had taken away her ability to read the tales in the stones since the days of Edirne, when she had deceived all with a shadow theatre devised to keep alive a man who was no longer living.

Those days, she had sung, spoken, eaten with the Padishah for seventeen days, caressed him, though she hated him. She despised him out of fear that his descendants would wage war among each other and shatter the empire, for he had not issued a *firman* against the fratricidal law. This is why everyone expected a crippled and dreary hour, when the mutes, the most feared executioners, would glide down the corridors wearing death around their waists in a silken girdle. The princes and their male descendants were all doomed to death by strangling, with not a single droplet of blood being shed, as no one had the power to spill the blood of Osman's lineage.

The servants left her alone, as she requested. Fireworks lit up the minarets and lit yellow, green, and red pyres in the windows of the Sultana-Mother's bedchamber. The food prepared in the morning had been cold for a long time; melted ice water ran down the sides of crystal carafes and dripped on the edges of carpets, on walnut and sandalwood floorboards.

She collapsed against the bed and began to weep with prolonged howls, shaken with sobs. Large tears stained her dress; she wrung her hands and banged her head against the edge of the bed, shouting like a stabbed animal. They heard her screams long after the sulfurous chrysanthemums of the fireworks died away, beyond the Princes' Islands, in Marmara.

In the morning, they found her asleep, still dressed, huge, gray, her face crumpled with despair. Aiyla, her dearest slave, approached her, woke her by tapping her gently on the shoulder, and asked if she would like to be helped with changing her dress, washing, and removing the imperial tiara from her hair.

TOMMASO

The plague came through her corridors. From Trabzon and Thessaloniki, from Bursa and Kayseri, from Aleppo and Ragusa, occupying the cities, emptying Stavros' inn of sounds and people. Few passers-by dared to walk down the narrow streets, once motley with the shouts of street vendors and shop boys running through the Covered Bazaar with hot tea.

Increasingly tired, Tommaso walked once a day through a city where death had colors. Black, white, grey, hidden in the decaying wooden steps, in the damp cellars, in the walls where cockroaches crawled.

Constantinople turned into an enemy, as in the days of the far-too-exhausted Byzantium, when the scattered treasures of the *basileis* and the thinner-than-thread silver coins of Constantine Dragas Paleologus had not saved all the descendants of the Comnenes, the Vatssians, the Nicephorians, the Latins, the Greeks, the Armenians, the Macedonians, all mixed together, noble families of a dying empire, forced to go into exile. No force could conquer the disease: not the precious icons, brought out from the altars, nor the useless whirling of the dervishes, nor the knees bent in agonizing prayer for which the Prophet with his face covered, for no one could know his face, neither appeared nor disappeared. In the plague-ridden city, shows became once more a thing of the past; dignitaries humbled themselves in public prayers; denunciations lost their power, and fortunes could not buy the lives of those melted under the fever. The rampaging Hetaera demanded ovations from destitute bodies covered in black stains, and horror was the lasting aftermath of human vanity. Her pestilential stench called them by name one after the other: vagabonds and dancers, odalisques and mullahs, poets, and courtiers. It inhabited them.

But it didn't inhabit Tommaso. Death had long had blue gums, blue fingernails, and blue skin in his remote world of opium. His companions, who knew him from his nights spent on Tophane teahouse's plank beds, had already encountered death everywhere.

Asif, the lame man, had met her at the foot of the Bulgurlu mountain, in the date orchards. Jacob the Albanian had claimed loud and clear that, on the contrary, Dev Dağı, the Giant's Mountain, was her host. Others swore that she floated beyond the Sweet Waters of Asia, and as for Ibrahim the fisherman, nicknamed Goatfish, nobody could get it out of his mind that her real place was among the steep, high hills that pierced the entrance to the Bosporus at the Black Sea.

To satisfy his hunger for such visions, Tommaso sold first his sable furs, then his Cordoba saddles. He drank the wine with Stavros.

"Don't go to the port, don Tommaso. Can't you see what a damn plague this is? They've got big pits where they're taking everyone."

"Yeah? I didn't know. Where?"

"On the other side of the strait, at Smyrna, and on this side, beyond Edikule, away from the city. That's where I put them. I've heard they set the corpses on fire, but I don't know if it's true."

"Everyone how? Christians, Muslims, Jews, all together?"

The universe had no contours, silhouettes soared into the air, hovered like unnaturally large butterflies, and nobody died in the opium realm from which Tommaso never fully awoke.

"Everyone, as I say. And no one picks the bodies off the streets; they lie there for days. They take them to the mass graves and throw them over each other when they finally find them."

"I've never heard anything like it. You're not allowed to do that; it's written in the Bible and the Koran."

"What do I know? I'm a poor innkeeper. I'm just telling you what happens. Don't go into town. You will get sick, don Tommaso."

And he didn't go, as there was no more opium to be found, only a coarse hashish — the poor man's grass — which the few sellers on the quays or under the bridges sold at double the price. When he couldn't find these sellers, Tommaso's whole body ached, and his arms and hands shook so badly that Stavros had to help him lift the spoon to his mouth or read the few epistles the merchant still received.

In the last of her letters, Catarina — in the rough Italian language of the innkeeper reading aloud — wrote of lotus flowers, low barges with reed roofs, and wicker baskets full of smoked fish and rice, of mountain yams baked in firewood, of blueish pagodas with red roofs, about trips to distant provinces, where she had gone to buy paper made from mulberry bark splinters, about Sichuan pepper or brown cardamom, about the painted faces of women she met on the shores of Lake Taihu in the Yellow River delta, about the easterly wind that always made her uneasy.

One November evening, the shadows of hurried passers-by, living and dead alike, blotted the walls. Stavros asked questions in Greek and tried hard not to stumble at every unintelligible word: *My dear, I will send you with the first ship to Constantinople the stone that fell from heaven. I think no one needs a miracle at this moment more than you do. I hope it keeps you from the plague, keeps you healthy, and that we meet again soon.*

Leaden eyelids covered Tommaso's whole body. Unable to reach him in the bewitched depths, Stavros folded the paper, and his voice trailed off.

MUSTAFA

A few months after the brilliant ceremony of the new Padishah coronation, the galleon Nossa Senhora da Vandoma, belonging to His Serene Highness the King of Portugal, anchored in the Golden Horn, next to Galata Tower, and the chest sent by Catarina arrived. Fernão Manuel de Cerqueira, the ship's captain, wanted to forget the bright-green forest of Poloveira Island's beaches, where he had almost run aground, the Canton prison, where he had lain for two weeks without being questioned by Ming dynasty officials, and the winds of the Malacca Strait, where pirates had attacked him three nights in a row. All he wanted was to reach his home in Ribeira as soon as possible and to see donna Beatriz. In the interval between voyages to the Indies, he had succeeded in producing three daughters, as plump as his wife, and a son, christened Afonso, in honor of the founder of the house of Braganza, with whom the Cerqueira family claimed to be distantly related.

The Fernandine walls, the wine glasses kept on ice, and the hot afternoons of the Iberian Peninsula were still a distant dream for Fernão Manuel de Cerqueira, who refrained from leaving the ship to enter the disease-ridden city. Instead, he sent a sailor to Stavros' inn. Tommaso had been nowhere to be found in the last three days. The Greek knew the whole talisman story, so he summoned one of his two last servants and sent him to the goldsmith's house.

The unpolished wooden box had traveled for many months among the *padrões*, cross-shaped stone pillars bearing the seal of Portugal, kept handy at all times to mark the boundaries of the new colonies born overnight and among goods of all kinds and the crew's clothes and food: flour, sardines, lentils, garlic, dried meat, plums, apples, fresh fish, and oranges — when they could find them — meant to chase away the scurvy.

The chest held few things. Several colored squares of silk, not too big, and the meteorite splinter. As Khalil had told him, the rock could look like anything: Constantinople seen from above, from a bird's flight, a sunken fleet of caravels, Piri Reis' maps showing undiscovered continents, the swathes of fresh water between the columns of the Roman cistern.

The stone appeared to flow in Mustafa's hands. He placed it back atop the prayer flags and chose not to store it in the workshop.

He pushed open the door into the room he hadn't been in for a year. Although he had closed all the windows, a puff of air brushed against the walls. The shivering flags on the ropes and those in the box rustled together.

Seraglio's messenger knocking on the door didn't frighten Mustafa anymore. His old fear sought to lift its head from the snake basket, but he refused to allow it, for he remained eager to hear the footsteps in Meryem's carpets or the slight, insignificant whispers of the tools she touched. The fear would kill everything.

As a result of his solitude, Mustafa could navigate into objects with the same ease that others moved through the rain.

He went back to a time when his forehead hadn't yet reached the height of the tables, and he envisioned the soul as a small, translucent sphere traversing a world teeming with metals, weaving through foliage, navigating their intricate networks, ascending into dispersing clouds, and eventually returning.

The next day, after the sunrise prayer, he put on his good clothes and set out for Seraglio, the same way he did in the old days, when the Padishah used to call for him. The goldsmith went behind the Conqueror's Mosque, past the water carriers with their empty large leather bottles, lined up beside the cisterns from which the water, dearer in the heat than the milk of the breastfeeding women, which flowed scarcely; past the doors of the empty hammams, at the early hour, behind which a *tellak* prepared the towels and the lavender-colored pieces of soap; past the *bedesten*.

His knees hurt. The walk to First Hill seemed longer than usual. *I should have asked for a carriage to take me to Seraglio, but now it's too late*, he told himself. Mustafa arrived sweaty and with his clothes hanging in disorder, in a hurry, despite having over an hour before his meeting with the Havva *Valide Sultan,* and entered the First Courtyard.

The morning bustle of the Sultan's University teachers, doctors, archivists, scribes, mint workers, storerooms, workshops, officers, and those filling the kitchens and bakery had begun. A coming and going of thousands of people employed to serve the chanceries, the barracks, the private apartments of an empire that stretched across three continents. No one noticed him, so he slipped through, slowing his pace. After he traversed the Second Courtyard, he requested the guards stationed at the Divan Tower to announce his arrival to the Black Eunuchs' Chief, as directed.

Before Mustafa could catch his breath, an agha emerged from the ground and led him towards the Fourth Courtyard, Gülhane Park, and the terraced gardens overlooking the Marmara. The fifty thousand fleshy tulips lined up like faithful soldiers; rows interrupted only by the artificial fountains and the white and pink pergolas of climbing roses.

Roses, carnations, tulips, and hyacinths, the flowers that brought good luck to the Osmanlı dynasty, bloomed everywhere. Lucky flowers, lucky jewels, lucky robes, the holy mantle, the sword, and the bow of the Prophet in the Treasury Hall. With all this divine protection, in Osman Gazi's family, people died much more than in other families; they died by law.

Mustafa had already been waiting for more than an hour near the marble pavilion where the Padishah usually took his *iftar* meals. Followed by the odalisques of the retinue, eunuchs, and slave girls laden with sherbet jars, water jugs, sugared fruit and sweets of all kinds, the Sultana advanced through the alleys like a small minaret on wheels, passing bronze vessels placed on tripods where they smoked the spices to ward off the plague.

After she crashed on a mountain of pillows, she urged him to sit on the lavish kilims, strewn all over the summer gazebo. A second wave of surprise struck Mustafa. By inviting him to sit down, Sultana-Mother broke the *kanunname*, the set of ceremonial rules of the Seraglio, crafted by Fatih Mehmed during a period of illness and melancholy to shield himself from dining with his viziers. Mustafa noticed Havva's disdain for etiquette and wondered silently about the motive behind it.

She ignored him until, at her command, everyone walked away. "Mustafa, you know I'm as good at stones as you are."

Like anyone else, he was aware of the rumors that the valuable gemstones spoke to Valide Sultan, who personally selected which ones would be embedded in the harem's furnishings, the plates, and the weapons of the Padishah. Furthermore, it was said that even the walls, mosaics, and tiles had a voice for her.

"Sultana, I'm not that good anymore. I'm not even one of the goldsmiths in the First Courtyard."

"That's because you didn't want to be one! And I can understand. It's better to stay away. There's so much going on here…"

She waved her hand in the air without finishing.

"I know everything, Mustafa. I know everything…"

At that very moment, Havva was lying. After so many deaths, her gift of seeing through stones had frozen. To the most powerful being in the world — as she unofficially held this title and not her son, the newly anointed Padishah, who had already displayed weakness and inclination towards vice, but at least listened to her — the basilica's walls had fallen silent, and the gates of Theodosius remained aloof and mute as she passed through them.

"How is the stone fallen from the sky?"

He appeared to be walking on ice and had to tread carefully. Mustafa took a deep breath.

"Do you want me to get it for you?"

"Not now. I'll see it when it's done. I want you to make another talisman for immortality. If you want, I can talk to the Chief Astrologer, get my son's birth celestial chart, but we both know you don't need it."

Mustafa nodded. No, he didn't need it.

"As for the remaining jewels, I'm considering what would be appropriate for Murad. Indian red diamonds, sure, black opal, chrysoberyl, rhodolite, maybe malachite from Moscovia."

With the intonation of the naturally privileged, the Sultana effortlessly selected very rare and precious gems, leaving Mustafa lightheaded.

With the voice of those who are born very rich and always will be, the Sultana strung out rare gems with an ease that made Mustafa dizzy. He wished he could interrupt her and inform her that the stones could not be chosen at random. To tell her about his long searches over the years. To tell her of the book about China's first divine emperor, the Son of Heaven, who dreamed of living as long as his kingdom, ten thousand generations, about the alchemists' eternal life elixirs containing liquid gold, arsenic, and mercury, of the herbs of the Taoist monks, of the Hindu astrology tome discovered by Khalil; but he didn't say anything. *What was the point?*

When the audience came to an end, the Sultana took out from under the black veils, edged with gold thread, a large, almost manly hand, adorned with rings on all fingers, which the goldsmith, kneeling, kissed. He had to return in three weeks with the drawings for the work. Mustafa knew that if Havva liked the talisman, the payment would be substantial, even though she hadn't mentioned money. This was how the imperial family treated their subjects, whether they were craftsmen, ambassadors, soldiers, or the King of Hungary.

Mustafa walked down the long street in front of the Palace and entered the city drowned in heat and dust. He thought he should walk to the *muvakkithane* to tell his friend about all this, yet fatigue hindered him. Minerals, seeds, fantastic animals, celestial metals, and potions swirled around in his thoughts. The poplars he passed by had fallen apart in the dry heat, and their shadows resembled stretched threads cast upon the ground. He turned back and walked home, with torpid steps.

At dusk, after the calls to the *akasham* prayer died down, he went into the workshop to look for his old notes. As he struggled once more to decipher the symbols representing the ascension of the planets, the movement of the haired stars, the sublunar spheres, and everything else, the Arab wrote about the stones that had fallen from the sky. He saw the brown stains on the backs of his hands. For someone working on an immortality talisman, he was too old.

EPILOGUE

In the second year of the plague, Tommaso died first, his body weakened and worn down by opium, followed by Khalil, who, anyway, had never known how to take care of himself or value his health.

Death found Mustafa in the workshop, alone. The neighbors called the gravediggers in a hurry, without changing his clothes or touching the little bag with the talismans he was carrying. The goldsmith's body ended up in the smoking pits on the edge of town, and the meteorite fragment returned to the flames from which it was forged.

Fulfilling Khalil's prediction without knowing it, Musa survived the plague wave in Constantinople, where he returned only once to sell his parents' house. An unchanged Pelagia opened the door. At Ariadne's request, she had kept the keys. She was still living at the orphanage, where the number of orphans had quadrupled as a result of the plague.

Returning to his residence in Spezia, the young ship-owner successfully marketed his colored-hued signal flags to the naval powers of England, France, and Holland. Red and white, yellow, and blue, blue, and white, black and white; just red, just white, just blue. All becoming the same language: "Man overboard," "I want to moor," or "I need help."

Near glaciers, on lakes, in the salty mist of the oceans, in bays and estuaries, at the entrances of harbors, in the long nights of the tropics, on rivers with waves, under the aurora borealis, in straits, near sandy shores or cliffs, in the shimmering waters of coral reefs, Musa's flags continue to talk with one another to this day.

ACKNOWLEDGMENTS

I WANT TO EXPRESS MY GRATITUDE to those who have stood by me in translating and publishing this book.

Nava Renek, Alexandra Carides, and the entire team at New Meridian Arts for their commitment to this editorial project, their profound reverence for literature, and their ceaseless endeavors to promote writers from diverse nations.

Carmen Firan and Adrian Sângeorzan for their unwavering support and generous friendship. They have been a constant source of encouragement and guidance.

I want to extend my thanks to Claudia Serea, Cristina Bejan, and Christopher Cervelloni for their invaluable help.

I feel blessed to have my husband, Bogdan Simion, in my life. Alongside his boundless love, he is always there to accompany me with his wisdom.

Last, but certainly not least, I would like to express my heartfelt appreciation to readers everywhere for their part in shaping the destiny of this book. Without you, no book would find its way into the world.

Anca Mizumsky

A

Ahar paper: special paper for calligraphy.

Akhet: annual Nile flood period.

Akşam namazı: evening prayer.

Alim: name for religious scholars and chief religious authorities, who often serve as teachers, judges, jurists, preachers, urban and rural imams, market inspectors, and advisers in various capacities.

Anne: mother (Turkish).

Asure: pudding with fresh or candied fruit.

Ayasofya: Hagia Sofia in Turkish.

B

Baba: father (Turkish).

Bailo: diplomat in charge of the affairs of the Republic of Venice in Constantinople.

Baklava: a layered pastry dessert made of filo pastry, filled with chopped nuts, and sweetened with syrup or honey. It was one of the most popular sweet pastries of Ottoman cuisine.

Bakhtiari: breed of horses, mainly bred by members of the Bakhtiari tribe in the Khuzestan province, southern Iran.

Bamiyeh: donuts with saffron and rose water.

Bardo: intermediate state of transition between death and rebirth (Tibetan).

Basileus: a ruler of the Eastern Roman Empire (plural basileis).

Bedesten: covered market or hall, traditional for the Ottoman Empire's cities.

Birinci kadın: mother of the Sultan's firstborn son.

Bülbül yuvası: sweet, ring-shaped doughnuts whose hole can be filled with nuts or pistachios.

Büyük baba: grandfather (Turkish).

C

Chador: long robe covering the hair and the body of devout Muslim women.

Cima: dish prepared from veal with peas, eggs, pine seeds, and herbs. Mainly eaten in Genoa as an appetizer.

Cirit: equestrian sport, popular in the Ottoman Empire.

D

Dilber dudağı: dessert made from egg, yogurt, milk, butter, sunflower oil, lemon, flour, and sugar.

Doge: usually a member of an aristocratic family, leader of a state-city in Renaissance Italy.

E

Edirne (Adrianople): first capital of the Ottoman Empire, before the conquering of Constantinople and the fall of the Byzantine Empire in 1453.

Efharistó: Thank you (Greek).

Ehl-i hiref: craftsmen's guild of the Ottoman Empire, which was under the authority of the Imperial Palace.

Eid al-Fitr: the festival celebrating the end of Ramadan.

Elif: letter of the Arab alphabet.

F

Farinata: thin pancake made from chickpea flour, originally from Genoa, typical of the Ligurian coast.

Felucca: narrow fast lateen-rigged sailing vessel chiefly of the Mediterranean area.

Fetva: legal ruling on a point of Islamic Law (Sharia) given by a qualified jurist in response to a question asked by a private person, a judge, or the government.

Firman: royal mandate or decree issued by a sovereign in an Islamic state. During various periods, such firmans were collected and applied as traditional bodies of law.

G

Gabardina: type of fabric.

Gheimeh: traditional Iranian stew of beef, peas, and potatoes with saffron, which is served over either white or spiced rice.

H

Hadith: collection of traditions containing sayings of the prophet Muhammad which, with accounts of his daily practice, constitute the major source of guidance for Muslims apart from the Koran.

Hafiz: Muslim who knows the Koran by heart.

Hajj: sacred pilgrimage that is required of every Muslim at least once in their lifetime — it is one of the five pillars of Islam.

I

Imam: the prayer leader of a mosque.

J

Janissary: a soldier of an elite corps of Turkish troops organized in the 14th century and abolished in 1826.

K

Kashbastı: diadem adorned with a stone in the center, usually worn by the women of the sultan's family.

Khenchen: title applied to the most respected Khenpo or to a senior Khenpo.

Khenpo: in the Tibetan Gelug tradition, the title Khenpo refers either to an elderly monk ordaining new monks or to the Abbot of a monastery.

Knafeh: sweet food consisting of layers of pastry and soft cheese in a thick liquid made from sugar, initially eaten in the Middle East.

Kolompeh: Iranian pastry baked in the city of Kerman, which looks like a pie with a mixture of minced dates with cardamom powder and other flavoring inside. Dates, wheat flour, walnuts, and cooking oil are the main ingredients. Pistachios or sesame powder are often used for decorating.

Kulliya: complex of buildings around a mosque, run as a single institution, often based on a waqf (charitable foundation) and consisting of a madrassa, hospital, kitchens, bakery, Turkish bath, etc.).

Kurban Bayrami: the festival of sacrifice, where millions of people sacrifice an animal to commemorate the Islamic prophet Ibrahim's willingness to sacrifice his son as an act of obedience to God.

Kuzu tandır: lamb roasted in an oven.

L

Lokum: also named Turkish delight, a family of confections based on a gel of starch and sugar. Premium varieties consist largely of chopped dates, pistachios, hazelnuts, or walnuts bound by the gel; traditional varieties are often flavored with rosewater, mastic gum, bergamot orange, or lemon.

Losar: Tibetan New Year and the occasion for the most important festival of the year in Tibet.

M

Madak: mixture of opium and tobacco, used as a recreational drug in China in the past.

Madrassa: Muslim school, college, or university that is often part of a mosque.

Manaqish: type of bread.

Melopita: traditional honey pie/cake from the island of Sifnos in the Southern Aegean. The base of it is fresh anthotyro cheese (or ricotta) mixed with aromatic honey and eggs.

Menemen: traditional dish made of eggs, to which tomatoes, spices, green pepper, and sometimes onions are added.

Mihrab: niche in the wall of a mosque indicating the qibla, the direction of the Kaaba in Mecca.

Minestrone: thick soup of Italian origin made with vegetables, often with the addition of pasta or rice, sometimes both. Common ingredients include beans, onions, celery, carrots, leaf vegetables, stock, parmesan cheese, and tomatoes.

Muezzin: Muslim crier who calls the hour of daily prayers.

Muvakkithane: room next to a mosque used by a person in charge of maintaining the correct Muslim prayer times, which will be communicated to the muezzin.

N

Nanmu: precious wood, unique to China and South Asia, used for furniture, and carving.

Nazar boncuğu: amulet in the shape of an eye, believed to protect against the evil eye.

O

Om mani padme hum: "Behold! The jewel in the lotus!" Buddhist practitioners spin large prayer wheels or small hand wheels while meditating or while chanting this mantra, also known as Mantra Mani.

P

Pansotti: variety of pasta (stuffed ravioli) specific to Liguria.

Pasqualina: pie filled with spinach, ricotta, and eggs; traditional Italian recipe served at Easter.

Pide: unleavened bread (Turkish).

Pigato: variety of white wine from Liguria.

Popolare: member of a lower social class in Renaissance Italian state-cities.

Predella: step and/or platform onto which the altar is traditionally placed. This component, as it relates to the Christian altar, was in evidence already by the time of Constantine in the fourth century.

Pulu: Tibetan wool fabric.

Q

Qottab: Iranian cake.

R

Rinpoche: highly respected religious teacher in Tibetan Buddhism; a term often used as an honorary title.

S

Sarma: a food in Southeastern European and Ottoman cuisine made of vegetable leaves rolled around a filling of grains (such as rice), minced meat, or both. The vegetable leaves may be cabbage, patience dock, collard, grapevine, kale, or chard leaves. Sarma is part of the broader category of stuffed dishes known as dolma.

Seraglio: palace of a sultan. The Italian word for serai or harem. The name of the imperial palace in Istanbul in the XVI century. At the beginning of the XVII century, the name changed to Topkapi Palace.

Sgabello: type of stool typical of the Italian Renaissance. An armchair with armrests usually was a chair of hieratic significance.

Sharia: religious law derived from the Quran, Islam's holy book. A set of rules that religious Muslims should adhere to, including prayers, fasting, and donations.

Shehzad: Prince.

Shemdap: Tibetan brown cloth skirt with a different number of pleats.

Sholeh zard: rice pudding with saffron.

Shükür Bayramı: The Gratitude Festival celebration.

Simit: ring-shaped bun, usually coated with molasses and sesame seeds before baking.

Spahi: a member of the Ottoman cavalry. The spahis were professional warriors granted a land fief in trust from the Sultan.

Sultanin: Ottoman currency.

Sura: chapter of the Koran.

T

Tafsir: Arabic term for the Koran exegesis.

Tellak: masseur in the Turkish baths, a young man who helped wash the clients.

Tespih: Muslim prayer beads.

Thangka: Tibetan Buddhist painting on cotton or silk, usually depicting a deity, scene, or mandala.

Torma: figurines made mainly of flour and butter, used as offerings in Tibetan Buddhism. They can be painted in different colors, often with white or red for the main body of the torch. They are made in specific shapes but are usually conical.

Tsampa: Tibetan barley, mixed with yak butter tea.

Tuğ: movable flag made of horsetail or yak bristles, of different colors, arranged in a circular pattern on top of a wooden stand.

Tuğra: monogram, seal, signature of a sultan, affixed to all official documents and insignia.

U

Ulema: Body of Muslim legislators, specialists in Islamic theology and laws.

V

Valide Sultan: title held by the mother of a ruling sultan of the Ottoman Empire.

W

Waqf: In Islamic law, a permanent donation made by a private individual for charitable purposes.

Y

Yashmak: veil.

Yiaourtopita: A traditional Greek cake recipe, made with yogurt instead of milk, which makes it extra moist and soft.

Yatagan: yataghan or ataghan (from Turkish yatağan), also called varsak, is a type of Ottoman knife or short saber used from the mid-16th to late 19th century. The yatagan was extensively used in Ottoman Turkey and in areas under immediate Ottoman influence, such as the Balkans and the Caucasus.

Yi Jing: also named the I Ching, usually translated as Book of Changes or Classic of Changes, an ancient Chinese divination text that is among the oldest of the Chinese classics. Originally a divination manual in the Western Zhou period (1000–750 BC), the I Ching was transformed over the course of the Warring States and early imperial periods (500–200 BC) into a cosmological text with a series of philosophical commentaries known as the "Ten Wings." After becoming part of the Five Classics in the 2nd century BC, the I Ching was the subject of scholarly commentary and the basis for divination practice for centuries across the Far East and eventually took on an influential role in Western understanding of East Asian philosophical thought.

Z

Za'atar: mixture of dried thyme, dill, oregano, sesame seeds, and
sumac.

Zergeran: goldsmith.

Zhen: additional brown robe worn by Tibetan Buddhist monks
that can be wrapped around the upper body for extra warmth.
When not in use, it is folded and draped over one shoulder.

"It takes a man with the heart of a lion to walk this extraordinary path; for the road is long and the sea deep and the journey is made in wonder, sometimes laughing, sometimes crying"

The Conference of the Birds, Farid Ud-Din Attar, Rosmarin Publishing House, 1999 (translated from Romanian by the author)

* * *

"He who enriches your cheeks with rosy light,
give me patience and rest.
And He who gave you beautiful and fragrant hair,
out of His mercy with gifts, has blessed me.
And if my hand is empty, I will not complain in vain:
my joy remains, and it is my wealth.
Treasures give to the kings, O Lord, and peace to the poor."

*Divan, Hafez, A92 Publishing House, 1996
(translated from Romanian by the author)*

* * *

"You're like the incense tree,
You are a sweet-tasting fruit,
You bear good fruit,
Mother of God, I have sinned before you…"

Incense tree, Armenian medieval hymn.